MEMOIRS OF A CORNISH GOVERNESS

Yolanda Celbridge

This book is a work of fiction.
In real life, make sure you practise safe sex.

First published in 1994 by
Nexus
332 Ladbroke Grove
London W10 5AH

Reprinted 1995

Typeset by TW Typesetting, Plymouth, Devon
Printed and bound in Great Britain by
Cox & Wyman Ltd, Reading, Berkshire

ISBN 0 352 32941 6

Contents

1

Chastised at St Agatha's

As a young girl, I was always embarrassed by my big bottom. My schoolmates would laugh at me, calling me a pear, though when I looked at my naked body in the mirror, I saw not a pear, but ripe downy peaches.

I followed the budding of my full young breasts with pleasure and excitement, for I saw that now my body displayed a voluptuous symmetry. I came to realise why I had been the victim of such unkindness: simple jealousy. A good figure is a girl's principle asset, and since men have the power to dispense the good things in life, it is only fitting that women should have the power to take from them. And as in all other business, the practitioner of the business of lustful pleasure must know the value of what she possesses.

How silly a young girl can be, not knowing herself. I was made to feel that at five feet and nine inches I was too tall; that my breasts, which had already developed to a ripe fullness when I was thirteen or fourteen years old, were ungainly; my waist too small. Women can be very cruel to other women, competing as we do for the lustful attentions of men, whose primitive desires we must try to fathom. We worry ourselves over the smallest details of appearance and fashion: is my dress too long or too short, too daring or too modest; are my breasts too pert or too pendulous; are my buttocks too tight or too flabby? Should I shave the intimate parts of my body, or is that too coquettish, even sluttish? And the question which makes us blush, giggle and whisper – should a girl trim her pubic bush, so that the thigh skin is left bare and creamy, or even shave the pubis completely, like a baby's? So many burning yet trivial issues! For one learns in due course that men, governed by the lustful organs they wield between their legs, are interested in one thing only, drawn to it like wasps to a honeypot.

Eyes are important; breasts, smile and hair are supremely beguiling; but all are adornments, advertisements for the pleasures of our silky warm cunts, for which men's cocks yearn as a traveller yearns for home.

And if truth be told, what do we women yearn for but the stiffness of a man filling us and making us whole? We may be seduced by the man of bravery and martial daring; by the cunning and power of the ruthless millionaire; by the peacock bravado of a prince or the eyelashes of a pretty boy; but if the cock does not stand hard in response to our bodies, if the balls do not have the vital essence to deliver to our avid wombs, why all these attributes are as nought.

I was always the outsider, and knew that I should have to fight to make my way in this harsh world. One feature of my body which attracted the cruellest and most jealous sneers was my skin. Now, my hair is a natural honey blonde. Not the pale wheaten yellow of the northern races, but a lush golden colour that is almost auburn. This, I was made to feel, was somewhat *louche* and sluttishly showy, although it is my natural colour. My eyes are not sky-blue, but a sparkling cat-like green, and my skin is not pale like an English rose, but creamy and sultry tan, with a hint of olive. A Mediterranean type, I suppose. This is due to my French ancestry, my ancestors being *de Comynge*, who arrived with Duke William of Normandy in the year 1066. My own name as a girl was thus an anglicised version of that borne by my grand forbears, the conquerors.

At any rate, this provenance, and my unusual physical features, earned me terrible taunts of 'darky', 'foreigner' and such like. For a long time, I stupidly envied my companions their alabaster white spotty skins!

But the worst of it was that I was an orphan. I remember my parents ; the fine house in Highgate; a life of servants and luxury, for my father was a wealthy man, with considerable and mysterious interests in the City. I suppose I have inherited his dark good looks, along with the voluptuous figure of my mother who was a very beautiful woman before tragedy struck.

One terrible day, when I was eight years old, my father shot himself. An unsuccessful speculation had ruined him.

I believe it was something to do with railways in South America, which were thought to be a certain source of profit at that time. It seems he had entrusted the bulk of his fortune to a man called Mr Volumene, and had lost it in murky circumstances.

The house was in an uproar and they tried to conceal the truth from me, babbling about an accident. But children are wiser than adults think. I knew the truth, for I had heard the terrible crack of the pistol, and smelled the acrid gunsmoke. Then I heard the crash as his body slumped to the floor. But they would not let me into the room to give my poor father a last embrace, and I wept bitter tears. Shortly afterwards, my mother succumbed to madness, and was taken to a hospital somewhere in Kent, where she later died, of grief I suppose. At any rate, she did not know me any more, her only child. So it was for me as though both my parents had died.

A trust fund remained of my father's wealth, which ensured my education at St Agatha's, a girls' boarding school at Wimbledon, south of the river. A pleasant place not unlike leafy Highgate. At the time it seemed as though I were going to the far end of the earth, although Wimbledon is no further from town than Highgate. Children's perceptions of distances in time and space are different from those of adults. I remember asking as our carriage crossed the Thames at Putney Bridge, if we had arrived in France!

But I got over my grief and decided to proceed with the business of life. Grief is sometimes unavoidable but there is no point in dying of it.

The other lesson I learned at this early age was to keep my coins in my own pocket.

I was not without aunts, uncles and cousins but they were scattered over the globe, and since I was now an orphan with no money, and a girl orphan at that, they found no reason not to ignore me. How different if I had been a boy.

I was lonely at school, although I came to relish my loneliness, and devoted myself to study in the well-stocked library. I discovered that I took easily to learning, and was at the top of my class in most subjects. This too made me the target of jealousy. We English tend to be suspicious of swots and brainy types, especially if they are girls. But I had my heart set on winning a scholarship to Girton College, Cambridge, which was for ladies only. Learning seemed to be the key to success, even at the risk of becoming a bluestocking. I belonged to no social set where I might find a man to marry, and the spitefulness of my

4

classmates made me feel that no one would want to marry me anyway. This caused me little of the unhappiness that it causes most girls who feel left out of a social life, for marriage seemed naïvely to me, as something bound to end in death and grief.

The worst times at school were the vacations, when I had nowhere to go, and the start of the new term, when I would listen to the other girls boasting about the splendid holidays they had enjoyed. Some of the teachers, old maids who were in the same situation as myself, made attempts to be jolly, especially at Christmas – whose enforced merriment I detested. But I preferred my own company, wandering through the mysterious hilly suburban streets of Wimbledon, or over the broad expanses of the common, which St Agatha's overlooked. I used to have long and merry conversations with myself in French, German and Italian, for which I discovered I had quite a proficiency.

The library, as I have mentioned, was well-stocked, but the choice of books very strictly censored, and restricted to the classics – Milton, Shakespeare (the bowdlerised editions) and so on. Of the moderns; Tennyson and Wordsworth were favoured as respectable. Byron, Shelley and Keats were viewed with suspicion as being a little *too* poetic.

But how different was the treasure trove of foreign books. I plunged deliciously into works of the absurd, the bawdy, the fantastic, the subversive, largely because none of the mistresses knew, or cared, what foreign authors might have to say. I devoured Boccaccio, Rabelais, Voltaire, the bawdy memoirs of the Abbé Brantôme, and much more. I did become quite friendly with Mlle Gryphe, the French mistress, who had a moustache, wore a lot of rouge, and sighed a lot. Her fiancé had been killed by a Prussian shell in the war of 1870, at the Battle of Sedan I think, and she tended to live in the past, or at least a fondly imagined past. I do not think she liked English life – she was always sniffing about 'this eternal cold roast beef and mustard' – but then she was not interested in anything that was not her gallant young officer, now mouldering in some heap of mud.

My acquaintance with Mlle Gryphe taught me not to dwell on the past but to get on with the business of life. It is too easy to treat grief as a pleasure and end in itself. To this day I am not sure whether Mlle Gryphe had ever lain with her gallant, or whether he ever existed at all outside her head.

My education in erotic matters was, as the reader may expect, precisely nil except for a few mumbled and embarrassed explanations when my menses began. But in the library I was lucky to find a huge leather-bound tome entitled (in French) *The Anatomy and Psychopathology of Human Sexuality*, written by one Professor Muffat of the Sorbonne, and published in 1853. I read it avidly, assuming correctly that the psychopathology and anatomy specifically under discussion were unlikely to have changed much in a few decades. The copious illustrations and accounts of the sexual act, or acts, were explicit to say the least, and dealt with the most bizarre variations of the human sex impulse and practices. I suspected that the good professor's interest in his subject was a little more than academic, and probably drew a lot from personal research.

Anyway, thanks to my reading, I had by age fourteen a profound, if as yet academic knowledge of matters erotic.

I used to visit Mr Izzard's chemist's shop in Wimbledon High Street, to obtain my monthly supplies of feminine requisites. Mr Izzard was a nice little man, although somewhat strange, and he always insisted on shaking hands with me and bowing formally with a soppy gleam in his eye. He never made improper advances to me, but sometimes to tease him I would put my arm round his skinny waist, blow him a kiss, or even brush against him with my thighs or breast. He would glow with joy. I realised what simple creatures men are, and how easy it is to thrill them.

I used to enjoy listening to him explain the various creams, pills and potions that he sold and manufactured; all of them having some arcane function involving what he called 'uro-genitary regulation'. He also had a wondrous selection of curious garments and appliances in leather, rubber or whalebone, for the same hygienic purposes, and I began to understand how complex the human body is, well, from the uro-genitary point of view at any rate.

'Sometimes, Miss Cumming,' he would say, 'folk like being cured of what ails them. And very often, where the uro-genitary system is concerned, they enjoy the cure even when they have no ailment at all.' And he would smile mysteriously, fingering a corset or enema tube. At the time, I did not understand such gnomic utterances, but I do now.

My schooldays, thus, while not being particularly happy, were not unhappy either. I felt, I suppose, like a soldier awaiting transport to his war, or a photographic plate waiting to be developed. It was a neutral time; my life would begin when, armed with my knowledge gained from eclectic sources, I should be launched into the world to fend for myself.

My favourite recreation was horse riding on Wimbledon Common, always under the supervision of a chaperone of course. The horses were kept at the stables beside the *Dog and Fox* public house in the High Street, and I loved the smell of animals; the odours of beer and cigars, dung and leather and sweat – the powerful reek of maleness – still excite me. We had to ride side-saddle, of course, the only decorous position for a lady. But I longed to straddle the horse with my thighs, like the gallant gentlemen in their smart boots and breeches and their whippy little riding crops dancing on the horse's flanks. But that would have been unladylike. The feel of a powerful steed between a girl's thighs, and the friction on her intimate parts, might cause unseemly sexual excitement.

Discipline was not unduly harsh at St Agatha's, despite its name – of which more later – and the mistresses, mostly spinsters, were distant rather than tyrannical, as though they had lost their way in life somewhere, and were marking time to no certain purpose. There were beatings of course, and they were as harsh, I suppose, as any other. But they were not frequent. Once I received what seemed to me at the time a ferocious and unmerited punishment: three strokes of a yew cane on my bare bottom (to add humiliation to pain). My crime was to have said that I thought the Greek gods and goddesses, and especially Selene, the moon goddess, whom I secretly worshipped, were far more interesting than the man on the cross and his twelve apostles. This was deemed blasphemy.

Miss Tubb, the headmistress, read me some prayers for the good of my errant soul.

We were in her study and she made me kneel to listen to her droning prayers. When she had finished, Miss Tubb closed the curtains, a rather ominous gesture, and ordered me to bend over the leather sofa, which I did. I was trembling in confusion.

My skirt rode up from my ankles to the backs of my knees, exposing the white calf-stockings which we

8

had to wear, as well as some inches of bare leg, which I remember seemed terribly shameful. Miss Tubb then remarked on the fact that it was the day after my sixteenth birthday.

'You are a big girl now, Cumming, and must take a big girl's punishment, especially for such a revolting offence. At your age, you should know better, and cannot plead childish foolishness as an excuse for this wicked thing. I intend, therefore, to give you three strokes of the cane. Have you anything to say to me, any excuse or apology?'

Clearly I was expected to grovel and plead, an especially humilating prospect when I was bent over with my bottom thrust in the air.

'Please, Miss,' I said in a tremulous voice, 'I meant no harm. I do not think I deserve a caning. Please do not beat me, Miss, I do not want to be hurt.'

'No one wants to be hurt, Cumming,' she replied. 'But have you thought of the hurt you have caused others by your impropriety? Your hurt will be small compensation.'

'*Please*, Miss . . .'

'Well?' she snapped, unflinching.

I realised that pleading was not enough. I was required to deny what I had said, and at that my spirit rebelled.

'I stand by my words, Miss. Those are my opinions, politely and fairly expressed, and I shall not take them back.'

'What!' she cried. 'Why, you impudent – you hussy – you. Oh, this is an outrage! Now, I shall cane you, Cumming. But, Cumming, you will lift your skirt over your back.'

'Miss?'

'Lift your skirt, girl, or I shall lift it for you! You will be beaten on your panties.'

9

My heart beat with terror and rage. I was alone and this woman represented all the authority in the world. Trembling, I obeyed and lifted my skirt.

I knew that by doing so, I would compound my offence. The air was cold on my exposed legs, and my bottom was protected only by a pair of satin panties – which were bright scarlet. I knew this was a flagrant breach of school rules. Our uniform was white blouse, dark blue skirt, white socks, and dark blue panties to match our skirts.

'Red!' she cried. 'Cumming, you are despicable. Remove the garment at once!'

'But, Miss, all the girls have –'

'Lower your panties this instant, young lady, I order it. Leave them down around your knees, for I will not have my carpet sullied with such a filthy thing. Come on, roll it down over your thighs, a girl like you cannot lay claim to modesty.'

I did as I was told, my face red with shame, and I exposed my naked bottom to her gaze.

'Very well. Three I said, and three you shall have, Cumming. But on your bare buttocks. You shall receive the cane on your naked unprotected skin. And when I have finished the punishment, you will replace the offensive garment and leave my sight at once. You will go straight to your dormitory and change into proper blue underthings, then report to Matron with that unlawful garment so that she may dispose of it.'

'Please, Miss,' I cried in despair. 'Not on my bare bottom!'

She ignored my plea, and ordered me to get my head right down in the sofa, and raise my bare bottom.

'I will tickle those wicked plums of yours, my girl, and how they will smart! I'll teach you, do you hear?'

What I heard was the swish of the cane. Three times it whistled and three times it stroked my bare bottom. It was horrid. It stung awfully, and I felt my bottom quiver but managed not to cry out.

When it was over, I did not wait to be dismissed, but rushed straight to the bathroom, where I dissolved in floods of tears.

When I had quelled my sobbing, I felt a sudden urge to pee, and lowered my panties once more. Before squatting to do my business, I turned to inspect myself in the mirror. The pain was strangely turning into a warm glow. I swivelled my bottom this way and that to look. It was beginning to feel almost nice, which I could not explain, for I had vowed to have my revenge on Miss Tubb for humiliating me. And yet I felt proud in a way; proud of having taken it without a murmur.

In fact my beating stood me in a good stead thereafter, for I gained a kind of respect from girls who had previously shown me none. No one could remember a girl having been caned bare before, and I learned to play a sly game.

Girls from whom I wanted favours would be granted a display, or even a touch, of my bottom, which impressed them greatly. I told them grandly that it had been nothing, that I had quite enjoyed my 'tickling' and so on. And in truth, alone in bed, I would allow my hands to creep up over my thighs to caress my bottom, and would feel a lovely smug glow of satisfaction. It was the humiliation I minded rather than the pain, and to my surprise I had to admit that I hadn't really minded *that* at all.

I was, however, quite serious about my adoration of Selene, the Moon Goddess. I loved her disdain for mere mortals; her icy aloofness. When there was a full moon, I would sneak out from school at midnight,

11

and go wandering entranced under the gleaming white moon. Unlike the sun, with its gaudy rays a symbol of puffed-up, extravagant maleness, the moon represented to me the power of the female: harder, brighter, and more baleful.

As I began to be more self-assured, I would go into the trees and take all my clothes off, running my hands over my nude body, washed in the moonlight.

Then, bolder, I would leave the concealment of the glade and prance quite naked on the open common, intoxicated by my nudity, by the frosty air and the cold light on my bare skin, and my solitude. In short, I felt thrillingly, nakedly alone, and free. It was during such a dance that I experienced sexual orgasm for the first time, that is, I 'spent'.

My body became suffused by a giddy, trembling, glow which turned to white heat; an unbearable sweetness flooded my belly, and I gasped with excitement as my heart fluttered. Then my fingers were irresistibly drawn to my wet cunt, where I found my clitty quite stiff with excitement, and I rubbed it. There was no male lover to cause me such delirium, just my solitude in the cold fresh air, the scented grass, and the light of the moon.

During my last year at school, I repeated this ritual at every full moon. Not for me the girlish games played under furtive bedclothes, the schoolgirl 'pashes' and 'crushes'. My love was the Moon Goddess herself!

My researches in the works of the good Professor Muffat had taught me that I was a virgin, like Selene, but that some day it was inevitable that my virginity would be lost when a man's penis, during the act of love, would pierce my maidenhead and make my blood flow, as a testimony to his virile puissance.

I resolved that only the goddess Selene should take

my hymen, and one night I laid myself naked on the grass, in love with being the only living thing in this dark world. My thighs were spread open wide to the moonlight, and I frigged myself voluptuously on the clitoris. I was so stiff, and so wet! Very soon I felt a spend coming, and with sharpened fingernails I drove into my hymen and ruptured it. The pain was sharp. I imagined myself pierced by Selene's spear – and I cried out, half in pain and half in ecstasy as my belly shook with the force of my orgasm. I felt the copious juice gush from my cunt, mingled with my hot maiden-blood, spill over my wrist and thighs. And thus was I deflowered – a wonderful, precious secret between my lover and myself.

One of the skills I acquired during my last year at school, was that I learned to type, with a machine and a book of instructions lent by the invaluable Mr Izzard. This was not because I wished to become a secretary or 'Remingtoneer' – at that time a common, but humble occupation for an unmarried girl – but because I wished to write books and dissertations of my own, on subjects as yet unspecified. This was thought highly suspicious and forward. A girl was supposed to write dainty letters on scented notepaper, not to put her words down in the hard clarity of cold print, unless, of course, it was at a man's dictation. She might even have ideas of her own! Armed with this liberating skill, I was impatient to have an end to school and venture forth into the world. This happened, but sooner and less agreeably than I had expected.

The blow fell shortly after my eighteenth birthday. At that age I was already ripe, with the figure and graces of a mature woman, and had lost my virginity into the bargain.

Miss Tubb, the headmistress who had flogged me, called me to her study. She was not alone. A middle-aged man in sombre business attire attended her, and I recognised him as Mr Lowe, my late father's solicitor and the administrator of my trust fund. Something boded ill for me, and I could tell that there was a guilty complicity in their glances.

After much preamble, evasive politeness and pious regrets about poor Papa, poor Mama, and so on, I learned that I was to leave school at the end of term; the term being Easter.

All the money in my trust fund had been exhausted. School fees, legal costs, disbursements here, disbursements there, Mama's medical bills, debts. In short I was overwhelmed with legal obfuscations which I had no hope of understanding (nor was I meant to), but with one clear import: no more St Agatha's, no Girton College, Cambridge, no more money whatsoever. I pleaded, and wept, but that stony fact stood unyielding.

St Agatha's, said Miss Tubb, was unfortunately, not a charity, and while they would do their best to see me settled with a position in the world, I should have to accept my fate and work hard to make the best of it.

Miss Tubb could not wait to see the back of a girl with no money! Our noblest and most venerated schools are businesses like any other and frequently the most avaricious. St Agatha's was then no exception, and nor is it to this day, when its function has subtly but not entirely changed . . . but I must not get ahead of my story.

To be brief: Mr Lowe had used his good offices to secure for me a position as governess and tutor in the household of Lord and Lady Whimble, near the village of Budd's Titson in Cornwall. Both Mr Lowe and

14

Miss Tubb advised me heartily to accept it, since it carried a salary of one guinea, or twenty-one shillings, per week, in addition to board and lodging and including hot water and laundry. Miss Tubb thought this arrangement most generous.

Cornwall. If they had said the planet Mars I could not have been more astounded. I had no doubt that Mr Lowe had chosen this godforsaken place to keep me as far as possible from London, where I could make trouble for him as he pursued his devious purposes with my rightful money, which, with righteous indignation, I imagined to be thousands and thousands of pounds.

I realised I had little choice but to accept, and did so with feigned gratitude. Since I saw no need for me to finish the term at St Agatha's, I said I was quite willing to take up my new post at the earliest convenience.

Miss Tubb bestowed on me a hypocritical blessing, and Mr Lowe gave me twenty pounds, which he said came from his own pocket, as a token of good faith. I accepted this unsmilingly.

Thus it was that the next Monday morning I boarded the West Country Express at Paddington Station, armed only with my suitcases and a typewriter, and game to conquer the world, in so far as Cornwall qualified as part of it.

2

Rakeslit Hall

I was full of foreboding as the coach jolted me across the misty northern edge of Dartmoor, and into Cornwall. My driver was a scowling old goat called Swivey (whether a name, or nickname, I never ascertained) who was well-filled with rum. It seemed he had been a retainer at Rakeslit Hall, seat of the Whimble family, for years or perhaps centuries, and I gathered that he regarded a trip beyond the confines of North Cornwall with as much fear and suspicion as others regard a trip to it.

My reading on the place had done little to inspire me. It seemed that the people lived by tin mining, or sheep farming, or smuggling brandy from France, and tended to die at an early age either from poisonous tin mining fumes, horrific ovine diseases, or revenuers' bullets. It was a desolate land, apparently haunted by all manner of pixies, hobgoblins and the ghost of King Arthur. The staple diet was clotted cream, which, I surmised, was because the people were too slow-witted to eat it when fresh. Their recreations were bible thumping, strong drink, and incest, and of the dismal cases brought before the courts involving illegal relations with farm animals, it seemed that those which were not in North Wales were invariably in Cornwall.

The landscape was a ragged affair of stone walls,

ditches and treeless fields, out of which surly peasants glared with vapid hostility. The villages made some attempt at the picturesque, with an abundance of flowerpots and shops selling the ubiquitous clotted cream. And their names sounded highly whimsical: Buttsbear Cross, Pancrasweek, Bulkworthy, East Balsdon, Chasty, Holemoor, Lashbrook and Dippermill.

Eventually we entered the grounds of Rakeslit Hall. The coach trundled up a gravel track that seemed to go on for miles, across a jumble of copses, lakes, fields, and moorland. Here and there stood curious little follies, half-finished structures in the Gothic style: summerhouses, pagodas and so on. There were also various attempts at ornamental gardens with fishponds, birdbaths and sundials. The whole effect was ramshackle but not displeasing. It was as though a multitude of hands had attempted to introduce some civilised influence to this wild land and had given up due to lethargy. The air was fresh and clean with the smell of the ocean and, in the distance, I could glimpse the grey waters of the Atlantic.

Rakeslit Hall itself thus came as no surprise. It was a large rambling place with stables and outhouses; overgrown flowerbeds with ivy and clematis snaking crazily over trellises and pergolas. Part of the house was Tudor, another Jacobean, another Doric and yet another Gothic revival. The dominant smell surrounding it was a hearty country aroma, one part flowers to four parts dung. I was glad I was wearing my thick leather knee boots. For the rest, my costume was a demure black satin dress, buttoned to the neck, which I thought looked suitably stern and governess-like.

But whom, or what, was I to govern? All I knew was that the Whimbles had a sixteen-year-old son called Alfred, who had proved difficult with previous tutors. It seemed that he could not apply himself to his studies, and needed to be disciplined somewhat so that he could pass the exams necessary for a cramming, final year at Eton, whence he would be propelled, it was hoped, to Oxford, and thence to the diplomatic service or the Guards, or both.

The coach pulled up by the front door, but there was nobody there to greet me, which caused me some annoyance, for my arrival must have been clearly visible. This was increased when the half-drunk Swivey unceremoniously dumped my cases into the mud and led his horses and coach away to their stable with only the curtest of salutations. For a moment I longed to be taken straight back to Exeter Station for the next train to London!

There I stood, clutching my parasol and hoping my wide hat would not be blown away into the mud. I decided that upon my first human contact – Swivey was only doubtfully in the category human – these people must be shown that I would brook no nonsense. It is tempting when in new surroundings to be over-friendly and submissive, in the hope that the friendliness will be reciprocated. But this would not be my way. I was here as governess, and I would jolly well govern, however lordly these peasants might think themselves.

Suddenly there was a furious whinnying and clattering of hooves, and a young man arrived, or rather erupted into view. He threw himself off his lathered horse and stood insolently in front of me, whip in hand. My heart fluttered. He was gorgeous. Like a young Greek god! He was as tall as myself, with a pretty face and a mane of lustrous blond hair that flopped over his brow like a girl's. His full, sensuous lips curled in an arrogant smile. He was in the first blossom of manhood, his chin scarcely scarred by a man's razor. I realised that this must be my charge, young Alfred Whimble. I sensed however, that beneath that arrogant bravado, there was a man, who like all men was soft and waiting to be tamed.

'So . . .' he drawled. 'You must be the new –'

I interrupted him sharply.

'Stable boy,' I rapped. 'Take my baggage inside and inform Lady Whimble that Miss Cumming the new governess is here.'

He stared at me, taken aback.

'I say, wait a minute!' he blurted.

'Are you deaf, boy?' I cried. 'Now hurry and do as you are told or it will be the worse for you.'

For a long moment our eyes met. I stared him down with a gaze of cold disdain until he blushed. A crimson glow suffused his lovely face.

'Yes . . . yes, Miss, at once,' he stammered. My heart pounded with triumphant joy as the young buck shouldered my heavy cases and led me into the musty vestibule of Rakeslit Hall.

It was a cavernous place, gloomy with cobwebs, dusty portraits of military Whimbles through the ages, and the carcasses of animals and fish which had perished by the Whimble gun or the Whimble rod. Various racks were stuffed with walking sticks, canes, umbrellas and the like, such as mysteriously accumulate in the hallstands of maiden ladies in Clapham or Golders Green.

The boy Alfred put down my things with a pleasing reverence.

'Actually –' he began.

'Where is Lady Whimble?' I snapped. 'I am expected!'

'Why, Mama is indeed expecting you, Miss, in the drawing room. She has arthritis, you see, and cannot move about very much. It is through this door,

19

please, Miss. I was going to say that actually I am Freddie Whimble, and you are to be my governess, I think.'

'You think, do you, Alfred?' I said curtly. 'Well, that is a start. Let us try and keep you at it.'

'Yes, Miss,' he replied, and smiled with another lovely blush.

'You are very muddy, Whimble,' I said. 'It won't do for lessons, will it?'

'I have been riding, Miss,' he explained.

'I can see that!' I retorted sarcastically. 'Riding, instead of studying. Why, I ride myself, but books come first, and don't forget it, if we are to get you into Eton.'

'Yes, Miss,' he said. 'You ride then, in London?'

'What is so strange? We do many things in London.'

'Oh, nothing at all, Miss. I just thought that perhaps we might –'

'And I think that perhaps *you* might have a bath and remove some or indeed all of that smelly mud, and then you will be fit to take a little French dictation before dinner. French dictation improves the appetite considerably. You do *have* baths in the country?'

'Why yes, Miss,' he exclaimed. 'I have had many baths.'

'And from now on, Whimble, you shall have many more,' I said firmly.

He showed me into a surprisingly cheerful room, with silken drapes and Persian carpets. There was the Rakeslit stamp of absent-minded clutter: bibelots, objets d'art, and mismatched pieces of sumptuous furniture strewn higgledy-piggledy. On the ottoman sat Lady Whimble.

At the mention of arthritis, I had assumed an aged crone, but here was a handsome, lissome woman of no more than forty, wearing a bright silk print dress and a splendid pearl choker. I could see from mother and son that the Whimbles were a handsome breed, and wondered what his Lordship looked like. Beside Lady Whimble, on a vanity table, stood a decanter of purple wine and some crystal goblets. She put down the illustrated paper she had been reading. From its cover it seemed to deal with hunting, fishing, and plumbing, the three great country preoccupations, and she waved me to a seat opposite her.

'Heard you talking to Whimble,' she said in a soft contralto voice. 'That's the ticket, firmness. He needs a good talking to. Look at the boy, he is all muddy. Mud all over my carpet that Whimble brought back from Afghanistan! Why doesn't the boy fetch you a glass of port wine instead of standing there like a big girl?'

She seemed to think of son and husband in the third person, as though neither of them was there. But Freddie Whimble leapt to get me a glass of port and carried it to me, making the carpet still muddier. I thanked him, and let my fingers brush his, upon which he reddened again, to my secret delight.

'Why doesn't Whimble go and make himself presentable?' she asked, of no one in particular. 'Miss Cumming has come all the way from London, where people are not muddy! People in London have a bath every week, don't they, Miss Cumming?'

She slurped at her port, and saved me the trouble of replying, by continuing:

'When Whimble was courting me – I was the toast of London, you know – we would ride in Rotten Row every morning, and he would go back to Knightsbridge Barracks and have a bath afterwards. At least I think he did. Men are such dirty creatures! Is that wretched boy still here?'

21

Taking the hint, Freddie backed sheepishly from the room, with his eyes on me, and crashed into a suit of armour, which clattered to the baronial floor. I felt I was getting quite an introduction to country life!

Lady Whimble now inspected me, unconsciously – or perhaps consciously – brushing back her short blonde hair, and smoothing her dress over her small, taut breasts.

'I like the look of you, Miss Cumming,' she said at length. 'The boy's last two governesses didn't last, you know. Crabby old Cornish spinsters. The boy ran rings round them. He needs someone more his own age, yet grown-up, like you, who will brook no nonsense and put him through his paces, punishing him when he needs it. And he often needs it, I think.'

'I will certainly brook no nonsense, ma'am,' I said politely. 'And as for paces, why, I shall be sure to put him through them.'

'That's the ticket. He is a handful. I can't look after Whimble myself when Whimble is away fighting in the mud of the tropics. Muddy fellow, Whimble.'

It seemed that both Whimbles shared a propensity to muddiness.

'It is the arthritis, you see,' she added. 'It comes and goes.'

She waved vaguely, indicating that arthritis that came and went encompassed each and every circumstance of her life. A gong rang mournfully in the recesses of Rakeslit Hall.

'Dinner,' exclaimed Lady Whimble, draining her port. 'I'll have Dorkins show you your quarters, as I expect you'd like to freshen up. No time for lessons just yet, I am sure you should get your bearings first. You are not muddy, I like that in a girl!'

She rose and, with the aid of a stick, showed me to the dining room where a young man, Dorkins, took charge of my things. Dorkins was good-looking in a sullen way, and he wore garments that might at one time have been a flunkey's uniform but which he had long outgrown, so that the muscles of his arms and thighs bulged invitingly under the tight shiny serge.

My room was under the roof beams, up four flights of stairs which Dorkins, nimble as a stag, ascended three steps at a time. The room was simple but pleasant, with a large comfortable bed, a mirror, table, jugs, bowls and so forth. He showed me the bathroom and lavatory which were situated at the end of the corridor. They were marvels of patchwork inventiveness, as though the fantasies of the Gothic revival had found their way into the art of plumbing.

However, the fixtures seemed to work, in an erratic fashion, and after squatting on the commode for a much-needed evacuation, I stripped and washed face, armpits, between my legs and buttocks, then applied powder and perfume, combed my hair, and descended to the dining room.

Lady Whimble sat at the head of a huge rosewood table, laden with silver and crystal, and big brass candlesticks. We were three to dinner, myself on Lady Whimble's left, and Freddie opposite me, though he had not yet arrived.

'Serve up the rations, Dorkins,' commanded Lady Whimble. 'If Whimble gets his cold it's his own damned fault.'

Dorkins and a buxom girl named Sally, who was a couple of years older than me, attended to the service; Dorkins poured copious draughts of wine while Sally ladled soup.

I drank the hot soup, which was a sort of lobster bisque, and was surprisingly good. Lady Whimble received a good drop of brandy in hers, but I declined.

23

'Hmm,' she cried, stroking her hair. 'Just wait till you have been in Cornwall a while, Miss Cumming!'

We made small talk while awaiting Freddie. I learned that Sally was in fact Dorkins' wife, and that between them they took care of the household, while Swivey was the outside man. Various villagers would help out the squire for urgent jobs; in the meantime, there was only this small staff for such a large house and I was not surprised at the abundance of dust and cobwebs. A large part of Lady Whimble's conversation centred on hard times, the cost of everything, and lack of money generally.

I realised that tutoring at Rakeslit Hall was not going to make me rich, and already wondered if there might not be other means to augment my income here in the untutored countryside . . .

We agreed that Freddie's lessons should begin the following morning, and would plan a timetable for him that evening.

I gasped in delighted surprise when Freddie made his entrance. He was wearing a magnificent uniform, bow tie and white jacket with gold piping, over tight scarlet breeches, with boots and spurs. He had dressed up for me.

'It is Papa's,' he explained with a blush. 'I thought you would like it if I dressed for your first dinner here, Miss Cumming.'

'Thank you for the compliment, Alfred,' I said, and gave him the barest hint of a smile, which made him glow with pleasure.

After an excellent dinner, comprising roast venison, some unidentifiable Cornish vegetables and strawberry tart with – yes – clotted cream, and all washed down with the finest wines, I told Freddie that we might as well start as we meant to continue, so he must go to his room and do some schoolwork, a French translation which I would correct on the morrow. He looked a little glum as I selected a book from my store and gave him a passage to work on, but he bowed gracefully and withdrew to his task.

Then Lady Whimble and I repaired to the drawing room with a decanter of port wine, of which she drank the lion's share, and devised a rigorous schedule of studies for the young man, covering all subjects fit for the education of a gentleman. I felt that milady's mind was not entirely on the matter, so followed my own instincts in setting up the curriculum, to her occasional nods of approval. She punctuated my explanations with loud sighs and cries of 'If only Whimble were here!'

I gathered that Lord Whimble was not at Rakeslit very much, if at all.

The household retired early, as is usual in the country, to save firewood and candlelight. By ten o'clock I was undressing in my upstairs room, listening to the creaks and rustling of the cooling building (so often mistaken for ghostly noises) and the whistles and chirrups of the night's furry and winged denizens out in the darkness amongst silent hedgerows and glades.

The moon was half-full; I stood naked in the pale light and looked out at the eerie beauty of the dark landscape, my thoughts in a turmoil. It was as though I were the only person in the whole world, a giddy feeling which I loved. Outside my window was a rusty old fire escape. Fleetingly, I thought of clambering down it and rushing out to dance naked in the fields, under the moon. I felt that the whole misty land belonged to me. But such boldness would have to wait until I had a secure position here.

My fingers crept to my breasts, and I began to stroke the tender skin of my nipples, very gently, until they rose and stood quite stiff, and my breath came harder and harder. Then my left hand moved across my belly and the thick curls of my pubic forest, to my clitoris, which rapidly hardened as I tickled it. I gasped at the pleasure which tingled inside me, and at the wetness of my cunt, and set myself to a firm frigging . . .

Suddenly I was interrupted in this lustful sport by footsteps outside, and a knock at the door. Panting, I slipped on my chemise and smoothed my ruffled hair.

'Who is it?' I called.

'It is I, Miss – Freddie,' came the reply.

'What is it you want, at this hour?' I cried in vexation.

'Oh this homework, Miss. It . . . it is so dashed difficult. There are some words I do not understand at all.'

'Well, Alfred, this is not the time for such matters,' I said sternly. 'I am undressed, wearing only my chemise with nothing underneath. I cannot possibly receive anyone in these circumstances, still less young men who should be sound asleep. Now be off with you and we will discuss scholastic matters in the morning, at the proper time. Good night.'

'Yes, Miss.'

There was a pause, while I listened for his departing footsteps. There were no departing footsteps.

'Alfred,' I said, 'are you still there, by any chance? You are not peeking, are you?'

'Yes, Miss. I mean, no, Miss, I would not peek. I just wanted to check that you were all right.'

'And why should I not be all right?'

'I mean, if you heard a ghost or anything.'

'There are ghosts here?'

'Why, oodles, Miss,' he replied enthusiastically. 'If you are frightened, just call, and I will come up the

26

fire escape. My room is directly underneath yours, and I will rescue you.'

'How can you rescue me from a ghost? Ghosts are insubstantial, if they exist at all, which I doubt.'

'Perhaps not in London, Miss, but here in Cornwall there are plenty. I would . . . I would comfort you, if you were afraid.'

I smiled. 'And how would you do that, Alfred?'

'Why, I . . . I . . .'

I could almost feel the heat of the boy's blushes, through the door.

'Once more, and for the last time, good night, Alfred!' I cried, and this time I heard his sorrowful footsteps sheepishly retreating down the stairs.

I was all tingly; I could not help imagining the enormous erection the boy must be carrying, excited by the thought of me in a state of undress, and I lost no time in climbing into bed. Then lifting my chemise around my neck, I resumed my caressing of my clit and breasts, and rapidly brought myself to a shuddering spend, my fantasy being of that wicked bulge in his breeches that I had ogled at dinner, and the naked stiff cock beneath.

Upon reading the anatomical explanations of the good Professor Muffat, I had perforce wondered what it would feel like as a man's stiff penis fucked me. Now I was sure that I should soon find out; on my terms, and under my control.

I drifted off into a happy sleep, full of lustful dreams, waking only once when, in the dead of night, I thought I heard a creaking of the fire escape outside and the sound of horses galloping away towards the sea.

I quickly settled into the rhythm of life at Rakeslit Hall. Mornings, and some afternoons, were spent in rigorous study with young Freddie. If he achieved good marks from me, he was allowed a little muddiness as a reward. I found I was a good teacher, the essence of teaching being discipline, and, as in all business, giving value for money. Freddie did not possess much discipline, but I possessed enough for both of us and the sternness with which I crammed his Latin, maths and geography into him, seemed to make up for his own dreaminess. I was nearer his age than I allowed him to think, and had to suppress feelings of my own! When I saw his eyes turn from his books to the freedom outside the window, or, more often, to my own demurely wrapped body, I was obliged to scold him with a severity I certainly did not feel. I began to feel a yearning curiosity to know the body of this lovely boy, nay his soul itself, so young and glowing with vital energy and possibility.

The French language, apparently so important for his future career (French being the international language of diplomacy and society in general) was something of a sticking point, as it is for many English schoolboys. Perhaps it is something to do with the vowel sounds, which seem shrill and forced to our English ears. At any rate, sometimes he would pout and sigh in exasperation, upon which I would silently rebuke him with a withering frown – enough to reduce the lamb to obedience – and when I deigned to smile, it was as though I had drenched him in golden light, enough to melt him to radiant joy.

Slowly but surely, I was making young Freddie Whimble fall in love with me.

Life was peaceful and very little untoward happened; indeed very little happened at all. Once or twice I was woken by those ghostly hoofbeats in the night, but I refrained from making flippant remarks about phantom riders, suspecting that it was in fact none other than Freddie, galloping off in his youthful exuberance to be muddy under the stars. This thought endeared him to me.

'Oh, Miss,' he would sigh, 'I don't think I can get the hang of this French. I'll never be a diplomat at this rate.'

'Nonsense, Alfred,' I replied. 'Your basic grasp is sound. It is just that you get mixed up with tenses, genders, and so on. You must concentrate, that is all.'

'But Miss, forgive me, but it is so boring! All this stuff about the pen of my aunt, and going to the *plage* with my bucket and spade, and visiting the grocery, the butcher's and the baker's. When should I need such stuff? That is what servants are for.'

'Well, Alfred,' I said at last, 'I take your point, and I shall see what I can find to make your progress more rapid.'

That afternoon, I took the carriage (reluctantly relinquished by Swivey – but I put my foot down and was backed by Lady Whimble) and went to Barnstaple, to see if the bookshops might have anything more suitable for a vigorous young man. Of course, I should have known better; there was scarcely a bookshop worthy of the name and, when I asked for books in French, I might as well have been asking for a primer in devil-worship. So, with a certain mischievous excitement, I resolved to use my typewriting skills and produce something of my own!

As I surveyed the stone walls of the meandering country lanes, on my return from Barnstaple, I noticed that many of them bore strange painted arrows in various colours. I assumed that these were some sort of agricultural notation, but when I asked about them, my innocent curiosity was rewarded with blank looks or hostile silence. I assumed that the

Cornish were highly jealous of their secrets of mulch and slurry and cast the matter from my mind.

My main diversion or amusement, apart from my gradual enslavement of young Freddie and his passionate youthful heart, was in taking solitary walks through the countryside, which I came to know and even love. Every now and then on my rambles I would come across these mysterious arrows painted on tree trunks or stones, but I thought nothing of them. I often strolled into the village of Budd's Titson, about a mile away, which was as pleasant as a Cornish village could reasonably hope to be. Often I took tea at Miss Chytte's Tearoom – 'Clotted Cream a Speciality'.

3

French Lessons

The high point of our week was the Sunday church service, at which the whole village would assemble. I would sit in the front, in the Whimbles' ancestral pew, decently garbed in black, and trying to stifle my yawns at the rustic caterwauling of hymns and the loud sermons of the Rev Turnpike, a good-looking man of about Lady Whimble's age, with mutton-chop whiskers, and as rough-looking as his parishioners, although he had a nice voice. I made it my business to become acquainted – decorously you can be sure – with all the men of the town: Mr Bragg the butcher, Mr Tannoc the baker, Mr Flett the grocer, and all the rest, together perforce with their dumpy, faded wives, silent eyes darting this way and that, as suspicious as mice.

On my country wanderings, I found myself drawn again and again to a particular wood about two miles distant from Rakeslit. It was a gloomy tangle of alder, birch, elm and oak, with a carpet of dark dank moss strewn with flowers. In many ways it was a sinister place, yet it spoke to me with a strange voice, that I could only dimly understand. I could imagine the goddess Selene taking human shape – my shape – and flitting naked through the dappled branches, her spear and arrows cruelly glinting as she stalked her prey. And, oddly enough, I learned that the historic name of the place was Sally's Wood. Why, I could not ascertain. Some thought that it had belonged to a Cornish landowner named Sally, which seemed as likely an explanation as any! There, too, the trees bore strange coloured arrows, but I could not work out what they were supposed to be pointing at, if anything, nor what agricultural mysteries could be concealed in the mossy ground.

One morning, I told Freddie that his French translation had improved immensely. He had been working from text of my own devising, and I approvingly read out a particularly good passage:

Yvette took off all her clothes and prepared to take a bath. She removed her blouse, petticoats, stays, chemise, corset, panties, stockings, garter-belt and suspenders and unlaced her boots until she was quite naked.

On her bathroom table were sponges, ewers, perfumes, oils, soaps, gels, creams and powders.

Suddenly her cousin Albert entered the bathroom, wearing his splendid uniform of the Fifth Mounted Belgian Hussars. He wore epaulettes, tunic, medals, riding boots, jodhpurs, sword, pistol and shiny brass buttons.

'Oh!' cried Yvette, trying to cover her naked breasts, belly, shoulders, thighs, elbows and feet.

'Yvette!' exclaimed Albert, his face red with embarrassment, desire, fear, hope, yearning and indecision.

'Why, Albert,' said Yvette, 'have you never before seen a lady in a state of undress, that is to say, bare, nude or naked?'

'No,' replied Albert.

'Well, you must leave at once, for to look on my naked body is dastardly, heinous and shameful,' cried Yvette. 'My fiancé Henri is expected any moment and he will surely kill you if he finds you here with me!'

At that moment, another soldier burst in impetuously.

'Yvette!' he roared furiously.

'Henri!' cried Yvette piteously.

'Albert!' yelled Henri menacingly.

'Henri!' riposted Albert apologetically.

'A duel on the sands at Knokke-le-Zoute at dawn!' challenged Henri. 'You may choose, select, favour, elect, or opt for sabres, rapiers, pistols, daggers, rifles or fists!'

'This is excellent translation, Alfred,' I said warmly. 'There is not a single mistake, and I see your vocabulary is well enlarged.'

'It is much more interesting than pens, bakeries, buckets and spades, Miss,' said the boy eagerly. 'I can't wait to see how the story ends. Where did you get it from, Miss?'

'Why, from . . . from a secret book, Alfred,' I replied, smiling. What a chump! As if a book can be secret, when the whole point is that it reaches the public. But men are so silly they will believe anything.

At that point the gong sounded for luncheon. But Freddie, normally an avid trencherman, stayed uncomfortably in his seat.

'Come along, Alfred,' I said brightly. 'The body must be fed as well as the mind.'

'I will follow you in a moment, Miss,' he said nervously. He was red as a beetroot. 'I . . . I have some things to do.'

'What things, Alfred?' I laughed. 'You have done them all.'

'Oh . . . just things,' he said, squirming. I looked down and saw that he was trying to conceal a massive erection of his penis, which bulged like a gorgeous pumpkin in the front of his trousers!

'Are you upset about something, Alfred?' I asked innocently. 'Feel free to tell me, for I am your governess, and not just for book-learning.'

And I put my hand tenderly on his knee. He trembled.

'Well, Miss, I felt awfully sorry for poor Albert in the story.'

'Why? Because your name too begins with A? Did you think he was meant to be you? A young man who has never seen a girl naked before? Why, I am sure you have seen girls before, Alfred, when they are undressed. It is well known that country morals are more cheerful and relaxed than in town. I mean, naked bathing and romps in haystacks and so on.'

I moved my hand a little way from his knee, up his quivering thigh.

'You are curious to see a girl's naked body, Alfred, is that it?' I said tenderly. 'Why, that is nothing to be ashamed of. Any healthy boy must have such curiosity, to see a fully-formed girl!'

'Oh, Miss,' he whispered, 'I don't want to see *any* girl. I don't give a fig for other girls . . .'

There was a long silence, as I slowly slid my hand up his thigh, looking him full in the eyes but not smiling. My gaze was that of a stern governess, but I admit that my cunt was wet. My finger brushed the tip of his erect penis where it strained against the trouser cloth.

'I can tell you are excited, Alfred. Do boys think they can hide such things from our curious female eyes? Now tell me the truth. Is it *my* body that you wish to see?'

He stared at me in terror.

'Well, answer, boy,' I rapped. 'The truth is always best.'

'Yes, Miss,' he stammered. 'Oh, yes, Miss. Very much.'

I touched the tip of his hard cock once more, and let my hand linger there as I looked deep into his eyes and allowed a long, slow smile to spread across my face.

'I am in charge of your education, after all,' I said. 'But I suspect it is more than education you desire.'

'Oh, no Miss, I swear!' he cried. 'Just . . . to see the beauty of your body would . . . would . . . Oh, I am so confused!'

'Beauty can be seen for nothing in the National Gallery,' I said sweetly. 'But living beauty, why that is another matter. It must be paid for, in brave deeds or in shiny coin.'

'When I am a great man, Miss,' he blurted, 'my glorious deeds shall be yours!'

'Shall be is the future tense, Alfred,' I said severely, 'and you cannot put the future tense in the bank. A coin, however, can be held in the hand. A coin is the here and now.'

He gazed at me in hope, yearning and confusion, just like my fictional Albert.

'Well,' I said briskly, rising to my feet, 'I hope your appetite for beauty has not spoiled your appetite for luncheon.'

As I opened the door, I stopped and pretended to think. He awaited my utterance with pleading eyes.

'Come to my room tonight, Albert – I mean Alfred – and bring a shilling for me, and we will see what we can do.'

His eyes almost popped from their sockets. He gulped for air and rushed out of the room, his magnificient erection bulging before him. At luncheon, the boy did not eat a thing!

That night, at eleven o'clock precisely, there was a soft knock on my door.

'Miss!' whispered Freddie dramatically.

'Who is that, at such a late hour?' I hissed.

'Why, Miss, it is I, Freddie.'

'Alfred! What on earth are you doing here?' I cried.

'But ... Miss,' stammered the poor lamb. 'You told me to knock on your door at eleven and bring a shilling for you. Here I am with your shilling, Miss. Please open the door.'

'Shilling?' I snapped. 'Whatever are you babbling about, boy?'

'Please, Miss,' he wailed. 'You said ...'

'I hope there is an explanation for this,' I sighed, opening the door. I was fully clothed, which perhaps surprised him, and he slipped into my room all gasping and flustered.

'Here, Miss,' he said, holding out a bunch of red carnations. 'These are for you.' I took them, frowning.

'Why, thank you, Alfred, but is it not a little strange to disturb a lady at eleven o'clock just to bring her flowers? It could surely have waited till morning.'

'And this, as you said,' he continued, and held out a shiny shilling, wet with his perspiration. 'As you asked ...'

I did not take it, but looked at him wonderingly.

'Alfred, I am just about to undress and go to bed. I hope your unexpected visit had no immodest purpose?'

'Miss, you cannot have forgotten. At our French

lesson – I admitted that like Belgian Albert, I had never seen a fully-grown woman's body before, and you said my education must be furthered, for a shilling. And here is your shilling, Miss, oh, please, please, take it.'

'And if I do?' I said. 'Then what?'

'Why,' he stammered, blushing. 'You are my governess, Miss. It is for you to decide.'

I smelled the flowers.

'They are very pretty,' I said distantly. 'Put them in a vase of water.'

'Thank you, Miss, thank you,' and he obeyed.

'Now then, show me this shilling of yours again.'

Very slowly, I reached out and took the coin from his trembling hand.

As I took the coin, I scratched his palm with my fingernail.

I could see in the candle's flicker that his member was swelling under his trousers, and this time he was too excited to try and hide it. I sat down on the bed and put the coin on my bedside table beside the candle, whose smoky flame illuminated us theatrically. Then I motioned him to sit in the armchair, facing me.

'I think you should cross your legs, Alfred,' I said primly. 'You are immodest.'

I was trying not to show my own excitement, for I was wet as I played this tantalising game.

I was wearing a pleated skirt of red satin, and a white silk blouse with a pearl choker, together with black lace-up boots, all of which I had put on specially for this occasion. The tight blouse showed my breasts quite dramatically, thrust upwards by a wasp corset of which my flat belly had no real need.

I took off the pearl choker and placed it beside my shilling, then slowly undid the first and second

37

buttons of my blouse. All the while I stared him in the eye, my expression stony and unfeeling.

Without shifting my gaze from his, I raised my left leg, stretched out and placed it on his thigh, with the tip of my high heel almost touching his bulging crotch.

'Unlace me, Alfred,' I ordered in a soft voice.

His breath was heavy as his clumsy fingers fiddled with my bootlaces, but at last they were loose. I placed my right boot beside the left and told him to repeat the operation.

When it was done, I said:

'Take my boots off, Alfred.'

He tugged delicately, as though afraid I would be hurt; my left boot came slowly free and now I allowed the heel of my right to rest firmly against the swelling of his manhood. My sheer white silk stockings were revealed. When both boots were off me, I cradled the tip of his penis with my toes and gave a little caress. He was panting hard, red in the face, and abruptly I swung my feet away from his lap and stretched my legs out in front of me, with a sigh of pleasure.

'Get my nightdress, now, Alfred,' I said curtly. 'The blue one, in the wardrobe.'

He stood up awkwardly, for his cock was quite immeasurably stiff. I could not help marvelling at what a big, ungainly thing he was blessed or burdened with. He reached for my thin silk nightdress and took it from its hook in the wardrobe, then handed it to me reverently as though it were the greatest treasure on earth. I took it, looking at him with a faint smile playing on my lips, and caressed the thin, almost transparent silk.

'Do you like it, Alfred?' I said.

'It is beautiful, Miss.'

'Hmmm,' I said, pretending to frown as I inspected

the garment. 'It is so thin that it scarcely hides my naked body. But then, in bed, there is no one else to see it, is there?'

'No, Miss.'

'So I had better get undressed and put it on. You may sit down, Alfred, and watch for a little while, until I get tired of you. 'Now, first, I must take off my stockings.'

Slowly, I lifted up my red satin skirt until it was rolled almost to my waist, showing the white suspenders that held my stockings to my garter belt. The boy's eyes were wide as he saw my creamy bare thigh skin.

'Now, Alfred,' I said, without looking at him, 'you had better make yourself useful. Undo the clips of each stocking, and roll them down – but without touching my bare skin, mind.'

He was shaking so much as he undid the clips that he could not help touching my legs, which in fact I found quite thrilling. When both stockings were freed from their straps, I lifted my skirt the tiniest fraction more, quite off-handedly, and for one fleeting moment he saw the silken triangle of my panties, where my mons swelled.

When my legs and feet were naked, I stretched luxuriously, and yawned.

'Heavens, I am so tired,' I said. Then, cruelly, 'Well, I have no further use for you, Alfred, and you may go.'

'But, Miss,' he blurted piteously, 'you said –'

'I have said nothing, boy!'

'Please let me help you with the rest of your clothes. Oh, I beg you – to let me put your nightdress on your sweet body, Miss, oh please!'

I laughed mockingly.

'You have had your shilling's worth, my boy! What

39

do you think a shilling buys you? I will not be used for your lustful pleasure.'

'Oh, Miss, I am sorry, I didn't mean any harm.'

'Well, there is no harm done, Alfred, you are only a boy and I know it is easy to get carried away. But you must go now.'

'Very well, Miss.'

And he turned, crestfallen, with a longing glance back at my bare legs. When he was at the door, I said softly:

'Alfred – if you would like to visit me again tomorrow night, you may help me undress. But you must bring another shilling.'

'Oh, yes, Miss,' he blurted. 'Thank you a thousand times!'

'Before you go, Alfred,' I continued, 'kneel down and kiss both my feet.'

Ecstatic, the boy knelt before me and showered my feet with kisses, taking my toes in his mouth and licking them fervently. I felt quite giddy and wet.

'Enough, Alfred,' I gasped at last. 'It tickles so, you naughty boy. Well, I will see you in the morning for lessons as usual, and of course you must not tell anyone about our little piece of playful fun.'

'Of course not, Miss.'

'Nor about my shilling . . . it is our secret.'

And when he had gone, I could not wait to strip myself naked, and, lying on my bed without bothering to don my nightdress, I clasped my swimming cunt and frigged my clit until I spent!

The next day's work carried on as normal, and I gave Freddie his lessons as though nothing unusual had happened the night before. Well, strictly speaking, nothing had happened. He worked very assiduously, desiring to please me and gain a smile from me, and

I gave him sincere praise for his industry, which made him glow with pride. Kind words cost nothing, I always say.

He came that evening, with more flowers, and I repeated my tantalising performance; pretending to be tired of the game, then reluctantly agreeing to take his shilling, and at the end allowing him to kiss my feet, and my naked legs too, but only up to my knees.

'Oh, Miss,' he begged, 'mayn't I just brush your lovely soft thighs with my lips? I will be so gentle.'

'Alfred, you must learn not to be so forward,' I replied sternly. 'Others might take it as impertinence. But I know what it is to be curious; I will lift my skirt up so that you may glimpse my panties. Would that please you?'

'Yes, please,' he cried, passionately kissing and licking my calves, and looking upwards with yearning in his eyes as I lifted my skirt to reveal my panties, where there was a large wet patch, and parted my thighs for him.

'I am more than curious, Miss,' he moaned. I laughed gently.

'I know you are,' I said. 'But it is time to go, now, before you lose control of yourself and say something foolish. You have had far more than a shilling's worth tonight! Why, to be vouchsafed a glimpse of my most intimate garment, my panties ... But you have been good – I think you may come again tomorrow night.'

'With a shilling, Miss?' he asked ruefully.

'With a shilling,' I replied.

On the third night, after he had removed my boots and stockings, I allowed him to unfasten my skirt and take it off.

I sat on the bed as usual, the straps of my red garter belt loose across my thighs. My panties too

41

were red, and I let him have a good view of my fat mons bulging against the wet silk, as I sat with thighs well apart.

'Oh, Miss,' he cried. 'You are torturing me cruelly. How I long to see what lies beneath your panties. It is a holy of holies for me and I dream of it nightly, yet in my wretchedness, I am the happiest man in the world. Why is it so? Am I in love?'

I laughed.

'You know nothing of love, Alfred,' I replied, 'apart from what you read in books, where you get all this hifalutin stuff. Lustful desire for a woman's body is not the same as love, you know. Feel your bulging manhood, which is plain for everyone to see. Does he feel love?'

'Yes, Miss!' he wailed. 'That is why he stands for you! Oh, please, Miss, when may I see your naked body? I shall behave myself like a gentleman, I promise.'

'That is what I am afraid of, young sir,' I replied. 'But you get ahead of our game. Who said anything about seeing me naked? My pile of shillings is not very high, is it?'

At that, I yawned, and spread my thighs wide, as far as was comfortable, holding them apart with my panties stretched taut across my swollen cunt lips. His eyes were riveted on my sweet wet place.

'Good night, Alfred,' I said firmly.

4

Red Roses and Silk Panties

And on his next visit, he brought *two* shillings!

I let him open my blouse down to the fourth button, and look at the soft swell of my breasts, but without kissing or fondling them. I sat on the bed with my knees against my chin and my heels on my bottom, so that he was afforded a voluptuous view of my cunt swelling against my tight panties. I allowed him now to kiss my thighs all the way up to the first curls of hair straying below the panties, and as he kissed me there, he sniffed deeply at the strong odour of my love juice, which I could not prevent from moistening the thin cloth that covered my labia.

'Oh, Miss, I am overcome,' he sighed, as he inhaled my most intimate odours.

I was quite overcome myself by this time.

'You may kiss me . . . there, on my panties, Alfred, if you wish. But just one kiss, a gentle brush with your lips, through the wet silk of my panties. Softly, now. There, you are a good boy.'

He did as I bade, and then I pushed his head away. My cunt was gushing; his lips glistened with my juices.

'Oh, Freddie,' I moaned, 'you may take my panties off, now.'

Without a word, but with awe in his eyes, he slid my panties down over my thighs and all down my legs until I kicked my feet free of them. Now the lower part of my body was quite bare. I smiled at him, and felt my composure return. Lightly, I stroked my mink, teasing him.

'There,' I said, 'I think you have had good value for your shillings, Alfred. This is what a woman looks like between her legs. Look, but do not touch.' I spread my lips so that he could see the glistening pink flesh and the stiff little clit. 'I think that is all you need to see for the moment.'

'I long to see *all* of you, sweet Mistress,' he said shyly.

I liked the sound of Mistress . . .

'You mean my bubbies? Why, a girl's breasts are a very tender and private place.'

'No more so than that beautiful pink slit between your legs, surely.'

'Let us not argue, for it will make me cross. You are not to see my teats, not tonight, anyhow.'

'Then I may hope?

'We may always hope,' I smiled. 'Here, Alfred, a gift for you.'

I picked up my damp panties and pressed them to his lips.

'Oooo . . . Mmmm . . .' he moaned. 'Thank you . . .'

'You may borrow the garment, as a memento of our little meetings,' I said, 'but on the condition that you wear them all day tomorrow. They will be very tight and uncomfortable on you, especially if you are unable to control the erection of your manhood. Why, your cock' – he thrilled as I spoke the harsh, lovely word – 'seems to grow bigger every time you see me.'

'I will do anything for you, Miss. Oh, to wear your intimate things . . . I will be in heaven. It will be as though I am part of you.'

'Come tomorrow night, Alfred, and I will inspect you. And remember, my panties may feel like heaven to you, but shillings are my heaven.' And I closed the door on him.

Teasing was part of the excitement of this game. By day, I was as cool as you please to my charge, striving to conceal my own excitement as I scrutinised the wicked bulge of his cock. To appreciate a treat, one must savour the anticipation, the voluptuous imagining.

The next day, I had to suppress my giggles at the awkwardness of Freddie's walk. Those panties must have been awfully tight on his crotch! Especially with that cock of his which flattered me by standing constantly to attention, although I noticed he now sported a long jacket to hide the tumescent part. I was most touched by the boy's labour of love.

That night, before I retired, I had a most unexpected talk with Lady Whimble, who invited me in for a glass of port. She was quite upset about something. I soon learned what this was, listening politely to all her cries of 'Disgrace!' and 'If only Whimble were here!' It had to do with Freddie, of course, and though I feigned maidenly reluctance to follow Lady Whimble's wishes, I eventually agreed, and promised to carry out her wishes to her satisfaction. I ascended to my room with mischievous glee in my heart and a spring in my step.

I awaited young Freddie in great excitement; I was splendid in my finest silk dress and stockings, my boots gleaming, a dab of perfume in all the intimate places of my body, and my legs and armpits freshly shaven. When I heard his shy rapping on the door, I promptly flung it open, but with a stony frown on my face.

He carried red roses and a whole handful of shillings!

45

I did not smile. I looked him coldly in the eyes, and before he could speak, plunged my hand brutally between his legs and cupped his manhood. His cock was not long in hardening to the full, upon which I nodded and withdrew my hand, as if in verification of some scientific experiment.

I ordered him curtly to put the flowers and money on the table. He obeyed, then stood gazing at me like a hungry pet.

'You have on my panties, Alfred?' I asked.

'Yes, Miss. All day, as you ordered.'

'Comfortable?'

'No! But my discomfort has been gorgeous, because it was for you.'

'You may now return them. Strip off your lower garments,' I said.

He fumbled at his breeches and boots, and soon was standing embarrassed with his great stiff cock almost bursting my flimsies. I nodded, and he took down the panties, then placed them in my outstretched hand. I threw them aside, and turned to look at him.

'Well, Alfred, you have seen my cunt, so it is fair that I should see this cock of yours that stands so stiffly for me. And I must say that it is a splendid big one. You are lucky to be such a virile boy.'

'Why, thank you, Miss,' he beamed.

'Now, sit down in the chair, and spread your legs wide, for I want to have a good view of that magnificent cock while I undress. You wanted to see me quite naked, and so you shall, for you have now brought sufficient money.'

I then ordered him to stretch his hands behind the back of the chair. Quickly, I bound his wrists together with his leather belt, to his great discomfiture. I smiled.

'For my protection, Freddie,' I said. 'You are strong and lustful, and the sight of my nudity may inflame you to actions we should both regret. Education must not be confused with lewdness.'

Before I began to undress, I placed the toe of my right boot underneath his balls, pressing them quite hard, which made him moan a little. But his cock was still rigid, I was pleased to see.

'It seems there is nothing we can do to make this cock of yours behave himself,' I playfully chided.

'I cannot help it, Miss. At the sight of you, he has a life of his own.'

'That I can well see,' I said matter-of-factly as I removed my foot from his crotch and unlaced my boots. I threw the boots carelessly aside, then peeled off my stockings.

I dangled my stockings in front of him, then stroked his belly with them, draped them across his mouth and nose, then caressed his penis with the delicate silk, warm and scented from my body.

'You are a temptress, Mistress,' he moaned.

'Then it is well that you are tied.' And in a businesslike, brisk way, I unfastened my skirt.

'I suppose,' I continued, 'that the sight of a woman's body causes uncontrollable desire in a young boy, and that lustful young boys have the deplorable habit of frigging themselves. Is that what you do, Freddie?'

'Yes, Miss, sometimes I just cannot help it.'

'Now, for instance?'

I stepped out of my skirt.

'Oh, yes, Miss.'

'And what would you do? Describe it to me, in detail.'

'Why, I should rub my ... my cock, Miss, and tickle the tip until I felt a lovely sweet spurt coming

47

from my balls. You are so beautiful that it would only take a few quick rubs before I spent. I . . . I have already done so, thrice, today, thinking of you.'

'What? And wearing my panties!' I pretended to be cross.

'I ejaculated my sperm just at the touch of that sweet silk that had been perfumed by your cunt, Miss.' I smiled.

'I wonder if there is any more sperm left in those tight big balls of yours,' I said mockingly. I stood before him in panties of sky blue silk, and my white blouse, with white garter straps dangling on my thighs. I undid the first four buttons of my blouse, and squeezed my breasts together to make a voluptuous cleavage, teasing him. Then I took the blouse off altogether, revealing my naked bubbies, pushed very full and high by my corset. I threw the blouse aside, after stroking it briefly across his penis, which made him gasp.

'You would love to suck my nipples, as you sucked your Mama's when a baby, wouldn't you?' I said, and he nodded.

I unfastened my corset, and let my breasts spring to their natural fullness, and soon I wore only the white garter belt and the blue silk panties, which were soaking wet. I unstrapped the garter belt then with little swaying movements of my pelvis I slid my panties down my thighs until for the first time he saw my nude body.

Grinning sardonically, with cruel amusement, I dangled the wet panties in front of his face, brushing his nose with them. I pushed the panties into his mouth, and wiped his lips with the wet silk, then abruptly threw the garment aside and pressed my lips on his mouth in a quick hard kiss!

'Girls, Alfred, are just as lustful as boys,' I said,

'and we frig too. I wager you did not know that. Here, this little button, this stiff pink fellow we call our clitoris.' I pulled back my cunt lips to show him, and began to stroke my stiff clit gently, which sent shudders through me and caused my nipples to swell to full stiffness.

'Sometimes we rub our nipples, too, for they are very sensitive, and connected to our clitoris. You see?' And I stroked and tweaked my stiff nips.

And as I caressed myself to madden the helpless boy, I saw myself in the looking glass, my eyes heavy, my face flushed, my lips full and red with desire. The honey welled in my belly, my spine tingled. I knew that this was the moment. I put my breasts to his face, and he began to suck and lick my engorged nips so passionately that I shivered and almost cried out.

'Bite harder,' I whispered, and he responded quite savagely. I felt a spend coming. But as I was about to straddle him I saw that a drop of white spunk had already appeared at the swollen tip of his engine.

'I think I am going to spend, Miss,' he moaned. 'I cannot help it.'

I had read about male excitability and knew that his time inside me would be too brief for my pleasure. As soon as he entered me, he would experience *ejaculatio praecox* and explode like a firework, uncontrollably. I resolved that when he did come inside my cunt, my pleasure should not be marred.

Therefore I knelt down and squeezed his penis between my breasts, and rubbed the shaft between my teats, making sure that my hard nipples caressed the sensitive base of his glans, or mushroom.

In a matter of seconds he groaned and gasped with a sweet little wail, as a jet of creamy hot sperm spurted from his cock and bathed my breast skin. Gradually, his moans subsided to a low 'Aaaah . . .', and I was enchanted with my success. As his penis subsided to half-erection, I rubbed the sperm into my nipples, and, stroking his balls all the while, brought myself to a satisfying spend in that manner.

'You see, Alfred,' I said, 'education can be a pleasure, if it is properly paid for. Now I am sure this thing of yours has some life left in him, or I shall be disappointed, for he has other places to visit.'

I bent down and closed my lips on his penis, kissing and licking the tip of the mushroom, and it stiffened again to a splendid hardness. When it was standing as proud as an oak, I took the whole shaft into the back of my throat and with bobbing pigeon-like motions of my head, I gamahuched, or sucked him. His pelvis began to thrust, as though he were fucking me in the throat, and I was afraid I would choke on that huge throbbing hot thing!

'Oh, yes, Miss, yes,' he moaned, straining against his bonds.

I disengaged myself and untied his wrists, then stripped off the rest of his clothes; now we were both nude. Then I embraced him standing, with my breasts squashed against his smooth bare chest, and my loins pressed against his cock, forcing it back against his belly. I could feel the glans tickling my bellybutton, which was most exciting. I rubbed my belly against his manhood while my hands stroked his buttocks, and now I kissed him full on the lips with my mouth open.

Our tongues met, and after a delicious bout of French kissing, I pulled away with a flushed smile.

'Your education must progress, Freddie,' I said with mock seriousness. 'There is always work for you to do!'

I lay down on the bed, with my thighs spread as wide as they would stretch. With one hand, I held open the lips of my cunt, and with the other, clasped his tight buttocks and guided his huge penis into my slit. I wrapped my ankles round his bottom and pushed him into me, trapping him tightly. It was heavenly, as though I were filled with life itself, my pussy so wet by this time that he slid in as smoothly as an oiled piston. There was no pain, nothing but sweetness and joy. I kissed him passionately, my tongue darting against his, while my fingers raked his muscled back and the soles of my feet slapped against his naked buttocks as they pumped up and down, and he fucked me with a brute savagery that left me breathless.

'Oh, God, I can't stand it!' I heard a voice howl, and recognised it as my own.

'Miss?' he panted, still thrusting vigorously. 'Am I hurting you?'

'Yes, yes . . . Oh, God, don't stop, hurt me, fuck me with that wicked cock, boy, fuck me till I scream. I cannot stand it. Oh, fuck me harder, more, more, split me . . .'

I was quite out of control, and loving every passionate moment!

'Feel how wet my cunt is for you, Freddie! How stiff my nipples have grown! Come up a bit – yes, that's right – now your cock is rubbing my stiff clit! Can't you feel it?'

'Yes, Miss, yes, God, can you feel how stiff my cock is for you, and you alone? I never dreamed I could be so stiff! And my balls are so full of spunk, at any moment I am going to pour my spunk into your hot sweet cunt, Miss, I cannot help it . . .'

'Spend, Freddie, spend into me!' I cried. 'Wash my cunt with your lovely spend!'

And together we mewled and gasped in a spend which for me was shuddering ecstasy – my body

51

shook as though from an earthquake – and, from his breathless cries and moans, was no less for him.

Afterwards we cuddled in my bed, under the covers, while the moonlight played on our faces. I lay there as pleased as pie, my body glowing, and his head on my breast like a little baby.

My hand cradled his balls, and after a period of somnolence, that cock began to stir again! Suffice it to say that before morning, Freddie had spent thrice more in my cunt, and once in my mouth. We fell into a contented sleep, and were awakened by the cock crowing at dawn.

'It is your cock I prefer, Freddie,' I said with a kiss, 'for it doesn't make any noise, and spurts lovely hot cream into my cunt.'

'Not forgetting your lovely mouth, Miss,' he said, and we both laughed and cuddled some more.

Then I became stern, once more the governess.

'You must know, Alfred,' I said, 'that to the world, you are my student and I your mistress, and nothing more. Such lustful passion as we have felt is for the moment only. Desire surrendered to must be enjoyed, but then brought back under control. Do you understand?'

'Yes, Mistress, but . . . I think I love you!'

'Love, Alfred,' I admonished him, 'can only take place between those of a similar class and financial standing. What you feel is mere boyish lust, pretty for all that, but fleeting as the morning dew.'

'Oh, Mistress, how can you say such harsh things? I will do anything for you, I swear!'

I put a finger to his lips.

'Hush, Alfred. I am your governess; responsible for your education and your discipline too. And now, in that capacity, which must be my only capacity as far as the future Lord Whimble is concerned, I have a duty – perhaps disagreeable – to perform. I have been instructed by your Mama; she does not wish to approach you and cause a scene, she would rather the matter be dealt with quietly, by me. And then you must go and humbly beg her forgiveness for your transgression.'

Freddie sat up, his face pale and shocked.

'Matter? What matter? What transgression? I don't understand.'

'Yes, you do, Alfred, do not dissemble. Your Mama has noticed the depletion of her purse – the missing shillings, Alfred, which only you could have had the opportunity to steal. She has not guessed what you have done with them and assumes you have been gambling or drinking in public houses, so does not expect the money back. But she insists that you receive a severe, private punishment. And I must administer it. I think you know what I mean, Alfred.'

He stared at me with wide, frightened eyes.

'A . . . flogging?'

'Yes.'

'And you would do it?'

'*Will* do it, Alfred. I have no choice. Your Mama pays my salary. So you see, this love for me that you profess, might not be so strong after the beating I am going to give you.'

He bit his lip.

'I took that money for you, Miss,' he cried.

'You took it for yourself, Alfred,' I rapped. 'To give to me in return for things you wanted, which is the nature of all commerce. Admit it.'

'Yes, Miss.'

'Now will you take your punishment like a man? For me, your only Mistress?'

'Mistress, it . . . it shall be an honour to take your punishment.'

53

I cupped his cheeks in my hands, and stared at him sadly.

'It will hurt very much, Freddie, my sweet.'

'I am ready, Mistress.'

'Today, then, we shall go to the wood and select a bundle of birch twigs, which you will bind into a whip. And tomorrow, after breakfast, I shall come to your room and give you two strokes on your bare buttocks. Afterwards, you are to go to your Mama and show her, then ask her pardon.'

Freddie was quite pale, and swallowed in distress.

I reached down and stroked his balls, very tenderly, and said:

'Well, Freddie? Am I your only Mistress?'

'Yes. Oh, yes.'

'And you realise that I must hurt you as hard as I can?'

'Yes, Mistress . . . but with the birch . . . and on the bare bum! Mama is so cruel!'

I got out of bed cheerfully and began to put my things on.

'Oh, no, Alfred, your Mama is not cruel. She wanted to let you off with a scolding.'

'You mean –?'

I smiled sweetly at his look of utter dismay.

'Yes, Alfred. This is my idea.'

5

First Kiss

The rest of that day passed as though nothing had happened to change our relationship. At lessons, I was stern and unsmiling, the businesslike governess and no more. At meals, he ate little; he looked frightened and gazed at me with pleading, bewildered eyes. That night, however, he knocked at my door.

'I do not recall inviting you, Alfred,' I answered, without opening the door. 'Have you any shillings for me, Alfred?' I said slyly. 'I suppose not, now that your source has been blocked.'

'No, Mistress, I haven't. But surely –'

'Then go away, you foolish boy. We shall be up early to go to the wood for your birch twigs. Then, after breakfast, well, you know what to expect.'

'I have never taken a birching before, Miss,' he said lamely.

'Then you have a new experience in store, haven't you? Now do not importune me further, unless you wish to receive an additional punishment for your insolence. Good night!'

'Good night, Miss,' he muttered sadly, and I listened to him slink away. I slept well that night!

The following morning, we walked through the dewy fields at sunrise, which was very invigorating. I had chosen this early hour so that none of the local folk should spy us. Even if we were surprised, I had a story ready about gathering botanical specimens, or some such, and had brought a long cricket bag to carry our birch twigs. It was already sunny, though the air was still fresh; the world was alive with the chirping of insects and birds, and I felt myself washed with a great joy at being part of its beauty. Freddie looked rather handsome in a sort of rough country smock, with Wellington boots, and was quite the rustic gentleman as he helped me over stiles and ditches. I smiled at him and chatted brightly, as though we were indeed going to collect mushrooms or butterflies, and not to make a whip for his body.

In Sally's Wood was a grove of birch trees; I pointed with my parasol to the twigs he should pluck, the hardest, juiciest ones. I made him snap them off to a length of about four feet, and place them neatly in the cricket bag, which he did with some nervousness.

All around us were the mysterious coloured arrows painted on the trees, and they seemed to point towards a large alder tree, whose bark was curiously bare, as though it were dead; yet it blossomed mightily with stout branches. I asked Freddie about the coloured marks.

'I don't know, Miss. But they say the wood is full of elves and pixies and other spirits.'

'Surely you do not believe that?' I laughed.

'The Whimbles have been here for thirty generations, Miss,' he said mysteriously, 'and we must live in harmony with the land and the tradition of the country folk. There are things into which it is unwise to enquire too deeply. Mama says the marks are to do with weather, crops and so on.'

'Very well,' I said. 'How many birch twigs have we got now?'

'Four, Miss.'

56

'That will do. Let us return.'

Impishly, I picked some bluebells and daisies, and put them in his hair.

'There!' I cried. 'You are as pretty as a picture!'

'You mock me, Mistress,' he said, but grinned sheepishly.

'Never,' I said quite seriously. 'I like you to look pretty for me, Alfred, especially when I think how your poor face will look when I apply four sturdy birch twigs to your bottom! Come on, do not look so downcast! Surely you have been beaten before?'

'Only with a cane, Mistress,' he said. 'And it stings so horribly, I am dreading the birch. It must be awful!'

'It is, Alfred,' I said, smiling merrily, 'it is.'

We retraced our steps and I asked casually:

'Did your Papa often beat you, Alfred?'

'Yes . . . on my pyjamas, usually with a strap, but sometimes with a cane. Then when he went away, Mama would beat me, but always with a cane. That was before the arthritis made it impossible.'

'When your father went away?' I asked, puzzled. 'Surely you mean whenever he was away.'

'Yes, Miss,' he corrected himself hurriedly, very red in the face. 'I mean, during Papa's absences, Mama would beat me. Gosh, Miss, you, a girl, I mean, you cannot imagine the pain.'

'I certainly can, Alfred,' I said coolly. 'Girls are punished too, you know, and I once received three strokes on my naked bottom when I had offended against the rules of St Agatha's.'

'That must have hurt horribly!' he exclaimed.

'It did, Alfred, but as not as horribly as this birch is going to hurt you,' I said pleasantly as we re-entered the portals of Rakeslit Hall. I was pleased to see that Freddie removed the flowers from his hair and instead of discarding them, kept them as a souvenir, kissing them fervently as he put them in his pocket.

We enjoyed a hearty breakfast, at least I did, and then we ascended to Freddie's room where I showed him how to fashion the birch, binding a handle with three lengths of wire so that it formed a grip about sixteen inches long. The remaining thirty or so inches of the twigs were splayed gracefully: a wicked instrument of discipline. I swished it once or twice on the leather sofa and he winced as the twigs cracked on the fabric.

'An excellent job, Alfred,' I said briskly. 'This should really give you a tanning to remember. Well, you had better undress. Take off all your clothes below your waist, and knot your shirt-tails high. I want a good wide view of you.'

As he doffed his trousers, I examined his comfortable, slightly untidy boy's room with some curiosity. I liked the manly smell of cricket bats, boots, sweat and leather, and the hint of . . . muddiness, which was quite exciting! Along with photographs, oars and sporting bric-à-brac, there was the skin and head of a flayed goat pinned most dramatically to the wall. When I remarked on this, Freddie, naked below the waist, was just knotting up his shirt above his belly button. I asked about it, and he said it was his pet goat that had died when he was little, so his father had flayed it for him and cured the skin as a keepsake.

'I was very fond of her, Miss,' he said with a sigh. 'Well, I suppose I am ready now.'

But as he stood before me, his cock trembled, then stiffened until it was fully erect, to his great embarrassment and my great amusement!

'Do you usually become stiff before a beating?' I asked severely.

'Sometimes, Mistress.'

'When your Mama was caning you?'

'Yes . . . but only sometimes.'

I slapped the stiff cock very gently with the ends of my birch.

He shuddered as the whip touched his skin.

'Well,' I said, 'I think that after the first stroke with this your cock will behave himself, don't you?'

'Yes, Miss,' he said miserably, 'but please, I beg you, strap me down, and give me a gag between my teeth, otherwise I don't think I could take it.'

'I suppose that is in order,' I said, rubbing my chin thoughtfully. 'You are young, after all, and it is your first taste of the birch.'

Soon I had him stretched across the table, his wrists and ankles lashed to its legs with strong leather thongs. His belly was pressed flat on the table top, and beneath the table, his cock still stood hard, his swollen glans stroking the wood.

I felt giddy with power at this delicious spectacle, and – I could not help myself – my panties were becoming quite wet. My heart pounded, and on impulse, I untied his shirt from his waist and lifted it over his neck so that his rippling bare back and buttocks were fully exposed to my lustful view.

I had in readiness a third leather strap with which to gag him tightly.

My hand reached out to caress his shoulders, and I marvelled at the smooth skin and the taut muscles beneath. Then my fingers crept down his spine, softly stroking him as they descended to the base, that sensitive acorn from which pleasure grows.

The room was still in the dappled morning light, silent but for faint birdsong and the sound of our breath: his, deep and laboured and my own coming nervously in little gasps.

59

I then ran my fingers down the cleft of his buttocks, almost to his anus bud, then repeated this action over and over, allowing my moist palm to stroke his tense smooth skin, comforting him with my touch.

'Oh,' he said, in a little choked voice as I caressed him.

'Well then, Freddie,' I said with a sigh, but I could not go on.

I continued to stroke his lovely globes, thinking all the while that I would soon be obliged to kiss them with my whip. There was a lump in my throat, for I could not bring myself to inflict such punishment on that sweet boy.

'Yes, Miss?' he said quietly.

'I . . . Oh, Freddie, sweet Freddie,' was my only reply. My heart had melted, and I was no longer the harsh mistress, ready to subdue my young naked buck, but a nurse, a lover. I wanted to release him from his bonds, take him to my breast and hug him. What a fool I had been!

'Please, Miss,' he said, 'hurry and get it over with. I can take it, I know I can.'

And my heart broke.

'No, Freddie, you shan't! I cannot do it,' I cried. 'I will release you. I will tell your mother a white lie, anything, I will say that you took your punishment and she will be satisfied and everything will be all right.'

'No, Miss,' he replied with surprising harshness. 'Mama has ordered me to be whipped, and whipped I must be.'

'It was my suggestion, and I have changed my mind!'

'Mama pays your salary, Miss,' he said coldly. 'And your duties include administering punishment to me when necessary. At this time you are to lay two strokes of the birch on my naked bottom. Why, it is only two! Do not insult me by suggesting I can't take them.'

'Two with the birch, Freddie,' I cried. 'Have you any idea how awful an engine it is? Not just a simple cane, but four vicious rods bound together. So one stroke alone is like ... Oh I cannot imagine it! To have to watch your sweet bottom squirm in torment, it is more than I can bear! Please do not make me, Freddie, I beg you!'

Tears sprang to my eyes, and I bent down to press my lips to his bare bottom, which I covered with kisses.

'Compose yourself, Miss,' he said severely. 'I have done wrong and must be beaten for it. I do not wish to report to Mama that you have been remiss in your duties.'

His peremptory tone stung me with its insolence, and brought me back to my senses. I stood up, drawing a deep breath, knowing that my moment of weakness had gone and I was once more the boy's governess. Now I stroked his buttocks, not with hand or lips, but with the cold rods of the birch. And I was pleased to see him flinch.

'Very well, Alfred,' I sneered. 'You think yourself a brave young whelp, don't you? Can you feel my birch rods tickle your bum? Slowly, gently ... that's nice, isn't it? How hard they are, how springy and strong! Four of them, four comrades waiting to kiss that soft bottom of yours. Think what it will feel like as I punish you for your wickedness, only two strokes to be sure, but each stroke will contain four of these *bâtons de correction*. I promise to lash you so hard you will want to scream; the first stroke will make you jump like a colt. The tears will flood your eyes, you won't be able to help that, and you will sink your

61

teeth into your leather gag. You will be right
ashamed of blubbing, and of your arse jerking at the
dreadful stinging, my boy. And then the really horrid
part will be waiting for the second stroke, for you
won't know when she is to come. I may wait a second, or a minute, or an hour. And in all that time you
will be alone with your fear and your humiliation. It
will make you think about your thieving ways, won't
it?'

But Freddie said nothing.

'Lost your tongue, boy?' I snapped.

Still he was silent.

'Well, sir, you leave me no choice but to punish
you with the utmost severity,' I said in as formal a
voice as I could muster.

He allowed me to gag him tightly without protest.

I seethed with fury at his haughtiness, and regretted
having assigned him a mere two strokes, although the
governors of Her Majesty's Prisons generally considered that punishment enough.

I took off my boots and stockings, so that my feet
would get a good grip on the polished floor, for I
intended to take a nice long run-up. His thighs were
well splayed, giving me a view of his balls, and that
impudent erection still in place. Damn him, how I
longed to touch him there! But I resisted the temptation, and positioned myself about eighteen feet away
in the corner of the room. I swished the birch in the
air and charged twice without delivering a blow, until
I was sure of my aim. How the poor boy flinched,
anticipating a blow that never came! My heart thum-
ped with joy.

'Now, Alfred,' I said slowly, 'I am ready to skin
you. By God how it will hurt! I will make you shiver,
sir, as you have never shivered; squirm under my lash
until your flogged arse dances with a life of its own.'

And still he made no sound.

I intended to approach him on the slant, the birch in one hand as high as I could raise it, then, at the last moment, to reach up and grasp it with both hands in order to bring it down on him with the full force of my arms.

I was panting quite hoarsely as I prepared to deliver the first stroke. I began to run slowly, then picked up speed, faster, faster, until I was right beside him, and – now – up with both my hands, the birch falling hard as a guillotine, to deliver a perfect stroke as I swept past him.

The birch whistled and its loud crack echoed through the room.

I skidded to a halt just by his shoulders and surveyed Freddie's naked body. The buttocks, livid, clenched madly, pumping in and out as though this frantic pressure would ease his pain. His eyes were shut tight and his breath growled deep in his throat.

I felt thrillingly, dangerously exalted, to think that my body could exert such power over another's. I gasped for breath and moved back out of his sight, watching him tremble. How I longed to flay that helpless body, to skin it alive, to reduce it to a single point of unwavering pain, and wrap myself in Freddie's skin so that he would belong to me forever! I was electric, and became aware of the moisture flowing between my thighs, the tingling in my breasts and clit, and the oily dampness of my panties.

'Well then, sir,' I gasped in what I imagined to be an imperious tone. I was surprised how weak my voice sounded.

'Mm . . .' he whimpered very softly.

I could not help myself. I lowered my panties to mid-thigh, and stood with my legs slightly apart so that the wet fabric was stretched between them like a drumskin. Then my fingers darted to my clit, all tingling and swollen and, as my hand bathed in my warm flow, I frigged myself very quickly and with fevered caresses. My breath was rasping, my whole body trembled, full of sweetness, and I knew I was about to spend.

Controlling myself with difficulty, I paused in my caresses and replaced my sodden panties, then withdrew to deliver my second stroke. I took a few minutes to calm myself, for I knew that if I brought myself now to orgasm I should be too weak and too unwilling to deliver the necessary punishment. A few minutes, I say, but it could have been a few hours! Time was still, and it seemed as though there were nothing else in the whole world but me and my sweet captive.

As last I began my second approach, padding on tiger feet that ran faster as I neared my victim, my whip held high. His bottom had stopped its ferocious squirming, but shivered a little, and I saw his buttocks tighten as my run quickened and my thudding feet were beside him, and the birch whistled its deadly wail and cracked on his naked skin with all the force my strong arms could muster. It lay on him for an awful split second, as though clinging hungrily, then slid across his reddened flesh in a lingering kiss before it was free.

Freddie began to sob, quietly and uncontrollably.

And I too was uncontrollable. I stood behind him, my wet panties between my knees, my fingers spreading the lips of my cunt and tickling my clit as I gasped, breathless with electric pleasure. But it was not enough, not right, somehow. I reached out to stroke his beaten buttocks, with no cruel whip but with gentle fingers. And then with my other hand I placed the wrapped handle of the birch, still moist from my palm, between my thighs. I squeezed it there tightly and rubbed it against my clit, making the cruel birch twigs soft and damp with my flowing love juice.

I did not know if Freddie was aware of what I was doing, and to this day he has never mentioned it, but I did not care. I stroked my clit ever so gently with that birch as I caressed the boy's skin which I had flogged, and came to an orgasm which made me shudder and cry out with tortured little yelps deep in my throat. My body glowed with fierce joy. I was so proud of Freddie, for taking his punishment like the man he was.

My cunt dripped with my love juice, and my nipples stood gloriously stiff, so excited was I by the sight of this helpless young buck whose naked body I had flogged! I put aside the birch and raised his shirt, to reveal a face knotted in anguish, his eyes welling with tears. He had half bitten through his leather belt. I took it from between his teeth, and gently knelt to unbutton his shirt. I stroked his hair.

'You are the bravest boy in the world, Freddie,' I said softly.

Then I unfastened his straps and helped him to his feet.

'Mistress,' he groaned, 'please give me the birch, so that I may kiss it.'

'Kiss it?'

'I want to kiss it to thank you for my punishment, Miss, and to show you that I am yours to command, to punish as you see fit. I am your slave, Mistress. Look – after all that pain, my cock is still stiff for you – because the pain was your gift!'

I allowed him to kiss the birch, and then made him lie on his bed.

He lay face down, with his thighs wide apart, and I sat behind him, admiring his body. He had taken *that* – and for me. Gently I slipped my hand between his thighs and under his belly, where my fingers found the swollen glans of his penis and began to caress it.

He moaned with pleasure, and I was very delicate in my frigging, for I sensed that he was not far from coming.

'You wish to be my slave, Alfred?'

'Oh, yes, Mistress!'

'Money is the price of a lady's favours or a lady's domination, Alfred. And if you have no money yourself, why you must get others to give it. If you, who are penniless, will pay a shilling to see my naked body, to feel my fingers stroking your naked cock like this –'

'Don't stop, please. It is so sweet!'

'Of course I won't stop, you silly boy, not until I feel your hot cream gush out all over my fingers. This is your reward for being such a brave boy. But think what wealthy men will give to see me, or . . . do more than look.'

'Mistress, I couldn't bear the thought of another man seeing your naked body!'

'Or even another woman,' I said thoughtfully, frigging him all the time. 'What does it matter, as long as I am happy? Eh, slave? You want my happiness, do you not?'

'Yes, Mistress. Please do not stop what you are doing . . .'

'Well, you shall achieve my happiness by being totally obedient. If you are naughty or fractious, I will have to give you another whipping, but far more severe, so you will not be disobedient, will you?'

'No . . .'

I laughed slyly.

'Not even the tiniest bit naughty? Tell me the truth, Alfred. Wouldn't you like me to flog you again, very,

very hard? Wouldn't you be naughty if you thought I wanted it? And then I should have to whip you until you begged me to stop? Wouldn't you?'

'Yes, Mistress. Oh yes!'

And with that his cock convulsed, spurting a fierce jet of hot spend over my hand.

Freddie was truly my slave.

Nothing further was said about the matter, except that as we were going in to luncheon, Lady Whimble said drily:

'Good girl, I believe we have made Whimble see reason. He'll be taking the next few meals standing up. Not up to these jobs myself, it is this accursed arthritis. How many did he take?'

'Two, Milady,' I replied, 'and he took them like a man.'

'Good,' she said, nodding, then sighed and shook her head.

'Ah, if only Whimble were here!'

6

A New Acquaintance

'I say, Miss,' said Freddie, 'this is really ripping stuff.'

It was a few days after his punishment, and he no longer grimaced when he sat down.

'I am glad you think so, Alfred,' I said, 'and you have done a good translation.' I read out:

The combat on the beach at dawn was furious, merci-less and untrammelled in its ferocity. Poor Albert stood no chance against the virile Henri, who stabbed, pierced and skewered him with his rapier until his stomach, heart and entrails gushed out. Albert collapsed on the blood-soaked sand, and his body was washed away by the tide.

Yvette rushed to embrace Henri her victorious lover, although if Albert had won, she would have embraced him just as fervently!

But Henri spurned her advances, pushing her to her knees on the wet sand and administering a savage thrashing with his sword.

'You are nothing but a whore, a slut, a hussy!' he roared.

'No, Henri!' pleaded Yvette, her flogged bottom smart-ing under her wet knickers. 'There was nothing between me and Albert. He was my cousin!'

*'Then you have committed incest, a sin and a felony.
And you shall reap the rewards of your sluthood! You
shall stand at the corner of the Rue de Coxyde in Zee-
brugge and sell your body to the matelots. And I shall
spend the money you earn on gambling, whoring and
drunken revelry!'*

*Thus was Yvette reduced to a life of sin, a common
whore who lifted her skirts for any jack tar who wished
to perform filthy practices upon her body. Every day
she was poked and rogered in the back rooms of dingy
taverns, and every night she was whipped ruthlessly on
her naked bottom by the drunken Henri, who had been
expelled from his regiment for debauchery, and lived off
her immoral earnings. Yvette had given up all hope of
a white wedding in the Cathedral of St Fiacre!*

'I think you will have no trouble gaining a place in
the Diplomatic Corps, Alfred,' I said warmly, 'although I am not sure about the word sluthood.
However, tell me – how are your wounds healing?
Are you comfortable?'

'I still feel ticklish, Miss, and it will be a while before I ride a horse again.'

'Well, I have received a package from my druggist
in London.' (This was the faithful Mr Izzard). 'I
ordered a special ointment which I think will be effi-
cacious. So come to my room tonight and I will apply
some to the afflicted parts.'

'Yes, Mistress. Oh yes!' he blurted.

'The purpose of the visit will be strictly medicinal,'
I warned him sternly. He was a little crestfallen, but
cheered up when I told him that I would personally
rub the ointment in – if he was a good boy.

'Why, Mistress,' he cried, 'I have already been a
good boy, as I am sure you will agree. I have spread

the word in Budd's Titson about your wonderful abilities as a mistress!'

'Hmmm . . .' I said. 'I am not sure if there will be many shillings in teaching French to the Cornish folk.'

'But I said that you were the most beautiful woman in the world, Mistress,' he continued eagerly, 'which is true. And that just to look at you, and breathe your perfume, was far more thrilling than any lesson.'

I was secretly pleased at this, but said:

'That was very forward of you, Alfred. Forward bordering on impudent. And on the subject of impudence, I can clearly see a bulge in your trousers as you talk to me. You have allowed your penis to stand, unbidden by me. It is quite insolent of you, sir! I think I shall have to find other ways of taming you.'

'I am yours to command, Mistress,' blurted Freddie.

'Till tonight, then.'

That afternoon I walked the mile or so into the village, to take tea at Miss Chytte's teashop. I was already on nodding acquaintance with many of the villagers, which was a great mark of respect in Cornwall, for I gathered that I would have to live there most of a lifetime before they actually smiled. I passed Mr Tannoc's bakery, where I saw the baker in earnest conversation with the vicar, and also Dorkins. They looked secretive, and did not return my salutation, but ignored me, which I thought rather hurtful, but did not dwell on the matter. I entered Miss Chytte's establishment, where I ordered a lavish tea with scones and cream from the serving girl, a pretty, sluttish young thing with a sullen country face.

As I was eating, Miss Chytte herself approached my table and asked if she could join me.

I accepted with pleasure, glad of the company. She was a handsome woman of, I guessed, twenty-five years; very slim, with a tiny bosom and a narrow waist which swelled into a bottom of rather alarming and voluptuous size. Her black hair was fetchingly cut short in a rather mannish style. Brown eyes sparkled with ready intelligence; the lips were thin and wide, the nose quite large and aquiline. She was in fact what the French call *jolie-laide*, meaning handsome but in a quirky sort of way, not according to the classical tenets of beauty. I found her quite intriguing, and she looked out of place in these rural surroundings. She would have seemed more at home strutting in Park Lane or Kensington, and had something of the courtesan about her.

She told me that she was here because she had been engaged to a wealthy gentleman of the locality whom she had met in London. But he had been killed by a fall from his horse, while riding near Sally's Wood and, after his estate had been settled, she found herself in possession of a little money. It was not enough to establish herself back in town (she was originally from Croydon, in Surrey) where property was expensive. But she had enough to buy the teashop, with the apartments above it, and professed to be happy enough with her lot, although I detected a great wistfulness in the manner with which she plied me for details of life in London.

She claimed, somewhat unconvincingly, that the teashop would serve her as a marriage portion, although even I could tell that Cornwall was not exactly awash with eligible young gentlemen of taste and breeding. My resolve was strengthened by this conversation, namely, never to let myself become dependent on the whims or availability of the male sex.

Eventually Miss Chytte came to the point.

'I have heard, Miss Cumming, that you give excellent tuition in the French language.'

'Very kind of you, Miss Chytte – I must assume that you heard it from young Alfred Whimble.'

'Why, yes, Alfred did mention it the other day. He comes in from time to time. I think he used to have a yen for my waitress Prunella, but now all he talks of is you, and what a wonderful mistress you are.'

'Well,' I replied cautiously, 'he is a very nice boy, but I fear he has a vivid imagination.'

'He said that he enjoys being . . . disciplined, Miss Cumming.'

'I am glad to hear that, Miss Chytte,' I replied coolly, 'for discipline, sometimes quite severe, is necessary in study as in all walks of life. And I am not one of those who shirks from imposing proper discipline on my charges.'

She looked at me with her lustrous brown eyes that sparkled hard as diamonds.

'The thing is, I have a little competence in that language, but it has gone rusty through disuse. I have in mind the current popularity of tourism as devised by Mr Thomas Cook, and thought that it would be an attraction to foreign visitors if they could visit an establishment such as my own where they might converse in their own language. Cornwall has always had close links with the French province of Brittany, across the Channel.'

'I see,' I said thoughtfully. 'You wish to brush up on your French under my tutelage, is that it?'

'Yes, indeed, if you could undertake the necessary amount of lessons.'

'In London, the rate would be a shilling an hour. But as we are between friends, Miss Chytte, shall we say ninepence?'

'Most satisfactory, Miss Cumming,' she smiled. 'Now, it is difficult, as you can appreciate, for me to leave my workplace during the day, and to visit you in your room at Rakeslit Hall might be thought indiscreet. Could you give the lessons here, in my apartments upstairs?'

'Why, gladly, Miss Chytte,' I said, and we agreed that I would attend her in her apartment the following afternoon.

That night Freddie came to my room. I admitted him without delay, feigning astonishment that the lustful whelp was perfectly, thrillingly hard for me. I tapped his manhood with my fingertip, quite hard, and he flinched.

'Something will have to be done about this, Alfred,' I said sternly. 'It is quite unseemly. I shall think of a suitable means of restraint, since you are evidently incapable of self-restraint. Now, though, to the business: take off all your clothes and lie down on the bed, and I will apply some of my special ointment.'

I took a bottle of salve from Mr Izzard's medical and hygienic box, and rubbed in a liberal portion of sweet-scented cream, allowing my fingers to linger voluptuously on his lovely bare bum.

'You should be as good as new tomorrow,' I said brightly. He sat up, his stiff prick pointing at me like a rampant serpent.

'But,' I added, 'there remains the problem of what to do about this.' And I gave his member a hearty tap. He moaned softly.

'It is because of you, Mistress,' he said. 'Whenever I think of you, my prick rises. It is always stiff, because I cannot stop thinking of you. Especially after –'

'Enough!' I cried. 'I am your governess, your mistress, and that is all. Hmmph! I suppose you have been frigging yourself on numerous occasions, unable to control your spermatorrhoea?'

'Yes, Mistress,' he said sheepishly, and blushed.

'How often? Every day?'

'Four or five times every day, Mistress,' he replied, not without a hint of pride.

'It doesn't seem to do much good, does it?' I said. 'There is too much spunk in those lusty balls of yours, young man. I think I have something in my medical box which will solve the problem of your uncontrollable erections. First, though, we must empty you of sperm.'

So saying, I cupped his balls in one hand and began to vigorously rub his penis with the other. I squeezed his glans hard between my thumb and forefinger, taking care to draw the foreskin back to its fullest extent at each stroke of my rubbing.

The sight of his engorged glans appearing like a huge glowing red mushroom, then retreating into the tight foreskin, only to emerge once more – over and over again – was tremendously exciting to me, and I felt my cunt become well moistened. I longed to feel him enter me with his cock, but restrained myself. At this moment, my hand ruthlessly milking his manhood of sperm, I was his mistress. He reached out to embrace me but I slapped his hand away.

'Obedience!' I cried. 'Well, perhaps . . .'

Casually, I raised my nightdress and parted my thighs so that he could see my swollen red lips and then I guided his fingers to my stiff clitoris and showed him how to rub it for my utmost pleasure. As soon as his fingers touched me there, he spurted a great jet of hot spunk all over my hand, and his frigging of my own clit became feverish, so that it was not long before I spent too, with a great moan of joy.

But I did not discontinue my frigging of his cock, much to his surprise. I carried on relentlessly, rubbing and tickling and squeezing until his engine was mighty and stiff again.

74

'Oh, Miss, how beautifully you do it. Please do not stop . . . I am going to spend soon, my balls ache to spend again for you.'

'Then keep your fingers on my clitty, Alfred,' I ordered, trying not to let my voice break with excitement, 'for that is pleasant too. Is your cock sore?'

'A little,' he admitted. 'But please don't stop.'

'Oh, I won't sir,' I panted, 'and neither must you, until I order it so.'

We sat on the bed, caressing each other in a fury of lust. He rapidly came to another orgasm, and I allowed his sperm to cascade over me without pausing for a moment in my frigging, so that his prick was not permitted to soften even for a moment. All the time, his frenzied fingers probed my soaking cunt and diddled my clit, and I lost count of the number of times my belly heaved in ecstasies of my own.

'Have you ever thought of other girls when you frigged yourself?' I demanded. 'Of Prunella in the village, for example?'

'Well, yes, Mistress, I admit it. Before I met you!'

I slapped him viciously on his balls, and he groaned.

'But now and forever I shall think of no one but you, Mistress,' he cried. I redoubled the vigour of my rubbing until my breasts shook. Freddie's face was red and covered in sweat as I made him spend for a fourth and last time, and his prick finally went all limp.

'I am so sore, Mistress,' he moaned, 'I do not think there is a drop left in me. Now I must make water, if you please.'

I gave him leave to go to the lavatory while I lay back, exhausted by my own spending, which tires a woman just as the ejaculation of sperm tires a man. When he came back, I wiped his cock dry, and held up the device I had fetched from Mr Izzard's box.

'This, Alfred, is known as a restrainer,' I said.

'It looks like a little horse's harness,' he said uncertainly.

'Yes – and you are going to be my little horse.'

The restrainer was a steel appliance which I fitted round the base of his penis and a chain which I looped tightly round the loose skin of his ball sac, just above those precious orbs. Then I snapped the lock shut and removed the key. He looked down at his trussed cock, somewhat puzzled.

'It is very pretty, Mistress,' he said doubtfully.

'Yes – but be warned, Alfred, that if your cock attempts to rise as a result of wicked lustful thoughts, the ring and chain will tighten viciously and you will feel the most horrible pain. It is a device to combat spermatorrhoea, or the wasteful emission of semen, whether by your own frigging or by nocturnal spurting during dreams. It is for your own good.'

'How long must I wear it, Mistress?' he asked.

'Why, for as long as I say, slave!' I cried. 'And for that impertinent question – quite unnecessary – you may put these on over it, for they will be an extra torment and temptation to overcome, and thus show your self-control.' And I threw him a pair of my panties, the pink silk ones, which I had omitted to wash. He breathed in their aroma, and then put them on over his tethered cock and balls.

'It will be awfully hard to avoid lustful thoughts while I am wearing your sweet panties, Mistress,' he said. 'Even now, I feel my cock stirring and the ring tightening on my balls. Surely I have done nothing to deserve such torment?'

I laughed cruelly. 'You are a man, slave, and that is offence enough. To purge it you must offer your complete obedience – to me, your only Mistress. Why, I have done you a favour, Alfred, by milking your balls until your cock is as soft as a rose petal. We will see if you have the strength to keep it that way.'

Unexpectedly, he bowed. 'Mistress, it is indeed the duty, the honour and the ecstasy of my manhood to submit to your every wish. Whip me, chain me, humiliate my manhood in a thousand ways, and the greater my suffering, the greater my pleasure, because it is for you. Not only do you possess my heart, Mistress, but with this device into which you have locked me, you possess my balls, my very essence, too. To be your willing slave is an honour greater than any I could have imagined.'

77

7

Awakening Flesh

Miss Chytte's apartment was tastefully decorated. She had the usual clutter of bric-à-brac beloved of single ladies, but mostly of an artistic, rather than a sentimental nature, with pots and vases whose voluptuous mouldings bordered on the erotic. There was an abundance of statuary, all of it depicting the female nude in classical pose.

Over a cup of China tea, we discussed her knowledge of the French language, which I found to be pretty fair, although she was rather confused on points of grammar. Nevertheless she did quite well with a passage from Michelet's *Histoire de la France* which I gave her to translate, which impressed me greatly.

'Why, Miss Cumming, this stuff is rather dry, don't you think?' she grinned. 'I had in mind a sort of guided tour of interesting places in our history, with all the murders, battles, love affairs and so on. In short, a somewhat racier vocabulary.'

'Well,' I replied discreetly, 'if you want to perfect your French, Miss Chytte, I am afraid this is the sort of thing French people write.'

'But Alfred gave me to understand he had some quite . . . vivid matter to translate.'

'It is true that I have texts which are not so dry, as you put it,' I said, and handed her a section of my personal course book from amongst my papers. 'But it is perhaps more suitable for the male student.'

'Why, I am sure you will agree that a woman is a match for any male where intelligence and taste are concerned, Miss Cumming,' she said, 'and perhaps superior.'

I looked at the sumptuous nudes which thronged her apartment, and smiled, as she began to peruse my copy.

'I cannot but agree, Miss Chytte,' I replied. 'Perhaps you would be so good as to translate?'

At once, she rattled off a near-perfect translation, and far from experiencing difficulties of vocabulary, she actually added bits! The passage is where Henri delivers a savage flogging to Yvette, and is interrupted by a rival panderer, who engages him in a bloody fist-fight and ends up by throwing him out of the window where he lands with a mortal impact on the cobblestones of the Rue de Dixmuide. She prattled in high excitement:

Henri's cane mercilessly lashed the succulent, naked buttocks of the squirming whore, whose breasts quivered helplessly as she writhed in torment ...

'Very good, Miss Chytte,' I smiled. 'But I fear that in your enthusiasm you have embellished things somewhat. For example, I do not see the word "succulent" to describe Yvette's buttocks.'

Miss Chytte's face was flushed.

'Oh, well, they sounded succulent, Miss Cumming. Just imagine, the plump young girl's juicy bottom, writhing under that scoundrel's cane. And I have no doubt that her breasts were big and lovely and firm ... like yours, Miss Cumming, if I may say so.'

She put her hand softly on mine, and our eyes met.

Without taking her gaze from mine, she suddenly overturned an ink pot, so that the page of text was spoiled.

'Oh, silly me!' she cried. 'I have ruined your pages.' But she did not make any move to wipe up the stain.

'It is nothing,' I replied. 'I have others.'

'But it is something! I am sure if young Alfred Whimble had been so clumsy, you would punish him.'

'Certainly, but –'

'How? A sound spanking, I suppose? Even a thrashing?'

'Well, possibly, Miss Chytte.' Her eyes were moist and glistening. 'Perhaps even . . . certainly.'

'Very well, Miss Cumming, you must not treat me any differently. Discipline is so important.'

'Why, you are not suggesting that a lady should spank another lady, Miss Chytte?' I said softly, with a sly smile.

'And why not?' she said. 'Many's the time I have pulled down Prunella's panties to spank her bottom when she has been clumsy. Besides, Alfred intimated that you were a very strict disciplinarian . . .'

How much *had* Freddie told her? Common sense, caution, and indeed my own personal tastes urged me to meet this woman's demands.

'Very well, Miss Chytte, I shall spank you. On your bare bottom.'

'More than a spanking, please, Miss Cumming. You must teach me a *real* lesson.' Her voice was soft and thrilled me.

She rose and went into the bedroom, telling me to wait until she called me in. Through the closed door, I heard noises of drawers being opened and the rustling of clothes. At last she called me to enter.

She lay face down on the crimson bedspread. Her skirts and petticoats were pulled up to her shoulders and her legs and buttocks were naked. A yellow cane with a curved handle lay on the bed beside her. Her buttocks were quite superb, muscled and smooth and rounded like shiny pears: but they were faintly mottled.

'Please, Miss Cumming,' she said in a small voice, 'flog me on my naked bottom.'

I picked up the cane and felt its shiny but rough surface, which I imagined would add pepper to each stroke.

'How hard?' I asked softly.

'Tight . . . very tight.'

I lifted the cane high and obliged her.

As I stroked her naked bottom, she moaned deep in her throat, and it was not a moan of pain. At length, panting, I put the cane aside and stroked her with my hand. Her skin was burning hot.

She was gasping and sighing, and her hips quivered, for all the world as though she were spending. I stood and watched her writhing buttocks, thinking that we must make a pretty tableau. At last she whimpered and her movements became nothing more than a gentle quivering.

'God, I needed that, Miss,' she panted. 'I have not had such a lovely thrashing for ages.'

'What a curious locution,' I replied. 'A lovely thrashing is surely a contradiction in terms, like . . . like a good pain.'

Miss Chytte turned her face from its pillow and grinned fiercely.

'Deep down, you know, Miss Cumming, I can tell. I mean, the ecstasy of the lash. God, the way you flogged me so tightly! The beauty of your strokes. I am sure your body yearns for the kiss of the whip.'

'I am not sure of that,' I said. 'Discipline and proper punishment, that is one thing, but –'

'I am not talking about punishment,' she cried. 'I mean the beauty of self-sacrifice, when the soul triumphs over the flesh, and thus frees itself. To be alone, supremely alone in a universe of pain, where all vanishes except the pitiless lash on one's naked skin . . . and afterwards, the sweet glow of pain endured and mastered. Be honest, Miss Cumming, when you were spanked as a child, did you not secretly enjoy it, afterwards?'

'I was not spanked,' I said. 'My father was a kind man.'

'Mine, too. He beat me on my naked bottom with a belt or crop, and afterwards was as loving as a father can be.'

Suddenly, I felt a surge of jealousy!

'How very fortunate, Miss Chytte. You are able to equate pain with love. It is not the case with me. I remember receiving three strokes of the cane at St Agatha's, my old school, and there was no love involved at all.'

'But afterwards,' she persisted, 'did you not relish the hot glow – look at yourself proudly in the mirror?'

'How did you know that?' I cried, blushing furiously.

'You and I are alike, Miss Cumming,' she said with an impish grin. 'We girls love to show off our bodies. For example, I adore feeling your gaze on my naked bottom, which you have just tickled so nicely. Don't worry – by dint of frequent floggings, my hide became tough as leather at a very early age. In an hour I will feeling nothing more than a lovely warm tingle.'

'Well, Miss Chytte,' I said, 'I trust you have had full value from your French lesson! There remains the matter of my ninepence.'

She burst out laughing.

'Take a shilling from my purse, Miss,' she giggled, 'for I am quite swell, you know, and tip handsomely for good service. You didn't think I got you here just to teach languages, surely?'

With a smile I told her that I supposed she was right. I had sensed her wishes, and realised they were my wishes too. I told her it would indeed be a shame to discontinue her lessons, and that for a shilling a session, I was prepared to provide the most intimate of tuition.

She agreed, and promised me that I too would in due course long to feel the lash on my naked body, a proposition to which I demurred for the moment.

But as I walked back to Rakeslit Hall, I wondered how long it would be before I too gave way to the yearning in my body, the desire to wash myself in an ocean of pain.

That night, I summoned Freddie to my room, for I felt mischievous and hot; the sight of Miss Chytte's magnificent bare arse, all red, would not leave me.

I admitted him and at once began to undress, as though he were not there. Matter-of-factly I removed my skirt and petticoats, and described my profitable day with Miss Chytte, including her punishment, though I made out that I had imposed rather than agreed to it.

The poor lamb goggled as he saw my yellow satin bloomers, which came to just above my knees and had a creamy lace trim. I saw the bulge of his prick tremble, and his eyes close in distress as he fought to control his erection.

I sat down on the bed with my thighs apart so that he had a good view of my intimate area.

'You are wearing my pink panties over your cock ring, Alfred?' I asked.

'Of course, Mistress. But it is dashed painful. I

83

have managed to keep myself under control, but it has been a battle. Even now I am trying not to look at the place between your legs with which you are so cruelly tempting me.'

I laughed, and my fingers strayed across the tight yellow satin, to my quim, which was clearly outlined. With slow, deliberate strokes, I began to tickle my clitoris as he watched.

'Remove your lower garments, Alfred.'

He took off his trousers, then the pink panties, and stood before me with his tumescent cock straining against the cruel steel thong. Calmly I frigged myself through the damp satin, my breath growing heavy as I watched that juicy young cock struggling to remain soft. The skin of his cock and tight balls bulged against the hard steel band, and he sweated in his confusion.

'Please, Mistress, release me I beg you, from my restrainer. It hurts so!'

'I am testing you, Alfred,' I replied coolly. 'If you have no self-control, why then it *should* hurt.'

His penis gave up the battle, and rose to full stiffness, creasing his face in pain.

'Flog me, Mistress, if you wish to torment me. But this is devilish!'

I was frigging myself quite rapidly – I could feel a spend coming and abruptly tore down my bloomers to reveal my wet swollen cunt. I carefully drew back the lips.

'Watch me,' I cooed. 'Don't you just long to plunge your stiff cock here into my love gash? It is most exciting for me to watch my naked slave, helpless and tortured by his lust for my body.'

'Please frig me, Miss, at least!' he cried. 'Touch me with your lovely fingers, and I promise I shall spend in an instant, and my cock will be soft again!'

'No, Alfred,' I replied. 'No ... and do not touch yourself there, or you will have the birch – and not a paltry two, either.'

I looked at his cock; it was monstrous and hard, with a bluish tint where the cock-ring was choking the blood from it. I felt myself on the verge of coming – and jumped to my feet. I proceeded to unlock his restrainer, at which he sobbed with relief. Then I lay back on the bed with my thighs wide.

'You have suffered enough, you lustful thing,' I said amicably. 'Now fuck me.'

He needed no encouragement; his huge cock was inside me before I could draw breath. Its base rubbed my clit as I had shown him, and I gasped with the raw, desperate force of his brute fucking. I cried out in a delicious spend almost at once. No sooner had he delivered a dozen or so strokes than he too spent with a great howl of ecstasy or despair, as my greedy cunt milked the spunk from his balls.

'Well,' I said, pretending to be cross, 'that did not take long, did it?' His cock went limp, and slipped from my oily cunt. 'I want more,' I added simply.

'I will be hard again in a moment, Mistress, I promise,' he said.

'You cannot fill a purse with promises,' I retorted, 'nor a woman's cunt with a soft cock. Very well, frig yourself and tell me when you are man enough for me.'

I yawned and reached for the newspaper, feigning indifference, although I was watching him out of the corner of my eye. I made sure he had a stimulating view of my open cunt lips and it was quite exciting to see his frigging. Like most boys, he was well-practised at the art of onanism, and he rubbed his cock quite skilfully as I nonchalantly riffled through the paper, pretending not to notice his grunting exertions.

One item caught my eye: the marriage was announced between Miss Daphne Tubb, headmistress of St Agatha's, Wimbledon, and Mr William Lowe, solicitor of Finsbury Circus. I filed this information in my mental book of accounts to be settled.

I put down the paper: Freddie's cock was nearly stiff, so I opened my blouse and bared my bubbies for his stimulation.

'Come on, Freddie, my sweet,' I whispered, tweaking my nipples to a tingling hardness. 'Let me have that great engine inside me, splitting me and spurting your hot spunk in my womb.'

Such talk excites men, or men's vanity. In no time he was rampantly stiff, and I knelt to present my arse to him. Then I showed him how to fuck me, doggy fashion, as I had seen demonstrated in my book. He performed superbly, clasping my breasts roughly with one hand while diddling my clitty with the other. I heard him roar as I felt the spunk jet inside me, and then I spent too, with his head sunk onto my perspiring back. It was quite delicious, the doggy position, but I had an appetite for something sweeter still, sweeter because forbidden . . .

I let him lie beside me, and he kissed my breasts as I cradled him in my arms, as though I were his Mama. I tickled his balls, and said that I thought there must be another lot of sperm to be emptied from them, so that I could replace his restrainer. He assented with a glum mutter.

'You have never done it with a girl before, Freddie, have you?'

'Not with a girl, Mistress.'

'But with boys? At school? Tell me – I know what goes on.'

'Yes . . . yes, we would frig each other, at night in the dormitory. We would climb into bed and fondle each other's penis, until it was hard.'

'And did the spunk come?'

'Not when I was very little, but later, yes.'

'And later, did you do *more* than frig? There is nothing shameful, for I know it is a phase boys go through.'

'Well ... as I got older, frigging did not seem enough. I longed to put my cock into a nice warm place ...'

'The bum of another boy?'

'Yes, Mistress. There were no girls, of course, so we did it to each other, in the bumhole. In the dark you can pretend that you are fucking a girl.'

'Did you take other boys' cocks in your own bum?'

He hesitated.

'Yes, Mistress. We took turns at being fucked. It hurt at first, but I admit I got to like it. Once I was ... fucked by ten boys one after the other. But you say it was not shameful?'

'Of course not, when you are young and immature. Did you like that? It must have been sore.'

'I did like it, especially when the spunk came. You see, I closed my eyes and imagined it was the matron. Every Sunday morning she would make the boys line up, and she would put a rubber tube inside us and wash our insides.'

'An enema.'

'Yes, that is what she called it.' He giggled. 'And I always got a hard penis when she did it. I suppose you think I am silly.'

I stroked his hair. 'Not in the least, you pretty slave. But that is all finished, and now you are a man. And what a man!' I felt his cock rise with pride.

I thought of those juicy naked boys, like hot young rabbits in the moonlight, and my cunt started to flow with juice. I could not wait. I had to have him ... there!

'Well, now, Freddie, your cock is pleasingly stiff again, and you are going to fuck *me* in the bumhole.'

I was rather nervous, for my academic knowledge of this unusual act was about to be translated into reality, which I hoped would not be painful.

'Does the idea frighten you or dismay you, Freddie?'

'Mistress,' he cried, 'I long to fuck you in your sweet bumhole, for that is your desire.'

I resumed my doggy position on all fours.

'First, Freddie,' I ordered, 'you are to kiss my arse-bud – my anus. I want to feel your tongue well inside me, so stretch my buttocks tight as a drumskin.'

He stretched my buttocks quite painfully apart, and got his tongue into my arsehole to a depth of about an inch, which was enormously ticklish and exciting. I frigged my clit gently, then playfully tightened my sphincter muscle and squeezed his tongue, before forcing it out like a stool!

As his tongue slipped out, I had the most exciting tickling sensation, and I longed to feel the same with his fat penis. I was still nervous – his cock seemed so huge to fit into that small place. But I guided him towards me, helping the engorged member towards the opening of my arse-slit.

I cried out as he pierced my anus with his cock. I experienced a sudden sharp pain, and then he was all the way inside me, fucking me very hard. The pain gave way to a lovely sensation of warmth and bursting fullness.

With my sphincter, I squeezed his cock as hard as I could, matching the tensing of my muscle to the forceful rhythm of his thrusts.

He was kneeling behind me, hands resting on my buttocks; I made him remove one from my bum and guided his fingers to my clit, which felt so stiff and excited! I had not realised that arse-fucking – together with the stimulation of my clit – could be such ecstasy! I felt so totally, wonderfully, in the thrall of that ruthless giant cock!

'God, Freddie, fuck me, fuck me in the arse until I burst!' I heard myself squeal. 'Feel how tight and juicy I am for you, better than any boy . . .'

'Better than anything, Mistress,' he moaned. 'Yes, squeeze my cock like that, it is so good . . . squeeze me till my spunk shoots into your lovely hole!'

I made him withdraw all the way out of my anus at each thrust, then tickle my arse-bud with his glans a while before plunging fiercely all the way into me. In this way my pleasure was prolonged maddeningly, as though – I am almost ashamed to admit – I were stooling again and again . . .'

'Spank me, Freddie!' I cried in a frenzy of painful joy. 'Make my arse tingle as you fuck me, please. Oh please!'

Then I felt a rain of heavy slaps on my buttocks, stinging red-hot, such was the muscled force behind them. To have his strong arms beating me was thrilling, and my clit throbbed; my belly heaved, and I lost control of myself and released a flood of my water! It splashed our thighs, all hot, and at that moment he cried out that he was going to spend. An orgasm shook me with its hot sweetness, and I cried out as though in torment:

'Yes, Freddie, sweet boy, fuck me and spend all your hot spunk in my bum, you cruel lovely beast! How you hurt me with your spanking, but don't stop, spank me, fuck me, please, tan my bum till she is as red as my cunt, all hot and swollen. Oh God yes . . .'

His fingers mercilessly frigged my clit as I felt his hot creamy jet spurt into my tripes, and then his spent cock slid from my anus with a delicious tickle, and we fell exhausted.

'Mmmm,' was all I could think of to say, or rather purr, and I kissed him on the mouth, my tongue searching for his.

'Gosh,' he said at length, 'I must have spanked you awfully hard, Mistress. I am so sorry if I caused you discomfort.'

I felt my arse, which was burning to the touch, both on the skin outside, and the sore anus hole inside. I glowed with pleasure.

'You silly boy,' I said, stroking his hair. How could he guess what I felt? The power of my spend as his hand cracked across my bottom had startled, even frightened me. God, I had needed that. For so long I had needed to be beaten!

After a while, I disengaged myself and told him it was time to retire to his own room.

'I think that your lustful thoughts will be quiet tomorrow, for I fancy I have well-emptied your balls for a while. But you will put on the restrainer just to be sure.'

I fastened the cock ring tightly, and then handed him my yellow satin bloomers, well-stained with my love excretions.

'Put these on, slave,' I commanded, once more the stern mistress, 'and do not wash your cock or balls until I give permission. Discomfort will teach you obedience.'

'Yes, Mistress,' he chirped joyfully, and obeyed.

I went to bed, but my mind was in such confusion that sleep would not come. The moon gleamed balefully, like a new shilling. I got up and inspected my arse in the mirror, marvelling at the livid red palm prints I had received from my sweet slave, who had spanked me with such fervour – knowing that I took his blows as avidly as he dealt them.

My marks seemed to be a reminder of the tenderness and lustful passion we had enjoyed; a testimony of love imprinted on the flesh, which is also a teasing foretaste of enjoyments to come. My arse still glowed. Impulsively, I took my silver hairbrush and dealt myself twenty fierce slaps, until it burned anew. Only then could I achieve a happy sleep, my whole body bathed in the love of life. My arse-fucking and my spanking had awakened in me desires which I had only dimly imagined before. I thought of Miss Chytte's voluptuous bottom writhing under my own blows; of her flushed lips and bright eyes, that fascinating mannish bosom, and wondered what would happen on our next meeting. Had she been right? That she and I were alike, were sisters?

To be fucked in the anus, I thought, and to be beaten – whether spanked or flogged with a whip – is to experience pleasure in utter degradation and humiliated submission. One is helpless, twisting in torment, yet feeling a damnable joy. It is the joy of freedom. The soul is removed from all constraints of dignity, of the self, and experiences the blissful scream of freedom, when all the cares of grown-up existence are removed; there is only the crack of the whip on bare skin, the thrust of the cock in our intimate and most private part, the anus.

I realised that from being the teacher, I was becoming the taught.

8

The Chinese Snake

The morning after my buggery, I was invited to take coffee with Lady Whimble. I duly presented myself, and found the Rev Turnpike in attendance. That afternoon, I was to have my second lesson with Miss Chytte, and was very much looking forward to it. I declined Lady Whimble's offer of a brandy livener with my coffee, but noticed that she and Rev Turnpike served themselves freely, so that they were really taking morning brandy with a coffee livener. Sally served us with her usual sultry surliness, and I wondered if this pouting, rough manner was a feature of rural inbreeding; as in the case of Prunella in the teashop, it seemed to conceal a sort of untapped, simmering wantonness which I found intriguing. I sat there and made small talk, smiling to myself. Little did they guess that my bumhole was still smarting from young Freddie's lustful attentions the night before.

'The Rev Turnpike is a godsend, Miss Cumming, in every sense,' exclaimed Lady Whimble, and the vicar smiled politely. 'He attends most effectively to my spiritual needs, and I find such solace more useful than all the doctor's pills and potions.'

I had no doubt of this.

It transpired that the vicar wished to invite me to tea that very afternoon, being most interested in making the acquaintance of his learned new parishioner. I inspected his florid but handsome countenance, and his athletic carriage, and decided he must be of an age with her Ladyship; but I wondered what he wanted from me. Something told me it was more than polite conversation. I eagerly agreed to come that afternoon, which in fact fitted my plans nicely: I could proceed from my appointment with Miss Chytte to the vicarage, which lay at the other end of the village. After this was settled, I returned to my lessons with Freddie.

Freddie was in a sulk! There was no doubt about it, his face wore a definite *moue*.

'Whatever is the matter with you, Alfred?' I demanded. 'Your mind seems to be elsewhere.'

He had just given me a translation of the latest instalment of Yvette's adventures, and it was surprisingly sloppy. It was the part where Yvette escapes from her savage new protector – the one who had thrown Henri out of the window – and finds herself rescued by a Javanese, who imprisons her in his Amsterdam brothel. With such exciting stuff, there was no excuse for an absent-minded translation, and I told him so sternly.

'You are going to see Miss Chytte this afternoon, Mistress,' he muttered at last. 'Do you like her?'

'And what if I do, sir? You are not jealous, surely?'

'Do you intend to . . . discipline her again?'

'Yes, as it happens, although it is none of your business.' But I continued, in order to tease and torment him: 'Why, yes, Alfred. I shall strip her naked, caress her for a while – you know, stroking her breasts and bottom, and perhaps allowing my fingers to stray between her legs – and then I shall give her a sound thrashing on her bare bottom. That is what I fancy will happen. And since the weather is so hot, I might even take my blouse off, to show her my

93

breasts. Perhaps my panties too, it depends upon my whim. There, does that answer your question?'

My tone was nonchalant, his face creased in sadness.

'Oh, Mistress, I cannot bear the thought of anyone else looking at you, touching you!'

'Alfred,' I rapped, 'your silliness, your stupid jealousy, has crossed the boundary of insolence. Come to my room again tonight for your punishment! Now, let us continue with our work, my conceited young buck.'

Punctually at two o'clock, Miss Chytte admitted me to her apartment. She wore a robe of black satin which buttoned from her neck to just below her mons, and was daringly slit at the side, giving a tantalising glimpse of her firm bare legs, which were without stockings or, as far as I could tell, panties of any kind. I was wearing only a loose blue blouse under my grey silk jacket, which I removed, saying that she must feel very hot in such formal attire.

'But I never wear underthings, Miss Cumming, which keeps me cool.'

'How very progressive, Miss Chytte,' I said, gravely.

'Practical too – you must try it, Miss Cumming.'

'Ah,' I smiled, 'you are never short of new things for me to try, are you, Miss? But let us to business. You have a nice shiny shilling for me?'

She produced the coin but when I reached for it, she snatched her hand away.

'Give me it, Miss Chytte,' I said. 'I will not be trifled with.'

'You must take it,' she answered simply. I grabbed her arm, but she resisted, and in a moment we found ourselves wrestling on the floor. I was slightly the stronger – or at least she let me be – and soon had her pinioned to the floor, her skirt having ridden up around her waist to reveal her naked thighs and minge. She had quite a silky, shiny forest of very lustrous thick hair, which was curiously straight, not curly like my own mink, and I longed to stroke it. But I prised the shilling from her grasp instead. We were both panting from our exertions.

I released her and stood over her exposed body.

'You are naughty, Miss,' I said with a smile.

'Will I be punished, then?' she whimpered.

'Yes.'

'Not the cane! I cannot bear it!'

'The cane it is, Miss, on your bare bottom.'

'Naked! No, no! The shame of baring my bottom for a flogging is more than I can endure.'

I put the heel of my boot squarely on her exposed cunt, and pressed quite hard.

'I want you completely stripped, to increase your shame. Undress for me, Miss Chytte.'

I released her and she stood, feigning terror, then unbuttoned her dress until it fell away from her body and she stood before me nude. I noticed that the nipples which crowned her taut little breasts were already stiff with excitement. The nipples, even in their quiet state, were a curious and lovely shape, not flat but domed like twin cupolas of a cathedral, and were deliciously out of proportion with the slim breasts they capped. But what surprised me was that they had been pierced, allowing two gold rings about three inches across to dangle from them. Well, I thought, if a lady may wear earrings, why not rings in her more intimate places too?

'You like my nipple rings, Miss Cumming?' she said slyly. 'Perhaps you would like me to pierce your own nipples, so that you may adorn yourself thus.'

'How insolent you are today,' I said. 'You shall do

no such thing. Get up, you wicked girl, and I shall tan your arse until you plead for mercy!'

'Please,' she begged, 'I cannot bear the cane! I am innocent, a stranger to the lash! My poor bottom would sting so! Do not be cruel, Miss, I implore you.'

I was thoroughly enjoing our little play.

'Oh,' I sneered, 'so you are a crybaby? Well, I think it is not worth chastising such a wilting violet, a cringing thing that would faint at a drop of cold water. You may dress again, Miss Chytte, for I see you are so sunk in self-pity as to be quite unworthy of correction.'

'No, wait,' she cried, as I turned to leave, pretending a great imperious scorn. 'I do deserve punishment, and I'll take it, Miss, I promise.'

'Not from me, you snivelling ragwort,' I sneered. 'Find some fool with hands of silk and a whip of feathers, for that is all you can bear. I come from a harsher school – why, one touch of my hand and you would quake with fear. Your rings would jangle like bells!'

'Let me prove otherwise. Touch me with your hand, Miss Cumming, please, touch my bare bottom and make it tingle.'

'How, then? A spanking? Is that all?'

'Hard, Miss. Make my arse all red and glowing as you spank my naked skin. Put me over your knee, sweet Mistress, and make my naughty bottom writhe and jump as you chastise her.'

I pretended to think.

'Hmmm . . . very well, Miss Chytte. I will sit here, on this French high-backed chair, which seems quite admirably suited for the job. You will please bend over my knee.'

'Please, Miss, may I first visit the commode?' she asked, her face all flushed with excitement. 'I am bursting to go, really I am.'

I saw that this was another artful part of our game.

'Certainly not,' I snapped. 'You are a big girl and must control yourself, Miss.'

'You are so cruel! How can I hold it in?'

'Enough complaining,' I ordered. 'You will position your upper body between my legs, bending your waist over my left thigh. Yes, that's right.'

I rolled my dress up to near my waist, and felt her soft skin slide against my thighs.

'Head right down, now, and legs slightly splayed. Good.'

I then placed my right foot firmly on her neck, grinding her face into the rug, and I could feel her shudder with anticipation. I stroked her bottom rather absent-mindedly, and I trembled myself, for I longed to smother that gorgeous pair of creamy globes with hot kisses, or cruel whip-strokes. I let my fingers wander in the crack of her arse until they found her anus bud set out very prettily like a little wrinkled hillock, and I began to tickle it.

'Oo!' she squealed in delight, her voice muffled by the carpet.

'What a hairy little hole you have, Miss Chytte,' I said gaily. 'It is quite uncouth. And look how the little scoundrel stands up so cheekily.'

I wiggled my thumbnail inside her anus, and slowly slid my thumb in up to its hilt. She squeaked again in evident delight and squeezed her anus muscle around my thumb so tightly that I could not take it out, and her buttocks began to writhe in a voluptuous dance around her filled anus.

The palm of my hand was beneath her squirming pubis, and my fingers pressed against the lips of her quim. I could feel her luscious thick mink, soaked in her oily love juice, and with my fingers brushing her clit, which made her shiver, I raised my free hand and delivered a mighty slap to her bare arse.

'Mmm!' she gurgled. 'Oh, yes!'

My slaps rained thick and fast, as hard as I could make them, until her bottom was all pink and squirming like mad. Her pubis, soaking wet, pumped on my probing fingers as fast as a piston.

Her whole body shook as I vigorously spanked her, and there were indeed little tinkles as her nipple rings clashed daintily together!

My hand grew sore from the spanking, but I did not care, for I was on fire with desire for that lovely squirming arse, glowing hot and red for me. Her bottom and my hand were partners in a quickstep of delight, as she jerked her bottom up to meet my downward slap in a beautiful mimicry of fucking.

But I wanted to see her arse dance in earnest, and for that it would have to be the cane. Before I told her of my decision, she cried out and slammed her pubis hard against my hand, trapping my fingers in her oily slit, and began to grind fiercely with her hips, whimpering uncontrollably.

I wondered if the patrons of the teashop down-stairs could hear their proprietress crying out in the ecstasy of a spend!

Gradually Miss Chytte's spasm subsided, and I desisted from the spanking, letting my hand rest on her burning bottom. I released her neck from my foot and she twisted her head up to look at me with a beaming blush. She panted, as though from running, and I could not help returning her smile, finding it impossible to maintain my play-acting role as implacable governess.

'Enough, Miss?' I said.

'No, Mistress,' she gasped, and I was pleased and excited.

'You see I am no wilting violet. Now *you* must prove your mettle, Miss Cumming. I require a sound whipping, with my Chinese snake.'

98

'Chinese snake? I have never heard of such a thing.'

'Well, you will soon see,' she replied, stretching her body with catlike grace, but making no move to get up from her submissive position.

The prospect of further labour excited rather than deterred me, but I was jealous of Miss Chytte for having enjoyed an orgasm while I was left wet between the legs and itchy with lust. I could not wait for this Chinese thing to appear, whatever it was. Keeping one hand between Miss Chytte's wet thighs, I kept the other, still smarting from her spanking, between my own thighs and began to rub my clit. My half-hearted attempt at discretion did not deceive my host and she purred in approval as she felt my body tremble.

'Don't mind the chair,' she said impishly. 'It has been wet before.'

But I scarcely heard her, as I could feel myself grow hot from the desire building inside me.

'Wet,' I sighed, 'how nice, Miss Chytte, how nice to be . . . wet.'

At that moment there was a knock on the door, and I jumped.

'You're late!' barked Miss Chytte.

The door opened, I heard a tinkle of tea things, and looked in confusion as the maid, Prunella, came in, bearing a silver tray.

'I'm sorry, ma'am,' she said rather petulantly, looking blankly at her employer's flushed naked bottom as though such a sight were perfectly normal.

Miss Chytte leapt to her feet and reached for her robe, while I attempted to hide my confusion by smoothing my dress decorously over my knees and removing my glistening fingers from my quim. I was rather annoyed at this interruption of my pleasure. What had Miss Chytte meant by late? Had she known, or arranged, that Prunella would interrupt us?

I was not long in finding out.

Prunella looked at me with a sulky *moue* on her bony, handsome face, but with sparkling inquisitive eyes. I realised I was very flushed in the face, and the knowledge made me blush still more.

'Do not get up, Miss Cumming,' said Miss Chytte formally, as she smoothed her hair and robe. 'I promised to show you my Chinese snake, so I will fetch it.'

'You said *I* could have it today, ma'am,' complained Prunella with a curl of her wide red lips.

'Be quiet, you cheeky girl,' snapped Miss Chytte, and I could not tell if her tone was serious or mocking.

'You are late with the tea, you have interrupted us, and now you are cheeky into the bargain. Oh, you are a muddle today. I think you know what to expect!'

Prunella raised her eyes in mock astonishment, and sighed. Then she resignedly lifted up her short waitress's skirt to reveal her naked minge, unencumbered by panties, and blessed with a fine thick forest of pubic curls.

'Shall I bend over the sofa, ma'am?' she asked in a matter-of-fact tone.

'Not today, Prunella,' replied Miss Chytte with a wicked gleam in her eye. 'Miss Cumming, as you see, has just taught me a very expert lesson, and I think she will apply the same care to your naughty bum. No, wait, a better idea is for you to continue her private pleasure with your nimble tongue, while I attend to your errant backside. Please remain seated, Miss Cumming.'

I did not know what was happening. My heart fluttered as Prunella's ripe body knelt before me. Miss Chytte lifted her waitress's skirt right over her back, to reveal two ample white buttocks, prettily framed by the black straps of her garter belt. Prunella's hair cascaded over her face, which disappeared under the hem of my dress.

I was quite mesmerised as I felt her strong country hands creep up my calves to my knees, which she gently parted, then over my thighs to my wet panties. There was a tug as they came away from my waist and were pulled down around my ankles.

I was intoxicated with desire and anticipation, and stared helplessly at Miss Chytte who was grinning mischievously. She held a flat leather strap of about three feet long, whose end was split into ribbons, rather like a very large bookmark. Her robe was open to below her breasts and she did not bother to cover her nudity.

Prunella's head was under my skirts, her hands holding my knees apart, and I saw the bump of her head moving towards my mons.

'Hurry, ma'am,' came her muffled voice from inside my dress, 'there are customers waiting.'

At once, I jumped as I felt sucking lips and a probing tongue in my wet slit. I swallowed and gasped, for a shudder of pleasure convulsed me as that sweet, rude girl expertly tongued my throbbing clit. My hands clasped her head, stroking her, and I moaned out loud.

At that moment, Miss Chytte lifted the strap and began to beat Prunella's raised buttocks. Her vigorous lashes made a juicy whacking noise, but I do not suppose they can have been too painful, for Prunella took a good dozen or more without flinching, or even seeming to notice. But the spectacle of her bare arse being beaten excited me so much that I could not contain myself any longer. Her sweet, rough tongue rasped on my tender clit until I cried out in a heaving spend, my eyes feasting all the while on Prunella's plump buttocks bobbing under the lash, their tops glowing prettily like two red mushroom caps.

'You naughty, naughty, girl!' cried Miss Chytte as she delivered the final lash. 'I hope that will be a lesson to you.'

I heard Prunella grunt non-committally.

I lay back, exhausted with pleasure, and Prunella disentangled her hair from my wet inner thighs. She replaced my panties on my mons, which was soaked in love oil, and eventually her head re-emerged from under my dress. She stood up and stared at me quite blankly, as though at a cow she had just milked, but with the hint of a pout on her glistening lips, which she licked with evident satisfaction. Then she curtseyed to both of us and impassively departed.

'I promise I won't be late tomorrow, ma'am,' she said as she closed the door.

'She is a good girl,' said Miss Chytte. 'She is always late. Now, perhaps you would like to pour us a nice cup of tea, Miss Cumming, while I fetch my Chinese snake, in preparation for further games?'

I poured tea and listened to her shuffling in her bedroom. When she returned she was barefoot, still wearing the same robe, with no sign of any snake.

'Where is this snake?' I asked.

'Why, here, for I am wearing it,' she replied, and let her robe fall away from her breasts. I saw that she was now wearing a sort of lustrous black bodice which came to just below her breasts, between which a snake's head peeped out! It was about the size of a pear, with a shiny red tongue, and a strange little collarette of rosebuds; the whole garment apparently being made of silk.

'This,' announced Miss Chytte, 'is the only undergarment I wear.'

My curiosity whetted, I leaned over my teacup and saw that it was not a woven fabric, but a coil of thin tubing that wound around her belly in a spiral. We stood up, and Miss Chytte threw aside her robe, and stood naked but for this curious garment, which evidently served as bodice and panties at the same time, for her mons was covered in a thin strip of the fabric, not enough, though, to conceal her forest.

She fiddled with the top of the bodice and released the snake's head. Then she stood on tiptoe and twirled around until she had unwound about three feet of the heavy black tubing, which was evidently the silken body of the 'snake'.

'Take this,' she said, handing me the snake's head, 'and I will dance for you, Miss.'

I held the silken snake's head and watched entranced as Miss Chytte pirouetted around the room, whirling in a strange ballet until half of the snake's body lay coiled on the carpet, and she stood breathless in the middle of the room, her face as red as her smooth, flushed bottom which I had so recently spanked.

The snake's tail was nowhere to be seen, until I realised that it was hidden inside Miss Chytte's vulva!

She laughed, and picked up the coils of shiny silk.

'A snake with two heads, you see. The Chinese are very ingenious. Squeeze him by the throat, and you will be amused.'

I did so and found that as I squeezed, the fat tongue flickered back and forth quite grotesquely, as though it were a little penis thrusting!

'Imagine what he feels like inside,' she said. 'A silken snake with a silken tongue, that is also a silken whip with a vicious backbone. You will please wear the snake's head inside you as you whip me with his body, Miss Cumming. I suggest you make yourself comfortable by removing your skirts and panties.'

My heart pounding, I was quick to strip off my nether garments and stood in only my blouse, stockings, garter belt and boots, as she took the snake's head from my hand and deftly placed it against the lips of my cunt.

I gulped, and with my own fingers parted my swollen lips. I felt the snake's head glide into my oily slit as smoothly as a gondola cleaving the waters of Venice. It was not smooth and hard like a man's penis, but lumpy, scaly, yet soft at the same time.

Miss Chytte gently unbuttoned my blouse and knotted the lower half beneath my breasts, making them thrust upwards.

'I think we must give our snake room to entwine your belly,' she said softly. 'And now let us dance.'

It was the strangest dance I had ever known. We both whirled languidly as the snake was uncoiled from her body and gradually covered me. With every motion of my dancing thighs, I felt the darting tongue tickle me deliciously, as though that silken thing were alive inside me, and the stiff rosebuds of the necklace rubbed maddeningly on my tingling stiff clit.

At last I had my own black bodice, and Miss Chytte was quite nude, with about six feet of the silken strand left between our bodies. She halted her dance, and plucked the snake's second head from inside her vulva, then kissed it and pressed it to my own lips.

'There is the tip of your lash, Miss Cumming,' she whispered. 'Please whip me well with him.'

I followed her into the bedroom, admiring the swaying curve of her bottom, which I knew she was rolling to entice me, with the desired result, for I felt intensely lustful towards her. Games and charades are so useful in fanning love's flames!

I expected her to lie down on the bed but she

ignored it. Instead she indicated a sort of stool, about waist height, with splayed legs beneath a padded leather seat, with straps and buckles at the foot of each leg.

'This is a very valuable antique, Miss Cumming,' she said. 'I believe it was once used by the Sisters of Mercy in Salamanca, in Spain, at whose nunnery the daughters of the nobility went to be educated.'

'Used for what?' I asked.

'Why, it is a flogging-horse.'

On Miss Chytte's instructions, I set to work to fasten her properly to receive punishment.

A golden chain was attached to each of her nipple rings, then stretched over her belly and tightly across her slit; across her anus and up her back, where it was clipped to a tight golden collar around her neck. A second chain stretched from her nipples under the flogging-horse to her braceletted ankles, and finally looped back to her nipples.

As a result of this chaining, the slightest movement was impossible without causing severe discomfort.

'I have never been chained so expertly before, Miss Cumming,' she said dreamily. 'Why, the metal caresses me.'

'Let's see how you like the caress of the whip, you slut!' I cried rather daringly, but she shivered with excitement at the taunt.

'Oh, it shall be a caress, Miss,' she cried. 'Have *you* never dreamt of being flogged by a silken whip? Its touch as light as a butterfly, or as hard as steel, for all is in the mind, a dream of pain, an ecstasy of pleasure.'

'I ... I am not sure,' I said, confused by the luscious tickling of the snake's head in my wet cunt.

'I am sure, Miss Cumming, for I think I know you. Now please lash my bare bottom with the snake, as hard and as often as you like. How I love it when he strokes me!'

I began to beat her, with long lazy strokes, and the harder I stroked her, the more my body swam with pleasure. I watched as her luscious arse became diffused with a gentle pink, that gradually deepened into a fiery red.

'That is lovely and warm, Miss Cumming. I think my bottom has been well seen to. Please let her glow for a while as you attend to my back. Chained in the position of the rising sun, my arms and legs stretched out like the cross of St Andrew, how often I have dreamt of being a sailor, whipped at the mast. The position of the rising sun is the position of the dawn, of submission to the kiss of the lash, the helplessness of the naked self before the vast universe.'

I thought this very pretty, and I knew that position, for that is how I would stand to worship my moon goddess, Selene. Miss Chytte rapidly gave me new orders. A line of rings hung from the ceiling, whose purpose I now understood. Now, Miss Chytte's legs remained fastened to the flogging-horse, but she was forced to stand upright, on tiptoe. Her nipples were attached by one chain to the ceiling rings, and her wrists by another, so that her arms were forced strenuously up above her head. Her body assumed a 'V' shape, of lovely and perfect symmetry which was embellished by the rippling of her back muscles as I flogged her.

'God, God, it is good!' she moaned. 'Whip me, Miss, oh whip me hard, purify my body with your lash.'

She began to writhe in a sinuous rubbing of her pubis against the leather of the flogging-horse, and I realised that she was masturbating, teasing her clitoris until with a frantic jerking of her hips, she cried out in the convulsion of a spend.

'God! I am spending, it is, oh God, so sweet, do not stop, flog me, beat me please, beat me, sweet Miss, make my skin burn with your rod. Oh flog me, hurt me, yes, yes . . .'

Her spasm subsided and her voice died down to a sob. I laid aside the whip and released her from her bonds, and we embraced lovingly.

Suddenly I realised I wanted to visit the commode. And it looked as though Miss Chytte had the same purpose.

'After you, Miss,' I smiled with exaggerated politeness.

'No, after you, Miss Cumming,' she gasped, then snorted in amusement.

'Oh, it is not necessary to be so formal. We can go together!'

And she led me to her capacious bathroom, where twin floor-level commodes *à la turque* faced each other.

We both squatted naked and did our business, holding hands and gazing at each other with dreaming eyes. To complete our toilette she handed me some pink paper, and our lips met.

'Oh, Miss Chytte,' I gasped, 'I don't know what to say. I am all wet for you between my legs. My cunt is quite overflowing, or so it feels. What a luscious body you have! I must taste it, Miss!'

All thoughts of impropriety at being naked and lustful with another woman had now left me. I felt giddy with desire for her sweet body, flushed and burning from my whipping.

I led her to her chamber and laid her on the bed. I lost no time in clasping her to my body in a fervent embrace, with my lips full on hers, and my tongue probing her mouth in a passionate French kiss.

For a minute or two, we were locked in this

passionate, silent embrace, our breasts pressed together and my thigh between her legs, rubbing her. Then I disengaged myself, and moved down the bed. I forced her thighs apart and kissed her on the cunt, as fully and firmly as I had kissed her lips.

'Oh, Miss Cumming,' she sighed, 'I knew . . . I could feel your aura . . . The way you whipped me: you are one of us!'

My tongue found her clitoris and flickered over the swollen thing.

'Turn round, Miss,' she begged. 'Sit on my face as you lick my cunt.'

I did so, adopting the position known as *soixante-neuf* and soon her nose was pressed against my ticklish little anus bud while her tongue busied itself with my own clit. I was flowing with juice, which she lapped up with grunts of joy. I wiggled around on her face, tickling my anus with her pretty nose, which was very thrilling. I squeezed it playfully with my sphincter muscle, and in this way we both achieved a hot spend. I clasped her bottom and kissed her cunt with all the passion I could muster, as I would kiss a lover's face.

We had time to repeat the operation, but with a slight variant: this time I sat upright, so that my whole weight pressed down on her face, and while she continued her tonguing of my clit, I pushed my foot between her thighs and rubbed her clit with my bare toes. At the same time I took hold of her nipple rings and pulled them up as hard as I could, stretching her breasts until she squealed in pain and pleasure. I thought it amusing that she should take a whipping without protest but should complain at a simple tension of the breast skin.

Her hands were free, and with them she spanked my bottom as I straddled her face. It was lovely! Hard, ferocious even, her stinging slaps reddened my

108

bottom and made me quiver. After a while of this sport, we both achieved another orgasm, after which I said it was time to go and to her displeasure, got off her face.

'Oh, I wish you could stay there, sitting on me and diddling my clit all afternoon, Miss,' she said. 'I knew Miss Cumming, that you belonged with us, the disciples of the poetess Sappho. Cannot we women pleasure each other more expertly, with more tenderness, than cruel men?'

'I cannot see the tenderness in the flogging I have just given you,' I laughed.

'Oh, but it *was*! It is so lovely to be helpless in your power, Miss, to feel myself your slave.'

'Slaves must pay a price for their slavery,' I said crisply, as I dressed. Miss Chytte still lay half swooning on the bed of our pleasure.

'Name it,' she said.

'First, there is the matter of my shilling.'

'Take it from my purse.'

I did so, then said:

'Those nipple rings – they are gold?'

'Twenty-four carat.'

'I think I will have them.'

'They are yours, Mistress,' she said. 'A good ounce in weight. You will wear them?'

'I will think about it,' I said briskly, as I detached the rings from her big stiff nipples. 'I am not yet a disciple of Sappho, more a curious party.'

I bent down and kissed her lips, then her nipples, and then her cuntlips, in farewell.

'I must be off to tea at the vicarage!' I said brightly.

'No!' cried Miss Chytte. 'I mean . . . watch out for him. He is a bad man.'

'The vicar? Surely not! Well, *au revoir*, my little slave.'

'Be careful, Mistress. It is I who, of all in this place,
am your true friend.'

9

Nude Model

The vicarage was a pleasant, rambling house, adjoining the church and looking like a miniature of it; with turrets, stained glass, arches and other Gothic style features. The vicar greeted me cordially, but excused himself for not taking my hand, as he had been 'at work'; he bade me make myself comfortable in the cosy drawing room.

'Mrs Turnpike will be with us in a moment,' he said. 'As soon as she has changed.'

'Dear Reverend,' I replied, 'I scarcely merit such formality!'

'No, no,' he continued. 'I am a sculptor, you see, an amateur of the classical, or Ancient Greek style and Mrs Turnpike serves as my model. I strive for authenticity in all things, and since the gods and goddesses of Ancient Greece were customarily represented in, ah, a state of undress, Mrs Turnpike kindly poses for me in the nude.'

The vicar then excused himself and I was shortly joined by Mrs Turnpike, who was a bright, bustling woman, full-bosomed and with a handsome, rather leathery, countrywoman's face, though scarcely my idea of a classical type. Her hair was a rich brown with flecks of grey and she wore a loose wraparound robe, tied with a belt, and satin slippers with curling, pointed toes. I surmised that she had not in fact

111

changed but simply slipped on this comfortable robe over her bare body.

The maid, who was addressed as Tess, brought tea things. She was about my age, slightly shorter in stature, and dressed in a pretty starched cap and a pinafore which did little to hide the sensuous full curves of her young body. She looked at me with a marked lack of friendliness; I put this down to the usual Cornish suspicion of outsiders – tinged, perhaps, with jealousy. Did she pose nude for the Praxiteles of Budd's Titson, and was she fearful of losing her place to me?

'You seem very flushed, my dear,' said Mrs Turnpike as tea was poured. 'It must be the hot sun.'

'Yes,' I replied, embarrassed, for my flushed condition had little to do with the sun. 'I have walked through the village all the way from Miss Chytte's.'

'Oh, the teashop? So you have already had tea?'

'Not exactly,' I said.

'Yes, Miss Chytte is fond of society,' she said.

We made small talk about cakes and calico, weather, dresses, dried flowers and so on, until the arrival of the Rev Turnpike rescued us. He sat down and helped himself to tea, then continued speaking as though there had been no halt in our conversation.

'I began as a painter, but nowadays turn more to sculpture. There is something much more vibrant and lifelike about the plastic as opposed to the purely representational art. And Hetty – Mrs Turnpike – is an excellent model. I shall show you some of my pieces. I wager that Hetty has been immortalised as a Greek goddess more than any other woman alive!'

'Oh, Rufus,' blushed Mrs Turnpike, 'Miss Cumming hardly knows us, she does not want to see such stuff.'

'But I do,' I cried, devilishly curious. 'With your

permission, of course, Mrs Turnpike. I am a devotee of the arts and love sculpture, especially the Greek. Why, the British Museum is quite worn with my eager footsteps!'

'Very well,' she smiled. 'But we must not fall into the sin of pride, eh, Rufus?'

The Rev Turnpike was stroking his chin thoughtfully, looking me up and down with a probing eye that made me rather nervous.

'You know, Hetty,' he said at length, 'I wonder if Miss Cumming here might not – but no, she scarcely knows us, as she has pointed out.'

Mrs Turnpike proceeded to scrutinise me herself, her eye wandering up and down my figure.

'I think I know what you mean, Rufus,' she said. 'Your artist's eye is never wrong. But this is hardly the time ... have some more tea, Miss Cumming. I say, Rufus, Miss Cumming has just been visiting Miss Chytte of the teashop.'

'Actually,' I blurted, 'I have been asked to give her instruction in the French language.'

'So I have heard,' said Turnpike. 'Your skills are highly praised.'

'Oh?' I said, taken aback. He smiled.

'Lady Whimble keeps me abreast of things,' he explained. 'I believe young Alfred is prospering under your tutelage.'

'That is very kind of you, sir,' I replied. 'But pray do not keep me in suspense. You have whetted my curiosity – what do you have in mind to suggest to me?'

'Well,' said Turnpike, 'since you seem eager – it strikes me that you have just the physique for my planned tableau representing Selene, the moon goddess. I should, in short, be most honoured if you would consent to be my model. Naturally you will

113

need time to think about my proposal, as it involves posing entirely nude.'

'Purely in the interests of art,' chimed in Mrs Turnpike.

'You would employ me as your model?' I asked, craftily emphasising the word employ.

'That's it! For proper remuneration, of course.'

'Why, sir, I accept your proposition with pleasure,' I cried. 'I am flattered to be thought worthy of serving art, the more so as a goddess! As for nudity, is not our National Gallery full of the most sumptuous likeness of the nude, both male and female? I am delighted to find such progressive thinking here in the country, so far from the metropolis.'

'Turnpike,' interjected Mrs Turnpike, 'holds rather progressive views on religion you see, Miss Cumming. He thinks the human body is part of God's creation, and should be worshipped as such, in its unclothed form.'

'Yes – in my work both as pastor and sculptor,' said Rev Turnpike enthusiastically, 'I am trying to create an awareness of the continuity between Christianity, the true religion, and its pagan forerunners, whose striving for the eternal verities was imperfect but none the less valid. And all around us, especially in remote country areas, we find traces of the old religion, which our Christian faith has absorbed and adapted for its own benefit. We must seek to understand these survivals, not to obliterate them, and the same truth applies to art. In Cornwall, for example, there are distinct traces of an ancient cult of moon worship; if such a thing were to exist in the simple lives of our village folk, my policy would be not to suppress it, but to build on it and incorporate it into our true Christian rites!'

'Well, sir,' I interrupted, 'I cannot but agree with

you. To come back to the matter of art, let me say that I am most eager to pose for you, naked or otherwise. The prospect is in fact very exciting.' And I spoke nothing but the truth. What woman is not flattered by the offer to pose as an artist's model?

'Splendid,' said the Turnpikes in unison. There was a pause, an awkward silence which I saw it was up to me to break.

'I expect, then, that you would wish me to disrobe so that you may . . . inspect me, sir?' I said coyly.

'Yes, Miss Cumming, if you are agreeable,' said Turnpike. 'First, though, you might care to see my little gallery.'

I was taken to a white-painted room, cool and shadowy because of the closed shutters, presumably for discretion. It was filled with statues, most of them life-size, and all of the naked female form. Mrs Turnpike, revealed in all her naked glory, was portrayed as Aphrodite, Nemesis, Hera, Ceres, Proserpine and other divinities: helmeted, winged or flimsily draped. There were other statues which represented the servant Tess, whose body was as fine and voluptuous as her tight uniform had promised; Rev Turnpike explained that she had been a suitable, but unsatisfactory model, since she had not the patience to hold still for long.

'Why, sir, Mrs Turnpike is, I think, as fine a model as you could wish for, and I am afraid my figure will hardly stand comparison with hers,' I said, modestly though untruthfully.

'Oh, you make me blush,' she laughed, but without blushing. Instead her eyes sparkled as she looked at me.

At the end of the gallery was a velvet curtain, presumably leading to more sculptures, and I made as though to pass through. But Rev Turnpike restrained me politely.

'There is nothing to see in there,' he said in a firm voice.

'In that case,' I replied, 'please show me where I may disrobe.'

'Yes – Mrs Turnpike will show you, and help you off with your things.'

Without replying mischievously that I had no need to be helped undress, I followed Mrs Turnpike into a back room overlooking a lush garden secluded by tall hedges. This room was the studio: it smelled of clay and the air was quite damp. Unfinished sculptures were scattered around on tables and the floor. I imagined myself in a romantic Parisian garret, and was quite excited, so that I felt an urgent need to visit the bathroom.

'Oh, there is no need to freshen up, Miss Cumming,' said Mrs Turnpike. 'We take each other as we are.'

'No,' I said, 'I mean I want to . . .'

'Of course,' she laughed, and showed me to the bathroom, where I sat on the pretty porcelain commode and delivered myself of a large evacuation, which gave me much relief in my excited state, although the passage of my stools reminded me rather piquantly of Freddie's attentions to my anus the previous night.

Back in the studio, Mrs Turnpike fussed quite unnecessarily with my buttons and straps, and in a short while I stood naked except for my panties. I looked surreptitiously to see if Miss Chytte's spanking had left any bruises, but there was no more than a dull flush which could have been caused by sitting for a long time, so with a flourish I stepped out of my panties and was nude. It was the first time I had undressed in the cause of art!

'You are a very pretty girl, Miss Cumming,' said Mrs Turnpike in a sultry voice.

I thanked her for the compliment. Rev Turnpike presented himself then, and clapped his hands in appreciation.

'Perfect in every detail, Miss Cumming,' he cried. 'You are a veritable Selene!'

'I am very pleased, sir,' I said, picking up my clothes.

'Actually, there is one other thing,' he added. 'You see, what I have in mind is a dual sculpture, a *tableau vivant* with two subjects. In this case, the goddesses Selene and Aphrodite, who are, ah, contesting the favours of the God of Love, known as Eros. It is a pretty pickle of a story, as some myths have it that Aphrodite was Selene's own mother, and Eros either her son, or Selene's son! I fear the Greek gods were sometimes a little confusing, not to say immodest, in their, ah, couplings. But would that present any problem? Aphrodite would be modelled by Mrs Turnpike, of course.'

'Why, it would, on the contrary, be a great pleasure, sir,' I said, looking at Mrs Turnpike. Now it was my eyes that sparkled, for I sensed excitements in store that were not purely artistic.

'Then perhaps you could both proceed into the garden, which is where I pose my models in the fine weather. It is quite private – the hedges see to that.'

Mrs Turnpike let her robe fall open; as I had guessed, she was naked underneath it.

She took me by the hand and led me into the garden.

'We are supposed to be having a sort of struggle,' she said with a little grin. 'You know, two rather passionate ladies fighting for possession of little Eros. I am not sure if Turnpike intends to have a third figure present, that of a boy. Finding a model might be a little difficult, perhaps even unseemly. You see,

117

the god of love would have to be represented in a state of . . . manly excitement.'

'Why, that is no problem as far as I am concerned, Mrs Turnpike,' I said. 'Artistic truth must come before all else.'

'Well, we shall see. In the meantime, Turnpike wants us to strike a few poses – grappling, or wrestling, you know – and he will take photographs, so that he may choose at leisure which one is suitable.'

The Rev Turnpike duly appeared with his tripod and photographic apparatus, which he set up on the steps of the French windows leading from the studio to the garden.

He explained that the warm, pink light of late afternoon, when the sun was low and cast vivid shadows, was perfect for the photographic art.

Both Mrs Turnpike and I were a little nervous at first, as we half-heartedly embraced in a variety of wrestling poses.

But as the camera clicked, our bodies grew slippery with sweat, and our poses grew less half-hearted. We acted for the eye of the camera itself, like an all-seeing god in the background. Our hands grew damp as we felt each other's bare skin; breasts, thighs and bellies touched as though by accident, although we both knew there was no accident, that our panting breath was as much lustful as combative . . . The bright light and the drowsy warmth quickened our playful sport and it became a fierce, joyful tussle.

'Come on, Aphrodite, come on, Selene,' cried the Reverend, as though from far away. 'Remember you are fighting for the prize of the pretty love god. Realism, realism!'

Suddenly, Mrs Turnpike put her foot behind my heel and tripped me so that I fell flat on my back! She fell on me brutally, pinioning me to the ground with

118

her breasts pressed against mine and her knee jammed between my thighs. I was winded by the fall, and taken aback by her ferocity. But then, in a sudden fury, I twisted her off me, and got her arm behind her, forcing her down on her belly with her face in the grass. I held her there, straddling her, with her head between my thighs and her arm bent behind her back.

'Yes, yes!' cried Rev Turnpike, as the camera clicked.

With a shriek that frightened me, Mrs Turnpike reared up with surprising agility; she twisted free, delivering a powerful blow to the small of my back. I lost my grip on her as she whirled round and locked her ankles on my neck so that I was pulled backwards, bending my back until I thought it would break. I was genuinely furious by now. The camera, the *tableau vivant*, were forgotten. There was only my naked opponent, and I wanted to hurt her.

With a tremendous thrust, I managed to free my legs and vaulted over her, so that I fell heavily on her in a position not unlike the *soixante-neuf* which I had so recently enjoyed with Miss Chytte! But there was no love here: I shrieked as she sank her teeth full on the lips of my cunt; in reaction, I lifted my pelvis and slammed it hard down on the bridge of her nose, which caused her to yelp in pain. We rolled over, scratching and kicking, until we stopped in the flower bed, which had unfortunately just been watered. We must have looked a strange sight, two vixens spitting and clawing and coated in sloppy clay.

I got myself on top of my opponent, and brutally slammed my knee again and again into her, which made her moan piteously, and at the same time fastened my teeth on her left nipple, which I chewed. It was a delicious nipple, big and brown with a sweet horny aureola, and I hated to harm her thus – but this was no longer in play! As I chewed, her sharp nails raked my back and buttocks most painfully, but she was weakening, her cries of anguish turning to sobs. At length I grabbed both her breasts, and pulled her to her feet by them, then slammed her body into the roses, shaking her against the spiky thorns. She squealed, as the dislodged petals cascaded prettily down her heavy breasts; I had her head down, and was forcing it towards those painful thorns, when she cried:

'Enough, for pity's sake! I am vanquished!'

'Wonderful!' exclaimed Rev Turnpike, whose presence I had forgotten. 'Selene has defeated Aphrodite! I must hurry to develop these most interesting photographs.'

We were left alone in the garden, both of us panting heavily. I released Mrs Turnpike from her thorny prison and we faced each other.

I realised to my astonishment, that my cunt was quite wet with an excitement that was purely lustful! I bent forward and said:

'A kiss for the vanquished, sweet Aphrodite.'

Then I embraced her and pressed my breasts to hers, kissing her full on the lips with my open mouth.

Her tongue darted into my mouth and filled it, and then our tongues wrestled as our bodies had. We held each other by the buttocks, pressing our cunts together in a tender embrace – and when I felt her hand between my legs, I guided her to my clit. I found that she was as wet as myself, and we clasped each other, kissing and stroking our wet cunts, with soft little moans in our throats, until we heard the Reverend Turnpike's returning footsteps.

'Well,' said Mrs Turnpike brightly, 'I expect we could all do with another cup of tea.' And we strolled back into the vicarage like two naked cherubs, our arms around each other's waists.

That night, Freddie presented himself to me as ordered. I was tired after the exertions of my most interesting day, so I gave him a lecture about discipline and self-control, and did nothing with him except make him lower his garments so that I could tighten his cock ring quite savagely.

'Ow . . .' he moaned.

'That will teach you,' I said curtly. 'And be warned that I have other, more severe restraints in my box, if that does not do the trick and stop this nonsense of constant erections.'

'Lustful thoughts are difficult to turn on and off like a tap, Mistress,' he said.

'And that is why we must learn to do so,' I replied. 'Self-control distinguishes us from the brute beasts. By the way,' I added, as he was dressing, 'I may have a job of work for you.'

'Work?' he said, in some alarm, 'I thought –'

'Yes, work. You have heard of the thing, I suppose. It will not be onerous, but will require discipline and obedience.'

'You have my obedience in all things, Mistress.'

I found his puppylike devotion very touching – men are such simple creatures – but as I always tell my girls, you cannot put puppylike devotion in the bank. I bade Freddie good night and settled down to a sound sleep, where I dreamt of a god of the naked Greek variety, except that his prick was a roll of five pound notes and his balls two huge golden sovereigns!

The next morning I treated Freddie to a further instalment of the adventures of Yvette. After terrible ordeals and degradations in the Amsterdam brothel, she is helped to escape by a mysterious masked man, who first forces her to perform the most humiliating erotic services imaginable. It turns out that he is none other than Albert, who did not die after all, and he takes her to Vienna, where he intends to sell her into slavery. Freddie found this very stimulating, especially the racier passages, but I saw that his cock gave no hint of an erection, and wondered if I had not tightened his restrainer overmuch. Still, I had other tests of his submission in mind, which could wait until I had proceeded with my newfound career as artist's model. That afternoon, I arrived at the vicarage as arranged, for my first proper posing session.

Mrs Turnpike greeted me gaily, with a light kiss on the cheek, and the two were bubbling with infectious enthusiasm. Rev Turnpike wore a sort of painter's smock with sandals, which gave him a rather Greek look. He explained that he liked to imagine himself as Praxiteles, or other masters of old, in order to achieve authenticity.

Over tea, I admired the photographic prints he had made of our session the day before. An untutored observer might have found them lewd, but I told the Reverend that they were very handsome. He assured me that the art of Greek wrestling, at the Olympic Games and so on, was always practised naked.

'I suppose that two animals wrestling looked much the same as two animals rutting,' I observed coolly.

At length we all agreed on a rather brutal pose which well illustrated the ferocity of the two goddesses' jealous struggle.

Selene has Aphrodite by the throat; Aphrodite is kneeling, her thighs parted, and her younger opponent has her head forced down so as to break her back. Selene is crouching, pressed against Aphrodite's breasts; Aphrodite has her forearm rammed against Selene's pubis, with her fingers viciously clawing her rival's back, trying to topple her. Both goddesses have their faces contorted in rage and anguish, looking at the boy god Eros and mutely begging him to intervene on their behalf.

My fee was to be two shillings per session. I took the florin proffered and slipped it into my purse, sealing the bargain.

We proceeded to the sunny, private garden, and when we had placed our clothing aside, Mrs Turnpike and I struck the desired pose, which was quite strenuous, though not painful. Rev Turnpike remained in the gloom of the studio, beside a large pile of wet clay; he had decided to make the tableau life-size, and preferred to work in the cool interior while we sweltered under the hot sun.

'Realism, ladies,' called Rev Turnpike. 'Remember you are trying to hurt each other! Claw and scratch and, most important, look longingly in the direction of young Eros, who for our purposes shall be represented by that rose bush – rose thorns are quite as sharp as love's arrows, as Mrs Turnpike can testify!'

'I hope you have forgiven me, Mrs Turnpike,' I said half-seriously.

'Why, no,' she whispered. 'That would spoil all our fun . . .'

We both strained hard, to make our pretended struggle look real, and in fact we were hurting each other quite severely. We were soon drenched in perspiration. Mrs Turnpike's ripe body was lovely in the sunlight; her thick bush glittered with droplets of sweat, like the candles on a Christmas tree.

'We should wrestle seriously, Mrs Turnpike, when we can be alone – amongst girls, as it were.'

'Yes,' she replied, 'a return bout. I want my revenge. Such impetuous young beauty as yours begs to be tamed . . . to be hurt!'

'It is agreed, then?' I grinned fiercely.

'Yes, Miss Cumming. Yes.'

We kept up the pose for twenty minutes at a time, followed by a five-minute break so that we could stretch, or visit the lavatory. I used each opportunity to make water, but I noticed that Mrs Turnpike, despite drinking prodigious quantities of tea, did not need to. But each time I returned from the bathroom, I saw that the sculptor's clay was supple, liquid and steaming. Well, every art has its tricks, I thought.

The session continued for about an hour, at which time we had all had enough for the day. The light and warmth were fading, so we hurriedly dressed and resumed our conversation in the drawing room.

'There is something not quite right,' said the vicar. 'I mean, in your expressions. I think that realism demands the presence of a third model, the god Eros himself. But what is to be done?'

'I think I have a suitable model in mind,' I said, 'who will be most willing to pose, if I ask him.'

'Who?' asked Mrs Turnpike, rather suspiciously.

'Why, none other than young Alfred Whimble,' I said smugly. 'He will accede to my suggestions without a murmur.'

'Freddie! Of course!' cried the vicar.

'He is like a young Greek god,' said Mrs Turnpike. 'But would his mother allow such a thing? It might seem . . . indecorous.'

'Believe me, Alfred will do exactly what I tell him, and keep his mouth shut, so that Milady need not know. Of course, there is the question of payment – another two shillings for his services.'

'That is not a problem,' said Turnpike, 'but I wonder if he is not a little old? His voice has broken, he is already a man.'

'A young man,' I replied. 'Scarcely more than a boy.'

'And a very pretty boy, Turnpike,' said Mrs Turnpike.

'I mean that his manly developments will be apparent. His body hairs for example, quite inappropriate to the androgynous figure of Eros.'

'Why, there is not a hair on Freddie's body,' I blurted, then realised my indiscretion.

Mrs Turnpike seized the point at once.

'And how would you know that, Miss Cumming?' she asked mildly.

'Well, obviously,' I blustered, 'as his governess, I have had to flog him on occasions.'

'You flog him naked?' persisted Mrs Turnpike, her eyes gleaming.

'Why, of course,' I said coolly.

'Surely,' she went on, 'his manly organ . . . there will be a sprouting of hair.'

I smiled.

'I can guarantee that will not be a problem,' I replied. 'And if you agree, I shall order him to meet us here tomorrow.'

'Agreed,' cried Rev Turnpike. 'This is splendid! But, Miss Cumming, is there not a chance that he will refuse to obey your order?'

I looked at him in astonishment.

'Reverend sir,' I exclaimed, 'what can you possibly mean?'

10

Godemiche

The afternoon's curious sport had left me very hot and tingly, and at dinner I drank more wine than I was accustomed to. It helped me sit through Lady Whimble's laments about money, although I noticed that there was never any shortage of meats or wines in the household, and the tradesmen delivered regularly and in good humour. Freddie was in a good mood and ate heartily. He obviously thought I was going to release him from his restrainer, but I had other more mischievous plans for my amusement.

The night was hot and once in my room I opened the window wide. Waiting for the hour of eleven, I entertained myself by preparing for Freddie's night visit. I stripped and washed the sweat and grime of the afternoon from my body, then dabbed perfume behind my ears, between my breasts and in my cunt lips, which I thought rather daring. I did not dress, but sat naked in the cooling breeze.

I pondered on the wayward nature of my desires when with Miss Chytte or Mrs Turnpike; I found that the lovely curves and orifices of the female body excited me; but now back at Rakeslit, within the aura of young Freddie, I wanted desperately to feel his strong body on mine.

Eleven o'clock crept nearer. I rummaged in Mr Izzard's box and, after checking as always my supply of spermicides and other anti-conceptual devices, as he put it, I found the item I wanted. Freddie's knock was punctual as always. I sped to the door and threw it open. He was amazed and obviously delighted at my nudity. I did not smile; I was a woman on heat, and ripped his clothes from him like a tigress!

When he was naked, and half-erect, I speedily removed his cock ring, then knelt and tongued him to complete stiffness. I noticed that the restrainer had left a vivid welt, but this did not stop his cock from growing to a monstrous size, and trembling, as I deftly tongued his pee-hole, which I knew he found very exciting. Without a word, I disengaged and pushed him roughly back on the bed, his prick standing above him like a great mast. I straddled him, opening my cunt lips to show the wet pinkness inside, and then fell on him in one swift motion, my bottom landing hard on his balls, which caused him to grunt. But I had his cock where I wanted it, to its hilt inside my cunt, with my clitoris well positioned for a rubbing. In this position, I bounced frantically up and down on him – I suppose his balls must have taken quite a drubbing – until I felt his hot cream spurt inside me, which brought me to a most satisfactory and relief-giving orgasm.

This urgent business settled, I could proceed calmly to the next matter. I leapt from the bed, and fetched a jug of hot water, also soap and a cut-throat razor. I took hold of his big soft penis as he lay with his eyes wide in puzzlement, then when I touched his balls with the razor his puzzlement turned to fear. At last I spoke.

'Do not be alarmed. I am simply going to shave your balls and cock, so that there will be no hair at all on your nice shiny body. And there is another reason, which is that I have a job for you, which will require your pubis to be naked, like a young boy's.'

'In that case you had better shave my armpits too, Mistress,' he said helpfully.

'Very well. Now lie still – I need not explain why.'

I lathered his balls, tickling them and squeezing them, which was lovely fun, and began to shave off the delicate scrub of hairs. To have a clear field of operation, I held his prick up to stop it getting in the way – but soon this was unnecessary, as the devilish thing stood up rigid of its own accord.

I then moved the razor to the shaft of his cock, carefully shaving off all the sweet gossamer hairs, and finally attacked his forest of lustrous curls. Soon he was as smooth as a baby.

To finish, I made him turn over and spread the cheeks of his arse, so that I could shave the inside of his thighs and his arse-bud. While I was attending to his lovely little anus, I could not help tonguing it, which of course excited him wildly, and (also of course) it excited *me* wildly and . . .

I did not need to tell him what to do when I cleared the shaving things and presented my buttocks to him: he gave me a royal fucking, first in the cunt, and then in the anus, where he spurted his sperm. I was growing to love the sensation of that hot stuff in that dangerous and intimate place!

As we cuddled afterwards, I asked him which he preferred, cunt or arse.

'I love both, Mistress. Your anus is so tight – but then, so is your cunt, and the hot oily stuff it makes is awfully exciting as it bathes my cock; it is like being bathed in love. The arse-hole is altogether harder, sinuous and more dangerous, and that is why it is exciting, because it is somehow forbidden . . .'

'But I do not forbid it, Alfred,' I said, 'and that is all you need to know.'

Then I explained his new job to him – posing as the

god Eros. I told him about my playful romp with Mrs Turnpike, and felt his body tense with jealousy, though he said nothing.

'Sometimes, Alfred, a woman needs the caresses of another woman, which are gentler and more thoughtful than those of the lustful male, who seeks only to impale us on his brutal prick.'

This was not strictly true!

'I will present myself at the vicarage as you order, Mistress. But I am afraid Mama will be displeased if she finds out.'

'Why? It is all in the service of art, you chump. And anyway, she is not going to find out. Because you are going to be discreet.'

I had not the heart just yet to impose my new restrainer on Freddie – it was an advanced type which Mr Izzard assured me would work wonders. He was very faithful, dear Mr Izzard, and I resolved to make good use of him in future; he would have a prominent place in the grand scheme which was now gradually taking shape in my mind. All those gifts that I had made to him, that is to say the worn panties which I would present to him with great ceremony, were certainly standing me in good stead! As I always emphasise to my girls, kindness costs little, and can pay off handsomely in the long run. Anyway, I sent sweet Freddie to his room with his cock fettered only by a fresh pair of my panties – the purple silk ones, which he would find bewitchingly tight. I settled down to sleep, my arse lovely and sore from his bumming, and my belly glowing with the satisfaction of my climax. But sleep would not come; I was troubled by strange thoughts.

Miss Chytte had fond memories of her stern father, who in a bizarre way had shown love by whipping her soundly; Freddie was closely bound to his handsome mother, in a way whose secret I could not even hope to penetrate. But had I ever really known my parents at all? I remembered the luxuries I had enjoyed, the trips to Paris and to the châteaux of our French relatives, but they had never raised their voices in anger at me, I had never been scolded or spanked, let alone given a sound whipping by my father. They had, in short, never cared about me enough to punish me. I felt so alone, then, and felt that I had always been alone. As I dozed off in a half-sleep, I imagined I heard the sound of horses' hooves drumming.

When I awoke in the morning, I was in a foul mood, and discovered that I was capable of feeling that most useless of emotions, jealousy! I was jealous of the place Milady occupied in her son's affections; I was jealous of Miss Chytte, who fondly remembered her disciplinarian father as I could not remember my own; I was furious with Freddie for having that monstrous, wonderful cock of his, and furious with myself for wanting it so much, and for the pleasure it gave me.

At lessons, I was perfunctory, even rude, to my charge, which quite bewildered him, though I did not care. I thought of his dismay when I would force him to wear the vicious, advanced cock restraint, and decided that for good measure it was time he had another whipping into the bargain. But I burned with desire to take out my frustrations on somebody. That afternoon, Freddie and I were due at the vicarage for our employment. Beforehand, I called on Miss Chytte. She was surprised and pleased to see me, and I ordered her to go to her apartment and strip off her clothing. Once inside, I slapped her face very hard, and told her that she was a lazy slut for not undressing fast enough.

'Punish me then!' she cried, peeling off her clothes.

I certainly intended to punish her, although the edge was taken off my pleasure by the knowledge that she wanted to be thrashed. To put back that edge, I resolved to thrash her so severely that she really would feel discomfort, and beg me to stop.

She was naked for me: I saw that she had replaced the nipple rings with a larger and heavier pair, and in addition, a third ring dangled seductively from the lips of her cunt.

'I shall never detach it unless you order me to do so,' she said proudly. 'That way, my sweet Mistress, you can be sure that a man's cock shall never penetrate me.'

'So, you are no stranger to amours,' I said curtly, with a sneer.

'Of course not,' she pouted – a little too perkily for my liking. 'But they brought me nothing but grief. The Sapphic way is the only one – for you, Mistress, too!'

'I shall thrash you well for your presumption, you common whore!' I cried.

Soon, two tight chains ran from her nipples to the ceiling, stretching her breasts upwards. A third was fastened to her cunt ring, and snaked between her buttocks, its end tethered to the chair's leg. In this way she could not move without experiencing severe discomfort in her tenderest parts.

I gagged her, stuffing one of her own silk stockings in her mouth, so that she was free to breathe only through flared nostrils. Finally, her arms were attached in a V shape above her head, the wrists shackled to the ceiling rings. She was helpless.

I selected a lovely whippy cane from her collection, an ashplant about four feet in length. Then I removed my own skirt and blouse for greater ease and, clad only in panties and chemise, I whipped her.

When I unbound her shivering, squirming body that I had made dance with my cane, she fell into my arms and kissed me, tears welling in her eyes.

'Oh, thank you, Mistress,' she sobbed. 'That was so lovely.'

I could not help smiling at her strange pleasure, and kissed her lips.

'Now, Mistress,' she said happily, 'I shall show you something to convince you of the joy of Sapphic pleasure.'

She fetched a strange object, which I recognised from Prof Muffat's book as a *godemiche*, or dildo.

It had four prongs, the shape of huge cocks, and looked like a sort of candelabra. Each end of the device had two cocks of polished oily teak, striated with notches and lumps. Between each end was a foot of stiff but flexible cable, so that the positions could be adjusted to the comfort of the user.

'A *godemiche*, eh?' she said happily. 'So I have learned some French today, at least! Look at the artful carvings on each stem – every one designed to give a woman pleasure, both to cunt and anus, while stimulating the clitty. Is it not ingenious?'

'Designed by a woman, I suppose?'

'By *me*,' she cried.

'Well, let us see,' I said. 'Lie on the bed while I undress, you cunning little harlot.'

She lay watching me, her thighs wide and her fingers shamelessly rubbing her clitty, while I divested myself of my chemise and wet panties. Then I seized the dildo and sank the prongs brutally into her cunt and arsehole. She had removed the cunt ring, although I imagine I could have twisted it painfully to get the prong through. She groaned delightfully, especially when I thrust the cock deeply into her anus; perhaps it was too big for her, but I did not care. I promptly straddled her and lowered myself onto these artful engines of pleasure until my cunt and anus were filled. The sensation was utterly delicious; the carved surfaces of the dildo tickled me almost unbearably.

I was quite rough with her, slapping her breasts very hard, and pulling on her nipple rings; she positively gurgled with joy. By rocking back and forth on that subtle machine, I was able to fuck her in cunt and arse at the same time as I was myself fucked. It was gorgeous.

'This is what the French call *faire la rame*, or rowing, Miss Chytte,' I gasped. 'So now you have learnt another piece of French.'

'And what sweet French it is!' she said.

We had that *godemiche* inside our cunts and anuses for a full sweet hour, during which we each climaxed at least thrice.

As I dressed to go, my hole gloriously sore, Miss Chytte said:

'I suppose you are going to the vicarage?'

'Yes, and why not?' I said, accustomed by now to the fact that everybody in this place seemed to know everybody else's business.

'Actually, I am going to pose for the vicar, who is making a sculpture on a theme from Greek mythology. I am to be the goddess Selene.'

'You will be nude?'

'Of course. Do not tell me that you have done the same.'

'Would that it were only that,' she muttered sadly.

She burst into a torrent of sobbing, and I stroked her hair and kissed her tenderly until she calmed down.

'Do be careful, Miss Cumming. You are so precious to me, even after such a short acquaintance, and I don't know what I should do without you.'

'Why, Miss Chytte,' I laughed, 'I am a big girl and can look after myself. If the vicar wishes to fuck me, well, who knows – it's an amusement!'

'It is no amusement,' she said darkly. 'Between them, the vicar and that witch of his have fucked almost every man and woman in the village!'

'Well,' I replied, attempting to sound light-hearted, 'perhaps he is very good at the sport, and I should be a fool to miss it.'

'He is not very good at it,' she said bitterly. 'He likes to watch. As for fucking, he is only capable of erection in one place, and it is horrible. Oh, I hate the thought! But having been in his power, I think I shall never escape it! Why else should I be tethered to this infernal place.'

I opened the door to go, thinking to myself that Miss Chytte was a trifle unbalanced by jealousy.

'Oh, come, Miss Chytte,' I concluded brightly, 'I think you have a rather vivid imagination. I cannot imagine why you think sweet Mrs Turnpike to be a witch!'

'I am not talking about *her*,' she replied bitterly. 'I am talking about Lady Whimble.'

11

Olympiad

I made my way to the vicarage, brimming with joy and confidence, thanks to my invigorating session with Miss Chytte. Does Shakespeare not say that 'appetite grows by what it feeds on'? I was eager for more sensual excitement! I dismissed Miss Chytte's unfortunate remarks about the vicar and Lady Whimble as the ravings of a jealous woman.

Freddie was already there when I arrived, taking tea with the Rev and Mrs Turnpike, and looking somewhat embarrassed.

'I have been explaining the situation,' said the vicar, 'and I think he understands what we are about. I do not think the sight of his naked form will cause any of us a surprise.' He looked meaningfully at me. 'After all, Mrs Turnpike used to suckle him at her breast when he was a baby, as his wet nurse.'

'Oh . . .' I said, puzzled. 'Forgive me, Mrs Turnpike, but I did not know you had any children to give you mother's milk.'

'Alas,' said Rev Turnpike, 'the soul of our own departed little one rests with the Lord.'

'I am sorry,' I said sincerely.

'There is no need,' said Mrs Turnpike. 'We have erased the painful memory – remember, the Lord giveth and the Lord taketh away. Now I suggest we concern ourselves with the here and now.'

We proceeded to the garden, and Mrs Turnpike and I were soon stark naked, as though it were the most natural thing in the world.

Freddie, however, was nervous, and he fumbled and shuffled until we took hold of him and playfully stripped him down to his panties, which of course were my own silk ones. I could see why he was nervous – his penis had grown stiff!

'What nice purple underthings,' said Mrs Turnpike, 'almost like a girl's.'

'Why, Mama gave them to me,' said Freddie, blushing deeply.

'Well, let's have them off, then,' she continued. 'Heavens, I have seen your manhood before, Freddie, although I dare say it has changed a bit since then.' She reached down and playfully tapped his bulging prick through its silken covering.

'I am sure it is a change for the better!'

The laughter occasioned by this remark broke the ice, and Freddie's erection subsided a little. He took off his panties, and his lovely prick sprang out, half-stiff, which is a very exciting spectacle.

'Splendid,' enthused Turnpike with an admiring look. 'I explained to Freddie that in the interests of verisimilitude the god would need to be in the, ah, erect state.'

Mrs Turnpike inspected Freddie's cock with an interest that was more than matronly.

'Well, it needs to be a bit harder than that!' she cried gaily. 'You don't mind if I help a little?'

And she gave Freddie a little tickle of his balls, upon which his cock rose to monstrous size, and he stood proudly, like a Greek god indeed; though more a lustful satyr than the boy-god Eros!

'It is so huge!' gasped Mrs Turnpike. 'I hope it is not too big, Rufus dear,' she giggled, then added,

'You have no hairs there, and your skin is lovely and smooth like a baby's. Surely, Freddie, you are of an age to sprout a good manly forest, if the size of your member is any guide?'

'I ordered Alfred to shave,' I answered. 'In the interests of verisimilitude.'

'That is most thoughtful, Miss Cumming,' said the vicar, as he donned his work tunic. 'Now, let us get on.'

Soon, Mrs Turnpike and I were locked in our grappling pose; Freddie stood as instructed, in a languid pose, a beautiful boy slightly bemused by the vicious ardour of his two rival suitors, yet unable to disguise his physical excitement. I myself was excited by looking at him, the more so since I could not touch. I wondered how that huge cock had ever penetrated my little anus!

Mrs Turnpike was no less excited than myself, I could tell . . .

Freddie wore nothing but a pair of golden sandals, but he carried a bow and a quiver full of golden arrows, which were 'love's darts'. He did his best to look nonchalant, but without much success. How could a young boy be nonchalant in such circumstances?

The vicar hummed a psalm as he slapped away at the clay, which I noticed was very well moistened. Mrs Turnpike and I sweated as we strained against each other; each of us was doing her best to hurt the other, and I knew that our rivalry for the attentions of our young Eros was not just playful.

Suddenly, Tess the maid appeared, and whispered something to Rev Turnpike, without casting so much as a glance at our interesting tableau. The vicar stopped working, and rose. It seemed there had been some sort of accident, and that he must hurry to visit the victim, who lived at the other end of the village.

'Time is of the essence,' he blurted, 'and I must go before it is too late, so I think it best to postpone our session. I may be some time away, so we will make arrangements for a later date, at your convenience.'

So saying, he left the scene, all of us feeling rather awkward – a trio of models with no sculptor! Mrs Turnpike and I exchanged glances.

Neither of us made a move to release the other.

'Well, Aphrodite,' I said through clenched teeth, for she was hurting me badly. 'We have our Eros. I suggest we fight for him in earnest.'

'Agreed,' she said, her eyes glinting. 'No holds barred?'

'What about Tess?' I said.

'Oh, she is no stranger to our . . . particular rites.'

'No holds barred, then.'

She twisted off me, looked at me with daggers in her gaze, then delivered a ferocious kick between my legs. I doubled up in pain, but as she lunged at me, I ducked and threw her on the grass, where I leapt on top of her and pinioned her. I sank my teeth into her breasts, and she screamed and groped for my eyes with her sharp nails.

We grappled thus, grunting savagely, until I was able to flip her on her belly and had my thighs locked on her neck. I grasped her ankles and bent her legs towards me, so that her back was arched most painfully. I got her ankles bent around my own neck, and she wriggled like a fish; then I plunged my face between her spread thighs and bit her cunt lips! Her face was pressed into the grass, which muffled her shriek. I released her and cried:

'Submit, Aphrodite, or I will break your back!'

She groaned furiously, and shook her head in refusal, and suddenly her calves kicked up around my own neck, and she toppled me. Now it was my turn to be trapped in a merciless leg-hold.

Her mouth found my breasts, which she bit tightly, and, maddened by this onslaught, I gathered all my strength and was able to free my hands which she had twisted behind my back. I groped for her neck, found it, and set about choking her. Her arms stopped their pummelling, and tried to release her throat from my grip, and this enabled me to prise my body loose and spring to my feet, my hands still around her throat. Bending above her as I strangled, I was able to deliver a good few kicks to her groin, and then, when she seemed to flop like a rag doll, I hauled her up by her neck – her face was quite purple, and with my strong arms, held her about a foot off the ground.

She hung in space, her eyes popping.

'Submit, damn you, Aphrodite!' I shouted. But still she shook her head in refusal, swinging her body to try and get her legs round my back.

I flung her body to the ground and, in her weakened state, she offered little resistance as I forced her legs back and trapped her arms beneath her. My own arms were locked behind her knees. I found myself sitting on her teats, holding her thighs open as though she were waiting for a fuck! And I realised the significance of what I was doing. I was blinded by sweat and pain, and panting giddily under the sweltering sun.

I did not know what to do. We were both immobile, gasping for breath, and I could see that Freddie was gazing at our pretty spectacle with lustful eyes.

'Well,' said Mrs Turnpike at last, when she had got her breath back, 'that was very nice, Miss Cumming! I hope I didn't hurt you too much.'

'Well, I think you should submit!'

'I am not ready for that. Aphrodite requires being properly humiliated before she submits. I suggest that you sit hard on my face, dear Selene. I promise not to bite . . . and then there is the matter of young Eros. If you know your Greek mythology, you will remember that there is one way for him to decide between us, and you seem to have me in the right position to be put to the test.'

I shifted my arse and sat on her face, whereby she lost no time in inserting her tongue into my cunt. I felt as though I were in a lustful dream of some god of old in his sun-kissed Greek garden.

I nodded to Eros.

He approached, knelt before Aphrodite's open legs, and kissed me on my open mouth, then, as our tongues met, he thrust his penis into her, and began to fuck her very gently. I felt my love juice flow over Aphrodite's face as she diddled my clit. Soon she began to moan as Eros fucked her, harder and harder now, until he cried out as his spend came, and it seemed from her little wails that Aphrodite also experienced a sweet climax.

'It is not over, Eros,' I said fiercely. 'Remember that for this glorious moment, this dream, we are immortal, and you are a young god with two goddesses to be pleasured.'

I remained in position and made Eros give Aphrodite a few juicy strokes on her bottom with his arrows of love, which proved admirable as implements of correction. Aphrodite squealed, but did not object.

Then I made him fuck the goddess in her anus.

After he had buggered her, I gave Eros a rest, while I assumed the sixty-nine position and licked Aphrodite's clit, clasping her arse as I buried my face between her thighs. Then it was Selene's turn.

I raised my buttocks, my face still busy between Aphrodite's legs, and, gloriously stiff again, Eros thrust his cock into my sphincter, while Aphrodite, to my astonishment, managed to get her balled fist inside my pussy, and frigged me very hard.

I tasted her salty love juice as it flowed over my eager lips and tongue; my own cunt gushed with juice as she stretched me with her fist, and Eros manfully attacked my squirming arse.

At last we were sated, we Olympian orgiasts, and lay entwined on the grass.

'Thank you so much, Selene,' said Aphrodite. 'I do believe I submit now.'

'It was my pleasure, Aphrodite,' I replied gravely. 'And I think young Alfred – I mean Eros – has acquitted himself well.'

'Yes, Freddie makes a very good Greek god. There is a Greek god; an old, lustful pagan, in all of us, Miss Cumming, and it is fitting that on occasion we should throw aside our cloak of respectability and purge ourselves of these lustful drives by releasing them, in what the Greeks call catharsis. The Bacchanalian orgies of which you have no doubt read, were of deep religious significance, you know.'

'I do not doubt it, Mrs Turnpike.'

At an upstairs window, a glint momentarily caught my eye, and I heard a little click. I realised that throughout our combat, that clicking noise had been in the background all the time. It was, of course, Rev Turnpike's trusty camera.

The summer was long and hot, and my appetite for experience was growing. By using Freddie to pander for me (a blunt term, but a true one), I considerably enlarged my circle of 'business acquaintances' to include half the men of the village! I discovered to my delight that the most respectable of men harbour the strangest and most whimsical lusts, which I was delighted to satisfy for the appropriate remuneration.

And these were married men, happily so by outward appearance. For fear of ridicule or contempt, they dared not confess their secret lusts to their spouses, and were grateful to confide in me; after all, I was a London girl, different, and a bit foreign as well!

My pile of money grew most satisfactorily and Freddie, cut off from access to his mama's purse, realised that he had to perform these services for me in order to receive benefit in kind, that is a fuck. Every couple of weeks I thrashed his bare bum with a good strong cane. Miss Chytte had kindly lent me a French book she had acquired, by a certain de Sade, which she recommended as a sound explanation of the flagellant philosophy.

My plans were taking shape, for I knew I could not stay here forever. Assuming a place was found somewhere for young Freddie, I reasoned that if there was money to be had from satisfying the lustful obsessions of the grunting Cornish citizenry, then there must be far more to be made by plying my trade in a great metropolis like London or Paris. The strange appetites I had discovered in Cornwall must surely be found throughout society, in more sophisticated (and lucrative) forms. Here, I thought, was a suitable career for an independent young lady!

We enjoyed a few more modelling sessions at the vicarage, but our playful orgiastic romp was not repeated, and neither I nor Mrs Turnpike alluded to Turnpike's spying on us with his camera.

I had a shrewd idea that behind that velvet curtain in his gallery was another, forbidden chamber, and burned with curiosity to see it, but I felt I must bide my time. I was eagerly and curiously awaiting a proposal of dalliance from the vicar, but so far I had had no indication that Miss Chytte was correct in her accusation of depravity.

Freddie's reward for posing as the god Eros was a good session afterwards in my bedroom. Naturally, there was no question of my handing over his two shillings, which I kept for myself, justifying what some might have taken for greedy mischief as a legitimate business expense! I thought it quite a good transaction to go home from a simple modelling session four shillings richer.

Mrs Turnpike did not refer to our scene of lustful frenzy, when we thought ourselves spirits of the antique world, but we became quite friendly.

We got into the habit of taking walks in the countryside, and sometimes we would make it our business to seek out a secluded stream or pool, where we would bathe naked, like nymphs. Afterwards we would lie in the shade, or the sun if it was not too hot, and make idle chatter as we caressed each other, cuddled and exchanged kisses.

Nothing could have been more innocent. Mrs Turnpike was a most agreeable woman, at any rate when she was not transformed into a Greek goddess, and her talk centred on cooking, sewing, and the like. She was unswerving in her devotion to the Rev Turnpike, and insisted that he was the soul of tolerance, and turned a kindly eye on her little games. I gathered I was not the only girl she took for walks to secluded spots, but it seemed that no male friends, only female 'chums' participated in these pleasant promenades.

There was only one occasion when we were roused from our gentle activities. We were cuddling and kissing, when we spied four strangers, who established themselves with a picnic about a hundred yards away. We were well-hidden in our glade, and watched with interest as they removed their clothing prior to dining. And we saw that they were no strangers, but none other than Dorkins, Sally, Tess and Prunella.

We suppressed our giggles and watched their picnic, which was quite a messy affair, since it involved frequent use of the human body and its various adaptable orifices in lieu of the normal cups and plates. It was quite comical to watch the muscular Dorkins kneel to slurp clotted cream from the cunts of his fellow picnickers!

But our laughter stopped when we watched the man pleasuring each female in turn in the most intricate combinations; every organ and orifice of the human body being put to the most inventive use. On that occasion, the languorous, almost nonchalant masturbation practised by Mrs Turnpike and myself became the most passionate and intense tribadism. We both had a lovely spend, and afterwards we were entertained by the culmination of the lustful picnic, where Dorkins received a vigorous thrashing on his bottom from all three women, shrieking with laughter, and belabouring him with rather pretty knouts of nothing more than twined ivy!

'You see some strange things in the country,' said Mrs Turnpike seriously. And who was I to disagree with her?

Meanwhile, I visited Miss Chytte twice a week, and each time gave her a sound whipping, sometimes with the silken Chinese snake, sometimes with a simple leather strap. On some occasions she demanded the cane. She could take the lightest or the harshest punishment and beg for more, at which I was amazed. Constantly she would implore me, with the sweetest of smiles and blandishments, to accept the kiss of the whip myself, but I demurred, insisting I was not yet ready to share that pleasure.

I feigned astonishment that these strange practices could cause her so much pleasure, and I suppose I was teasing her. But I knew in my heart that I was also teasing myself.

I craved a beating. But I was afraid: not so much of the body's voluptuous torment under the lash, as of the nakedness of the soul. I loved to administer punishment, playful or otherwise, since it gave her so much satisfaction, and I adored the play-acting with which we dressed our scenes. But I still remembered the shame of my punishment at St Agatha's, and knew that only when I had liberated myself from that painful memory, and accepted with joy the beating I craved, would I be truly free.

In the meantime, Miss Chytte was the most inventive of lovers, and enticed me with good spankings on my bare bottom, using her hand, or a hairbrush, or all manner of delightful things, which had us very merry: a butter pat, a carpet slipper, a little walking stick made of Brighton rock, which of course soon shattered into sugary pieces which we licked up from each other's tummies.

But I refused the whip or the cane, and I would not be chained. She accused me of not trusting her, so to mollify her, I agreed to let her pierce or infibulate my nipples and later the lips of my sex, in order that I could wear the big golden rings she gave me. It did not hurt to have this done, apart from a sharp prick and afterwards it was most exciting when, both of us ringed like slave girls, we kissed and rubbed our bodies together in joyful tribadism.

We spent much time idling in her curious bathroom with its Turkish twin commode, and its great bath with room for two or even three people. All of these things she had ordered from Paris. We amused ourselves by dressing our hair, trying lotions, scents and so on, amidst vases of sultry flowers. She said she had the idea for this bathroom from reading of the harems of the sultans of Turkey and Morocco, where the women would spend each languorous day in the steam baths, gossiping and flirting and gorging themselves on sherbet and sweetmeats.

We would lie together in that bath for hours, drinking wine or eating titbits. One of us would occasionally get out to squat on one of the commodes under the amused gaze of the other, or sometimes we would squat together, opposite each other and hold hands as we gossiped. It was quite a comfortable position once I got used to it, and I found it quite delicious to share such an intimate occasion with my friend. Poor Prunella was obliged to run up and down the stairs from the kitchen with buckets of hot water, and if she did so with good grace she would be allowed to join us in the bath, where we had great fun washing each other with soapy bath oils. Prunella liked to be spanked on her wet bottom, which made a tremendous slapping sound like a fish on a slab, but she would not use the commode in front of others, saying that it was 'not nice'. I refrained from asking her if she thought eating clotted cream was nice.

When Miss Chytte desired a more serious punishment, then her mood was far from playful. Normally she was nude, but sometimes she wished to receive a caning while wearing a pair of thin silk panties. This was in order that the cane should tear holes in the panties. I queried this at first, as it seemed a waste, and anyway Miss Chytte did not wear underthings. But it turned out that the shredded panties were for me to keep as a memento. I wore them with secret pride, for there is nothing so devilish as to sit in polite company knowing that one has on the most scandalous underthings, or indeed no underthings at all. However I never showed them to Freddie, lest it put ideas into his head.

Sometimes Miss Chytte liked to take punishment wearing a curious garment of tight black leather, all in one piece, which covered her entire body except for mouth, breasts, arse and pubis. I had to chain her so that she dangled from the ceiling with her feet just off the floor, her arms straining with her whole weight. Then I would take the Chinese silk snake and lash her on the arse and the naked breasts, or even tickle her minge itself. It was for her sins, she insisted, because the places that give the sweetest pleasure are those which must suffer the hardest pain. But I do not think there was as much pain from the Chinese snake as there was in the idea of pain; and the hardest punishment she took in wearing her 'martyr's surplice' was a caning on the buttocks only.

I loved attending to her in this costume, because her cries and movements were so exaggerated and wonderfully theatrical. It was best when she carried what she called full regalia, which meant that she hung from her wrists, with two additional chains lifting her nipple rings to the ceiling, and a third chain fastened to her cunt ring. This chain snaked very tightly into her anus before passing up the cleft of her arse and joining its fellows on the ceiling. Her ankles were chained to the floor, so that she was on tiptoe, perpetually straining in frustration to allow her legs to take some of the strain off her arms. And to complete the picture, she wore a metal gag, of the type known as a scold's bridle, which was locked around her jaw and lips, with a steel flap that depressed her tongue, allowing her plenty of room to breathe but to her discomfort no room to talk!

She could hang happily in this costume for hours, squirming and whimpering and sighing with happiness.

'I do so wish you would let me whip you, Miss

Cumming,' she said one day after I had released her from her leather prison. 'I mean just with the cravache or riding crop, at first. I won't try and make you put on my martyr's surplice, not immediately. But after a few juicy tannings with a good cravache, why, you will beg for the cane, I know, perhaps you will even want to be trussed in leather too.'

'You know I am not ready, Miss Chytte,' I replied crossly. 'Perhaps I have not committed as many sins as you.'

'What?' she blurted somewhat intemperately. 'Why, Miss Cumming, surely you cannot be serious. The vicar has had you. I and the whole village know. We all see how thick you are with him and Mrs Turnpike. The man is the very devil!'

'Miss Chytte, I will have no jealousy from you. My relations with Mrs Turnpike are one thing, and none of your business. As for the vicar, well, it is simply not true.'

Her impertinent tone secretly decided me to accept the vicar's advances as and when I could arouse them, because to be fucked by a demon sounded quite a novel excitement. But I did not tell her anything of this.

'I am sure he has taken photographs of you,' she persisted.

'If you must know, yes. I am proud to have served the cause of art,' I replied.

She groaned sadly.

'Then he already has you in his power,' she said. 'The vicar, you should know, is no ordinary Christian. He is a follower of the Manichaean heresy, which holds that the flesh is evil, a mere trap for that point of light which is the imprisoned soul. With his camera, or by modelling your form in clay, he believes he can take possession of that point of light

148

which is your soul. Certain religions, such as the Mohammedan, forbid the photographing of the human form, and for good reason.'

'Well, what then,' I retorted crossly, 'so he has me in his power? I think I shall give myself to him, just to show you what an ass you are, my jealous little slave.'

'No! No! You mustn't!'

'But if I commit such a sin, why then I might feel guilty enough to let you flog me as punishment! Isn't that what you want?'

'Do not make fun,' she wailed, clutching my arm, and gazing at me with tormented eyes. 'Miss Cumming, the vicar has fucked me.'

'I cannot believe it,' I exclaimed.

'It is true. He has had me many times, always and only in his cemetery, lying . . . lying on a dank, filthy tombstone, for that is the only place, amongst decay and death, that his filthy manhood can become stiff. Oh God, that prick of his is ice, for he cannot be human. Oh, I should not tell you this, but I must, you are my true friend. But I was – am – in his power, and can never escape.'

'In his power?' I scoffed. 'How can that be so? These are phantasms of your imagination, Miss Chytte. If you have given your body to a man, once or a thousand times, why I find no sin in that, even though he is a priest. What power can he possibly have over you?'

'The power to ruin me. The power of blackmail, Miss Cumming. You do not know, you cannot guess, what lies behind the velvet curtain. It is a collection of pictures, photographs, all of the vilest obscenity, and whose disclosure would ruin reputations throughout society, not least my own. I helped him begin his evil collection. I was his mistress, Miss

149

Cumming! I lied to you and everyone else: it was he who brought me here, not my mythical fiancé. He met me in London, speedily found out that I craved, well, the torments that you know I crave, the ecstasy of the lash, and more. He brought me here, purchased these premises for me, and used me for every manner of perversity. Then, at scarcely more than twenty-one, I became too old for his dark lusts, and I must now serve him, under threat of exposure, as procuress of young girls.

'Tess was my employee – I broke her in, like a colt, accustoming her to the whip, awakening her Sapphic desires until the flesh was just a plaything, to be caressed or tortured indifferently. Prunella will go the same way, and there will be others! I cannot escape, because if the contents of that secret room are published, I will be ruined . . .'

'Well, I must have a look in this secret room,' I said. 'I enjoy a good mystery.'

'Impossible,' she said. 'The vicar lets no one inside, and he keeps the key in a pouch beneath his clerical vestment, strapped round his waist, which he never ever takes off.'

'Not even when fucking?' I asked impishly.

'Not even then.'

'Well, there is a first time for everything, Miss Chytte,' I said, and smiled.

12

The Vicarage

It was the easiest thing in the world to seduce the vicar. Not long after my conversation with Miss Chytte, I was posing once more, this time for a series of photographs on the mythological subjects so dear to him. I was nude, holding flowers, with a filmy shroud draped across my shoulders, and striking a pseudo-heroic pose to represent some Greek nymph or other. He snapped away with that camera of his, wearing his artist's smock. I thought it all rather funny, having an idea that my likeness was probably going to end up on the sort of postcards sold furtively in Port Said or the Boulevard Montmartre. But I did not care. If men wanted to feast their eyes on my unadorned beauty, and if my nakedness inspired them, then I think I was rather flattered than upset.

Without warning, I raised my leg and positioned my bare foot on the stone balustrade of the steps that led from the French windows.

'I think this is a more vivid pose, don't you agree, Reverend?' I said coquettishly.

He said nothing. As he watched, I saw the front of his smock swell as his penis rose for me. A thin smile played on his lips, for he was well aware of my intention.

'The nymphs of Ancient Greece, sir, had other things on their minds beside art, I think,' I continued.

'What do you mean, Miss Cumming?' he said.

'I think you know what I mean, sir,' I replied. 'Mrs Turnpike is away in the village, I believe, and we are alone.'

'And Tess?'

'She is a servant, sir – well trained, if I understand Miss Chytte rightly. She is discreet, is she not?'

'Yes . . . but still, let us not test her discretion unnecessarily.'

I wrapped myself decently in the filmy robe, and stepped up to him, smiling mischievously. Boldly, I touched his stiff penis through his tunic. He breathed deeply. I got my hand around the thing, and was surprised to find that though it stood a good seven or eight inches, it was scarcely more than half an inch thick! I clutched it like a handle, and led him by his prick until we were in the graveyard adjoining the church.

'Here?' he said, feigning surprise.

'Let there be life amidst death,' I said gaily, lying down on a crumbling old tombstone that was covered in moss. It was cold, but I removed my robe and spread my legs for him.

'My cunt, vicar, has had enough of the camera's eye,' I purred. 'It wants a helping of *your* one eye . . .'

He grunted, red-faced with lust, and hoisted his smock so that I could see his spindly stiff cock. His balls were almost hairless, and the spectacle was unusual, as though he were but a strange mutation, a tapir or a sloth or a pink ape. The strangeness was increased by the fact that he was circumcised: his big purple glans swelled from his shaft without any foreskin to cover it, and the effect was, I must admit, both menacing and at the same time very thrilling. That huge, top-heavy glans spoke to me of all dark virile power . . .

He prepared to mount me. I looked at the church clock, and noted the time.

'Wait, sir!' I cried. 'I am naked for you, and I want you to be naked also! Otherwise there is no pleasure.'

'Very well, Miss Cumming,' he said, and took off his smock.

'That ugly thing too,' I said, pointing to the key pouch that was fastened round his waist.

'Why, I never take that off,' he said. 'It contains a very precious keepsake.'

'What? A lock of hair? A beetle in amber? Some pagan gewgaw, without which you cannot fuck? Then I shall have none of you, and you may sit in this dank graveyard and frig for all I care!'

I sat up, as though to go, but I made sure that he could get a good look at the pleasures which were being denied him. He gurgled in confusion, and gently I unfastened the belt, throwing it out of sight behind the gravestone, along with our clothing.

'There,' I said brightly, 'that was not so difficult! We are naked and alone – no one will come, except you, dear Reverend! You will come in my willing wet cunt, won't you? Or would you prefer . . .?'

And I spread the cheeks of my arse so that he could see my anus bud.

'*There* . . .' he growled.

'The fee for cunt fucking is two shillings, but in the bumhole, well, that will be four shillings,' I said coolly.

'You minx!' he cried.

'Take it or leave it, sweet sir,' I said. 'Pleasure, like salvation, must be paid for.'

'You shall have it,' he replied in a voice choked with desire.

'Two or four?' I persisted.

'Four shillings, damn you!' And without more ado,

he plunged his spindly cock right up to the hilt in my anus. It was like being buggered by a pencil! Three or four quick thrusts, and he grunted as his spend shot into me. As he was squealing in his ecstasy, I looked at the church clock. Right on time, I heard a rustling in the bushes behind our bed of passion. But I gasped, for Miss Chytte had been right – his spend was icy cold, and my body was shivering in fear rather than lust. I wanted the business over with, and as soon as he had finished, I jumped up and retrieved both our garments.

'My pouch,' he cried. 'It is gone!'

'Nonsense,' I replied. 'It was wrapped in your tunic, sir.'

'It is not here. Where have you hidden it, miss?'

'Why should I do such a thing? It has probably fallen in the nettles.'

He scrabbled vainly for his precious pouch, but of course it was gone. Cursing and sweating, he stood up with fury in his eyes.

'It is a trick!' he shouted.

'It is no trick, sir,' I said. 'A furry beast or grass snake must have carried the thing off to its lair. No doubt you will find it, once your gardener has cut down these rank weeds. Or else,' I added slyly, 'your Tess is not as discreet as you think. These country girls do like their little pranks, do they not?'

He stormed into the house, bellowing for Tess.

'I must depart,' I said, 'but first, there is the matter of my four shillings, plus my two shillings for modelling. Total, six shillings, sir.'

He was none too pleased.

'Come, sir, you have had a good fuck in my poor arse, which is very sore from your attentions. Six shillings, if you please.'

'Sore, is it?' he said with a thin smile.

'Yes, terribly,' I lied. 'I do not think I can sit down without pain, or walk comfortably.'

'Well, good – very good – you have earned your money, Miss Cumming, and I thank you.'

I duly got my six shillings, and was glad to leave that place which, far from being the garden of warmth and sweetness I had known earlier, was now eerie and ominous. As I hurried, I heard squeals and roars behind me, and the sound of leather on bare flesh. Poor Tess was learning the painful rewards of being innocent!

'Very good, Alfred,' I said, as I placed the vicar's shiny key in my drawer. 'You will make a good thief.'

'Thank you, Mistress,' he said. 'Gosh, how those nettles stung! The vicar should have them cut.'

I smiled, because I had devised a rather bizarre and lustful scene for our night's sport. I had bent young Freddie to my will, having uppermost in my mind the plans which I had formed for him, and I wanted to see how pliant he was. I hoped he would bend all the way to my desires without snapping.

'Well, you are going to sting a little more, Alfred, because I am going to beat you. You cannot be a thief and get away unpunished. I haven't thrashed you for a while, and my wrist needs the exercise. You will undress while I fetch the cane.'

I took a nice springy yew, and bent it back and forth with great relish as I watched him strip. His penis bulged beneath his panties, the yellow ones I had given him the night before, and I made him peel them off.

'Now you will strip me, Alfred,' I ordered.

'With pleasure, Mistress,' he beamed, though not without a nervousness in his eyes as they followed the swish of my cane through the air.

'Your pleasure does not count, boy,' I rapped. 'Only *my* pleasure is important.'

'Your pleasure is mine, Mistress,' he blurted as his clumsy fingers disrobed me, fumbling with the buttons of my blouse; my camisole and straps, and peeling off my stockings and panties.

'Now, Alfred, we are going to play a little game. I think I have gone some way to making a man of you. Now let us see if I can make you a woman.'

'I . . . I don't understand.'

I laughed.

'Why, you are to put on my clothes.'

'I have never been dressed as a girl,' he said wonderingly.

'Well, I am sure you will enjoy it,' I said, 'and who knows, we may find out something about you that neither of us knew. First, put on this hair slide. It will give you a nice girlish look. That's right – now the blouse, the stockings, the camisole . . . not the panties, for I am going to cane your bare bum.'

He caressed my garments and sniffed them as he put them on.

'Do I smell nice, Alfred?'

'I smell like you, and it is wonderful!' he cried joyously. 'It is as though I have become you!'

'Good, now touch your toes, for I am going to flog you, my sweet young girl.'

I gave him a very tight beating on his lovely quivering bottom, and I was hot with desire, my cunt helplessly wet. It was as though it was *my* bum taking those stinging cuts!

I made him – her – lie on the bed, facing me, with thighs bent over the belly so that I had a clear view of the anus.

From Mr Izzard's hygienic box, I took my own godemiché, a less elaborate one than Miss Chytte's in that it only had two prongs, but effective: the cocks were giant things. I strapped on the machine. The polished teak penis slid easily into my soaking slit; I straddled Freddie, and tickled his anus bud with one hand, while I rubbed my clit with the other.

'You deserve a good arse fucking, you wicked girl!' I cried.

'Oh, please don't fuck me with that huge cock of yours, Mistress,' he pleaded, and I could not tell whether he was serious or entering into the spirit of my play-acting. 'It will split my bum right open!'

'Exactly what I want, miss,' I replied firmly, and pushed the gleaming brown dildo right into his arse-hole, with a very hard shove that made him jump.

'God, how it hurts!' he moaned.

'Nonsense, you silly girl,' I snapped. 'There is nothing so lovely as a filled arse, a fat brown cock sitting warm and snug in your girly's hole.'

I began to thrust with my loins, fucking like a male.

I guided his hand to my very female clit and made him rub it; at the same time I began to frig his stiff cock which lay on his quaking belly like a huge tree.

'What a stiff clit you have, girl,' I cooed. 'And so big! I wonder if I can make it spurt white creamy stuff, for then it would be a magical clitty indeed.'

'It is stiff, Mistress, because your sweet clit is fucking me in the arse,' he answered. He *was* entering into the spirit of the thing. 'God, yes, fuck me harder, split my arse in two, I beg you!'

I knew that he was about to come, for a drop of sperm had appeared at his pee-hole. I kissed him on the mouth and fucked him with all my might, at the same time as I furiously rubbed his naked glans. His fingers were frantic on my throbbing clit; we both cried out as we spent together.

His spunk spurted in a lovely creamy jet all over his belly, and I rubbed my fingers in it, then painted my stiff nipples and my breasts with the hot sticky stuff.

'Mmm . . .' I purred. 'Was that good, Freddie? Do you like being my girl? Has Mistress fucked you well?'

'It was indescribable. That big clit of yours, sliding so hard in and out of my hole. God, how well you fuck me!'

And he burst into tears! I stroked him, and pressed his lips to my breasts which were still sticky with his own hot sperm. 'Yes, Freddie my dear,' I whispered, 'you really are my girl, aren't you?'

I had decided that Miss Chytte and I would break into the vicarage when the village was at morning service, the first Sunday after my encounter with the vicar and his cold penis (the thought of which still gave me the shudders). We would plead illness, or the time of the month, to explain our absence, and I overcame Miss Chytte's objections by pointing out that no one would know we had inspected the secret gallery.

I felt rather sporty that Sunday. After breakfast, I waited until Freddie had performed his morning ablutions, then summoned him. I told him that I had decided to be indisposed with a slight cold, and that he must keep secret about my real task that morning. Then, for my amusement, I locked him in Mr Izzard's *Super Uro-Genitory Regulator* which I thought looked tremendous fun. It was an undergarment made of leather, like a pair of panties, tightly enclosing the penis and balls except for a little hole through which the tip of the cock was allowed to peep. The garment was so cleverly moulded that any erection would be awfully painful, if not downright impossible. And I knew that the growing hairs of Freddie's new pubic forest would itch quite abominably, and he would be unable to scratch himself through the thick leather. The crowning touch was a bull's pizzle about six inches long sewn into the underside of the garment, and which was inserted fully into the anus.

'This is the very latest thing, Alfred,' I said. 'It is a perfect regulator. Now, you may only move your bowels with my permission, although you are permitted to sprinkle whenever you want. I wish I could see you sitting in church with that great pizzle stuck inside your bum! Only I have the power to unlock you, of course, and that shall be our little secret. You might like to know that I tried it on myself before I gave you it, and I know the pizzle is quite a corking one!'

He smiled, all soppy.

'Thank you, Mistress,' he purred.

When the coast was clear, and everyone had departed to church, I made my way to the village, but took a devious route for concealment. I skirted the wood, where I noticed that the ground seemed to have been tidied and cleared; it looked as though some diagram had been painted on the soil in ochre, rather like the lines of a cricket pitch. I did not give it much thought, because I was so excited at the prospect of viewing the vicar's depraved collection, not least because I scented opportunities for – persuasion. Blackmail is a rather distasteful word.

Miss Chytte was quite agitated, and said she had changed her mind and did not want to go through with our plan. I told her not to be silly, that there was no risk, and that I knew just the thing to set her mind at rest. And I was right – a quick, juicy set on the bare bum with a pickled elm rod, and she was as happy as a bird!

We walked through the deserted village, dressed in sombre black satin and clutching prayer books, as though going late to church.

'Tell me, Miss Chytte,' I said casually, 'do you not

miss the lights and hubbub of the great metropolis? Budd's Titson must seem very quiet after a while, not to say dreary.'

She sighed.

'You know what keeps me here,' she replied.

'What you *think* keeps you here,' I corrected. 'Perhaps you are afraid of breaking free, one reason why I want you to face reality, and view this depraved collection of our dear vicar.'

'You may be right, Miss Cumming. And yes, I yearn for the worldly wisdom and tolerance of London, where ladies of my – our – persuasion are free to seek their pleasures without censure or hindrance. But it is academic, money is the problem, how can I sell this business of mine, and get enough to establish myself back in London?'

'Money might not be a problem, Miss Chytte.'

And as we passed the various shops and business places whose owners I regularly serviced, I gave details of their erotic penchants, of which whipping was by far the mildest!

'Yes,' I said gaily, 'the butcher, the baker, the candlestick-maker, I have had them all, Miss Chytte, and grown quite prosperous as a result. These Cornish folk like to look poor, but they all have money under their mattresses, and a lot of it has now found its way under my mattress!'

I told her of the various indecencies that I performed for money, sometimes charging ten shillings or even a guinea. She listened, open-mouthed.

'Yes,' I said merrily, 'Mr Treglown the bank manager always gives me a guinea, and I do not even have to fuck. He likes me to . . . to stool on his penis. Is that not strange? I think there must be some connection between ordure and money. But my point is: if these crude country folk can harbour such bizarreries, think how much more sophisticated and sensuous will be the erotic pleasures demanded by the jaded, wealthy inhabitants of London?'

'Would that I were there,' she said, with another sigh. I decided it was time to tell the direct truth, and took her by the shoulders, facing her with an intent stare.

'Come with me to London, Miss Chytte. There is nothing for us here. I intend to set up the most bizarre and exclusive house of pleasure in town. There! What do you say to that?'

'You mean . . . sell my body, as a whore?' she stammered. 'Why, Miss Cumming!'

'As a *specialist*,' I insisted. 'Your tastes are Sapphic, my dear, but you do not need to be fucked by any man: there are plenty of rich women who will pay for discreet Sapphic pleasure. And you like to take the whip; why, London is bursting with men and women who long to whip and be whipped. Miss Chytte, your tough hide can be your fortune! Society is full of hypocrisy concerning the profession of gay girls. If lustful practices bring you pleasure, as they do me, then why not do them for money? I have had nearly every man in this village, one way or another, and I am not ashamed! But the market is limited, whereas in London there is an unending stream of clients to pay for their satisfactions. I am not talking about the sordid life of a streetwalker, but a life of luxury, friendships and even power. You know what influence is wielded by the famous Parisian courtesans, the *grandes horizontales*, who became the mistresses of princes and generals. Why, the same applies in our own country, you can be sure. Come with me, Miss Chytte. Freddie and I will be so happy, together we shall conquer the gay world of London!'

'Freddie?' she gasped. 'You mean –'

I put my finger to my lips and grinned.

'Yes, my charge, young Alfred. I have been training him in obedience and to enjoy uninhibited lustfulness at my direction. But he does not yet know what I have in store . . .'

She gulped, and swallowed, and took a deep breath.

'Yes, Miss Cumming – Mistress – I will gladly come with you to London. Oh, I am so happy!'

And, merrily, we entered the silent vicarage.

Once inside the familiar house, I was not exactly scared – it was evident that the place was empty – but I suddenly felt an overpowering urge to stool! I have learnt that this is a common nervous reaction amongst those who burgle houses, although I did not consider myself a burglar. I made straight for the commode, where, just in time, I evacuated my bowels quite copiously. This achieved, I busied myself with the matter in hand, and slipped the key into the locked door behind the velvet curtain. Miss Chytte was trembling, but I was quite calm now, and before she could have any more doubts, I pushed her into the room.

We were in half-light, the heavy shutters admitting only a dim luminescence. Around us stood an eerie array of life-size sculptures, as it seemed, for they were shrouded in canvas. In one corner of the room stood a large chest of the seafaring type, and beyond that a velvet drape, about twelve feet by ten, hung on the wall, evidently covering some portrait or other painting. I opened it, and saw there a tableau depicting the torments of naked, martyred St Agatha!

'Do not be frightened, Miss Chytte, after all the vicar is a minister of religion,' I said somewhat sardonically. 'His fun may be obscene, but it is only fun.'

'A minister of *what* religion?' she replied in a tremulous whisper.

The first sculpture I unveiled was certainly obscene: it showed Mrs Turnpike, nude, being taken in both orifices by two horned devils, one of whom was Mr Tannoc and the other the servant Dorkins. I hurriedly replaced the cover, and went on to the next, and the next. All depicted scenes of the most horrific debauchery, pairs, groups, and trios and whole groups of both sexes or the same sex, engaged in every debauched practice imaginable: and all with contorted, grimacing faces that were the faces of the vicar's doughty parishioners!

In the centre of the gallery, towering over these clay orgiasts, stood a tableau that was larger than life size. I reached up, my own hand trembling now, and pulled away the covering.

Two nude figures leered at us. One was Lady Whimble, and she wore a crown of leaves, thorns and berries, carrying a wand, or spear, about six feet long. Her hair was a nest of snarling serpents.

Beside her stood the Reverend Turnpike himself, his prick erect and Lady Whimble's hand cupping his balls while his own paw was buried inside her. The skin of a flayed goat draped his back, so that his head appeared to wear horns; his feet were goat's hooves. The eyes of both statues had been painted crimson.

'He is the devil,' moaned Miss Chytte, 'and we have both lain with him!'

'He is no devil,' I rapped, 'just a wicked man with deluded fantasies.'

She pointed at the chest.

'Open that!' she cried. 'I do not dare . . . the photographs!'

There were eight leather-bound photographic albums in the chest, and I inspected them all. I was in there, of course, singly and with Mrs Turnpike or with Freddie. I thought I did not look half bad; at

163

least I seemed to be enjoying myself, unlike the other photographic orgiasts, whose contortions seemed to take place in abject fear and self-loathing. At any rate, the photographs left nothing to the imagination, least of all those depicting poor Miss Chytte. She was right – any respectable woman would be ruined by the publication of these things. However, my plans for myself and Miss Chytte did not involve respectability; a state I wished to transcend.

Under the albums was another box, containing the photographic plates. This pleased me. I put everything back and closed the chest again, having decided to steal the plates prior to my return to London. What pleasant material they would make for a little persuasion, or insurance! For there were faces there which were not of the locality, or even Cornwall: faces which I half-recognised, dimly, as though from some old illustrated paper. I had no doubt that these ladies and gentlemen would find the plates, or at least my silence about their existence, well worth a modest financial investment.

And as a bonus, I would have Mr Izzard make some prints of *my* likeness, for the vicar was not a bad photographer at all!

I told Miss Chytte a white lie: that there was nothing of her in this collection, and she sighed with relief.

But there was one photograph out of sequence, and I could not tell where it was supposed to fit into this gruesome procession of lust. A man fucked, or buggered, poor Miss Chytte, while Lady Whimble and Turnpike looked on. His face was vaguely familiar, but I could not place it – then it came to me. I had seen his portrait in Rakeslit Hall, and it was none other than the absent Lord Whimble.

I knew then that I must quit this sinister household

as soon as possible. One thing that troubled me was how to explain such things to my dear young charge, for it was obvious that he could not be aware of these goings-on. Unless he *did* know, and by some strange infantile mechanism of the brain, had suppressed the awful knowledge in order to keep his sanity.

Summer gave way to autumn; the days became sombre and gusty, and, wrapped in warm clothing, hat and scarf, I could hardly remember the abandon with which I had sported naked in the vicarage garden. It had seemed so natural under the golden sun. Now, our mood was decorous and even chastened. Oddly enough, I still took tea with the vicar and Mrs Turnpike, and it was as though nothing of the summer's events had taken place at all! Sculpture and modelling were not mentioned: the vicar, to be sure, did not allude to his rather expensive buggery of me on that gravestone. And I, of course, let no hint drop that I knew the contents of his bizarre gallery. To seem cold or unfriendly would arouse suspicion, and I was sure I was the object of enough suspicion already. My meetings with the gentlemen of the village carried on – income is income, whatever the weather – but were of necessity less frequent, due to the rain and cold.

The vicar talked now, not of art, but of church business: the festivals to be celebrated, and especially the imminent night of Hallowe'en. I told the vicar that I thought this was a pagan rite, with hobgoblins, witches, and so on.

'Originally, yes,' he enthused. 'But I try to incorporate what is good and natural in such superstitions into the good works of our own religion. There is a kernel of truth, a yearning for the absolute, in even the most debased rites of paganism.'

I gave no hint that I knew a lot about his good works – debased rites seemed nearer the mark. Yet, such was the tranquil normality of the village and its inhabitants that I wondered whether the horrible things I had witnessed in the secret gallery had not been a figment of my imagination.

In the meantime I prepared for Freddie's 'big day', fast approaching, when I should escort him to Eton, where he was to be examined for entrance. My visits to Miss Chytte continued, and I found that I was becoming very fond of her. Our sessions took on a jovial, even friendly mood. On the other hand, I strictly rationed my visits from Freddie. I did not want him to become jovial, but wished to keep him in a constant state of lustful hunger for my body.

Freddie was doing well, especially at French. I derived great amusement from the continuing saga of Yvette, who by now found herself one of the hundreds of concubines of the Emperor of China, where her feet were bound and she had to endure horrid floggings from the court eunuchs! I had to explain to Freddie what a eunuch was.

I considered that he was by now disciplined enough to discontinue the treatment with restrainers, although I must say I had enjoyed removing his pouch and anal retainer every morning so that he could hurry to the bathroom. The poor boy's cock hairs were growing into a wonderfully thick new forest, and of course itched abominably.

I decided that his brain must be stimulated as much as possible, and to this end employed a technique of the yogis called *karezza*, which I had learned from the pages of Professor Muffat.

This is a method of fucking without the male's achieving orgasm, and involves tremendous self-restraint, so that a yogi can pleasure a woman in this way for hours!

This means that the vital energy is not dissipated in a spend, but is directed up the spinal cord into the brain, producing great wisdom and spiritual power. I did not know how far Freddie was capable of progressing along the path of spiritual power, but I thought it might do his French homework some good. So, every morning, I would give him a good spanking – about thirty with my hand on the bare bum – and then frig his cock until he was just about to spend; then seize the shaft of his penis between my thumb and forefinger and squeeze it very hard, which would make it subside again. It made him incredibly frisky, and I could see that he longed to come, whether in my hand or in my cunt, but I was very sparing indeed with those favours. I am sure it enriched his brain immensely!

It was hard to restrain myself, but if I wanted, I had a ready supply of clients in the village who would pay me for their pleasure and my own. I always gave – and give – good value for money, which is the soundest business practice, for it is not the first purchase that counts, but the second, third and so on. I allowed Freddie to shave my bush, which he enjoyed mightily, although Miss Chytte was peeved that I had not let her do it, so I promised that she could do it the next time, if she behaved herself. My customers liked the novelty; and I found that I was very intrigued by my silky bare mons when I chose to pleasure myself with a clit rubbing.

Another thing I discovered, is that it is generally powerful men who like to be whipped. And if this was the case in the society of Cornwall, where power was measured in cows and acres, then how much more would it be in the fabulous wealth of London society! Exercise of power demands humiliation and pain, so as a balance I decided it was time to endure a whipping myself.

I went to sleep wondering whether to submit to Freddie, or to Miss Chytte. But my mind was made up for me. Around midnight I heard the sound of a horse galloping, and I knew it must be Freddie, on his way to the beach at Damehole Point. Without pausing to reflect, I leapt from my bed and dressed hurriedly, not bothering with panties or stockings. Then, wrapped in my warmest cloak and holding my boots, I tiptoed downstairs and out of the dark house, towards the stables.

It was the work of a moment to secure a steed, and soon I was galloping towards the ocean, the full moon gleaming on the empty moorland and the fresh smell of the sea filling my lungs.

I knew that this was to be the moment. For the first time, I would give myself to Freddie, and for this night, I would be his.

Onward I rode, my hair streaming behind me, taking walls and ditches at a gallop, my heart pounding. At last I halted at the top of the cliff.

Below me stretched an immense silver strand; a track wound tortuously down to it, and at the bottom of the track, beside the looming cliff, Freddie's horse was tethered. Freddie's white body jumped and cartwheeled exuberantly in the crashing surf, and when he at last emerged, dripping from the ocean, I knew he had seen me. He was lovely to watch, like a young colt frisking.

He stretched out his arms to me, and my heart went out to him.

I rode down to the beach, and tethered my mount, then crossed the sand to his side. The sea crashed, and the silvery powdered sand was cool between my toes. The smell of the sea, of life itself, filled my body.

Under my cloak, I was naked.

Miss Chytte I loved, but I knew, as I had always

known, that I must be whipped by a man. By my man. By Freddie.

'Mistress,' he said in a low voice. 'You have come to me.'

'Yes, Freddie,' I replied. 'It is time.'

Gravely, I withdrew the birch from beneath my cloak and handed it to him.

He took it and held it before him, gazing at me with wide eyes that were sad and joyous at the same time. His manhood was stiff for me, gleaming proudly in the moonlight, and I thought I had never desired anything so much.

'Whip me, Freddie,' I said softly. 'Whip my naked body. Do with me what you will, for this night I am yours.'

He took my cloak from me, and laid it on the sand. I placed myself face down upon it, my arms and legs outstretched in a cross. He knelt and kissed me, all down my back, and on my feet and buttocks.

His breath was hot on my shivering skin. I felt the wetness in my cunt; my heart pounded with fear and excitement and desire. I longed to feel his lash on my naked skin, punishing me, reducing me to nothing, making me exist only through his rod.

'Oh, Freddie,' I sighed. 'Didn't you know I would come, one of these days?'

'Yes, Mistress, I knew.'

'It's just that I was not ready. I needed time.'

He stroked my back and caressed the nape of my neck, while his lips played on the cleft of my buttocks.

Then he lay down on top of me, his arms and legs stretched like mine, but upside down, so that my hands clasped his toes, while his cock nestled in the cleft of my arse, and he bent my legs back to take both of my feet in his mouth, where he licked my toes with his hot wet tongue. He stayed in this position for an age, and my cunt was so hot and wet I could hardly stay still.

At last I could wait no longer. 'Whip me now, sweet Freddie,' I moaned.

He whipped me then, with hard, tender, loving strokes that made my heart dance and my flesh with it. I was electric with joy, and my whole body sang, and I thought I had never been so alive before, as my moon watched me being flogged.

Freddie was my hunter, my conqueror; his fierce gaze made me melt with fear and lust. My body was feeble with pain and with my overpowering desire; he saw that I was helpless in his power, and smiled cruelly.

'Please . . . fuck me,' I begged.

Suddenly, his mouth was on mine, and his cock was ramming my cunt with a fury I had not yet experienced; as though he wanted to tear me apart, like an enemy. And I wanted it too. I had never felt so wet, so deliciously helpless; I moaned and babbled as my jerking pelvis matched his rhythm.

'Oh, fuck me, you beast, fuck me harder with that giant cock, fuck me till I burst . . . I am your slave!'

He howled as his seed spurted into me, and I cried out with him, for at that moment my body was consumed by a heavenly fire and I experienced the most powerful climax I had ever known. His roaring was quite superhuman, as though I was draining the very essence of his manhood from his bucking loins, and afterwards, he sank to my breast, exhausted.

'Oh . . . Mistress, Mistress . . .' he sobbed.

I cradled his head and stroked him, whispering:

'Come to me, sweet Freddie,' and I smiled, for I knew that I had him in my power, now and forever . . .

13

Household Cavalry

It was the great day! A misty October morning saw Freddie and me packed off to Exeter, there to board the express train to London. Freddie looked adorable in his top hat, bum-freezer jacket, and tight, striped trousers, with his unruly blond locks cascading deliciously over his starched collar. A uniform on a man is so exciting, as it hints at the naked male power beneath!

For myself, I had chosen a stern costume of black satin that buttoned up to the neck and wrists, and felt every inch the stern governess. It was a bumpy, bone-shaking journey: I amused myself by flirting with Freddie, using only the teasing of my eyes to make his trousers bulge, and his face flush. I longed to caress him there, but I decided there would be time for that later.

Instead, I reminded him gently that I carried a restrainer in my case, and a cane too, in case he should need discipline, so as not to disgrace himself in the learned company he would shortly encounter.

There were not many passengers on the train, and we quickly found a first-class compartment to ourselves. I set Freddie down to study a further instalment of Yvette, where she is rescued from the Chinese Emperor's harem by a dashing English officer, and taken back to London on the Trans-Siberian

Express. Unfortunately they are captured by a band of Cossacks, who proceed to whip her soundly and then fuck her one after the other – about fifty of the ruffians – while her protector is obliged to watch helplessly! He manages to free himself and uncouple the carriage from the train, so that all the Cossacks plunge to their deaths in the icy waters of Lake Baikal. But the Englishman has now acquired a taste for lustful practices, and after forcing her to whore for him in Warsaw, Berlin, and Paris, he sets her up in an apartment in Bayswater as a martinet, or whipping-girl, for the delectation of the sophisticates of London.

While he was avidly reading this gripping stuff, I made myself comfortable by taking off my boots and stretching out my legs so that my stockinged toes rested on his manhood, which I stimulated with gentle little tickles. Of course he got hard. He was in this noticeable state of excitement when, at Taunton, a middle-aged lady entered our compartment. There is nothing more disagreeable than being disturbed in a railway compartment one has thought one's own, so I began to frig Freddie's cock quite voluptuously and blatantly.

'Oh!' cried the good woman, understandably shocked.

'Don't mind his Grace,' I said cheerfully. 'You know what these dukes are like, rampant as sin. He hasn't had a fuck since this morning, and already he is lusting for more. You couldn't oblige, could you, Ma'am? It is just that I am so sore between my legs.'

'Oh!' she squealed again, and hurried away – but not before curtseying in the doorway with a shy murmur of:

'If your Grace will excuse me.'

And we laughed all the way to Paddington.

I made Freddie act as porter and carry our luggage from the platform at Paddington into the Great Western Hotel, where I proposed we should take tea before taking our train to Windsor, the station for the village of Eton. We went up into Praed Street and in through the front entrance of the hotel, for I wanted Freddie to see the clusters of gay girls, or prostitutes, plying their trade all round the station. He duly noticed this feature of metropolitan life, and was amazed. I myself was so glad to be back in the grimy but exhilarating air of London, and decided it was time to explain a few of the facts of life to my charge.

We ordered a splendid tea, with hot buttered crumpets, jam and cakes and scones, and set down to eat with hearty appetites. I was entranced; inside, warmth and comfort and food, and outside the autumn twilight, never so sweet as in London, blowing the leaves around the swirling skirts of the street girls.

Freddie ogled them, and I must admit that some of them were uncommonly pretty. It was evident that he had some dim inkling of their purpose, as they accosted gentlemen emerging from the station.

'They, Freddie, are prostitutes,' I said.

'You mean, they sell their bodies for money? How awful that must be!'

'And why, Alfred?' I asked. 'Does not every working man prostitute himself when he takes an employer's shilling? When you had shillings, which you stole from your Mama, then I was your prostitute.'

'Do not say such things, Mistress,' he cried. 'That is different.'

'It is not different. All life is a series of transactions, of buying and selling. And a person who has no assets, meaning, land, money, property or influence, must sell what they do have, which is their body.

173

These ladies here are selling their most valuable asset, and it has the advantage that it can be used and sold over and over again. Imagine a cornfield which, when the crop is harvested, at once produces a second crop, and a third, and so on indefinitely!'

'But why should a man pay for it when it can be done for nothing?'

I laughed.

'Alfred, you have much to learn. There are men who find themselves without a wife or mistress, and wish only to perform the brute act, without all the pleasant flirtation and flattery, outings and presents, which some ladies think indispensable to an amorous friendship. Some men want variety, or require services that their wives find indecent. Some crave the thrilling anonymity of the streetwalker, or else the opulence of a brothel, where a man can choose amongst a whole array of beauties, or have them all, indulging his every whim, like a child presented with an inexhaustible chocolate box.'

I withdrew a silver cigarette case, and extracted a Balkan Sobranie, which a waiter promptly rushed to light. I let the fragrant smoke dribble from my lips in a lazy, sluttish way.

'This is London,' I said coolly. 'And ladies smoke. They do all kinds of things. Did you know that there are brothels – houses of pleasure – for ladies as well as men? Here in the heart of the metropolis there is an abundance of discreet houses where every variety of pleasure can be obtained; where ladies may pay for a virile young boy like yourself, Alfred; where men buy the services of Chinese or Negro girls or bugger pretty boys. There are places specialising in the lash, where both men and women go to whip and be whipped. Such is the ungovernable perversity of human lust that the list is endless!'

I blew smoke in his puzzled face.

'In this mechanised and soulless age, men require ever more bizarre stimulations for their jaded senses. Stimulations, Alfred, for which like everything else, money must be exchanged. For example, it may surprise you to know that I have fucked almost every man in your village, and for money. Which is why I can afford tea at the Great Western, and cigarettes . . .'

'Oh,' he muttered numbly, his face a picture of sadness.

'Do not act thus, Freddie,' I said, taking his hand. 'I sold my body as a commodity. It was a transaction. And by treating my body as nothing more than a fleshly machine, I use it to amass wealth, and thus am free of its dictates. And I believe that a good prostitute, one who can offer the subtlest pleasures, the most refined tortures and humiliations – for that is what men want, the poor lost things – can be the freest of women. She does not have trade, like these street girls, she has suitors.'

I pressed his fingertips to my lips.

'Discipline, Freddie, is the thing,' I said softly. 'We must use our bodies, not allow our bodies to use us. Only your cock gives me pleasure, my boy, because it is not just flesh, it is manhood. It is you. For the rest, it is just a mechanical business, nothing more than –'

'A transaction, Mistress?' he said with a wide grin.

I lit another cigarette and inhaled deeply.

'Alfred,' I said, blowing ribbons of smoke, 'there is a possibility that you do not gain entrance to Eton. What would you do then?'

'I hadn't thought. Anything to be near you, Mistress! Perhaps the Guards. If you are in London, then that is where I must be also.'

'Very prettily said, my boy,' I smiled. 'Well, be

175

assured that I will have plans for you. They may not be your mother's plans, but what I would have in mind is that you become a sort of partner in my transactions.'

'I will do anything to please you – you know that.'

'Good. For what I have in mind, Alfred, is to become very rich. And to do that I intend to open the most voluptuous and degraded house of pleasure in all Europe!'

At about five, we left the hotel and proceeded to the rank of cabs. We had to cross London to Waterloo Station, whence the trains departed to Windsor. But before selecting a cab, I instructed Freddie to accost, or let himself be accosted by, one of the street ladies, simply to find out what she charged for her favours.

Sheepishly he obeyed. And I watched with some amusement as he engaged in embarrassed conversation with the whore, then politely tipped his hat and returned to the cab rank. The girl looked none too pleased at this small waste of her time, but in business one must always be prepared for promotional costs which might not seem profitable in the short term. We got into a cab, and since we had ample time, I instructed the driver to take us the long way to Waterloo, past Piccadilly, Trafalgar Square and Parliament, for Freddie's instruction.

'Well, Alfred,' I said. 'Tell me what you have found out.'

'She seemed quite businesslike, Mistress,' he said. 'She told me that a short time was five shillings, a long time ten, with an extra five shillings for fucking in the arse or sucking the penis, and ten shillings for a caning. Or all together for three pounds, for the whole night.'

'Very interesting,' I mused. 'She should have a card

printed with her tariff, it would save time. And never forget, Freddie, that a prostitute, like every other worker, is paid for her time as well as her services. Time is money!'

On our way to Waterloo, I explained the sights of the city, and Freddie was suitably impressed. 'You shall be my consort in pleasure and debauchery, Alfred,' I said. 'A lifetime cannot exhaust the wonders of the appetites of this seething metropolis, appetites which I shall play my part in feeding and inflaming. The humblest London street, whether in Crouch End or Collier's Wood, conceals lusts and secrets beyond the most fantastic imagination. In the country, all is open, everyone's business known. But the city, my dear, the city is mystery, awe, the beauty of a million nightmares!'

We arrived at Windsor shortly before seven o'clock and proceeded to the Cloisters Hotel in Peascod Street, just across from the magnificent Windsor Castle, and a short walk from Victoria Barracks, where the cavalry lodged. I showed Freddie the River Thames which lay at the bottom of the High Street, and Windsor Bridge, over which we would walk the next day to the village of Eton and its college.

After a light supper, I sent Freddie to his room, which was on a separate floor from my own, and told him to be in bed asleep by ten o'clock, for a good night's rest. I myself had other business.

I hurried downstairs and handed in my room key, explaining that I wished to take a walk on this cold, clear night, and view the moonlit splendours of Windsor.

'A lady may safely walk our streets at night,' said the crone proudly. 'It is not like London, where all sorts of vile persons throng the streets. As long, of course, as you keep away from the public houses where the rough soldiery go.'

177

'Why, I have no intention of visiting such places,' I said truthfully.

I made my way to the High Street, where I turned right into Sheet Street, away from the sparkling river, and towards Victoria Barracks. There I took up my station.

I took out my nice yellow yew cane, which I had concealed in my cloak, and began to stroll nonchalantly along the opposite pavement for a distance of about fifty yards, then turned and retraced my steps. All the while I tapped the ground with my yew cane, and gave it an occasional swish in the air; to a casual observer, it would look like a walking stick, but I was not looking for any casual observer.

It was a bright, clear night, and there were plenty of passers-by both male and female. Some of the men gave me looks, and I noticed that a few of them passed me several times in each direction.

Whenever an officer left the barracks, I looked at him coyly, and whistled a little tune. And it did not take long before a tall young man in the uniform of a major stopped and addressed me.

'It is a cold night to be out,' he said with a smile. He was quite handsome, with splendid curly moustaches. I smiled back and replied that the beauties of Windsor made a promenade worthwhile.

'You are a visitor?'

'Yes, from Cornwall.'

'A long way indeed. But Windsor! Why, you should see the beauties of London. That is where I am normally stationed, in the cavalry barracks at Knightsbridge – next to Hyde Park, you know.'

'I believe the riding is very good there, sir,' I said softly.

'You are fond of riding?'

'In the right company, sir.' I gave my cane a little

178

swish. 'There is nothing more exciting than the crack of a riding crop on the haunches of a fine stallion.'

'I dare say you are lonely without a stallion, then.'

'I admit it, sir. But where can a lady find a mount at this time of night?'

I swished the cane again, and he breathed in deeply.

'Perhaps I may offer my help,' he said.

'Oh, I doubt it, sir. To hire a suitable horse would cost at least five pounds, I mean, a horse that bucks well, and can take a good thrashing.'

'Five pounds, eh?' he said, stroking his moustaches. 'I am sure that can be arranged, Miss –?'

'Cumming, sir.'

'Well, Miss Cumming, perhaps we could discuss the matter over a glass of wine in my apartments, which are in King's Road not far from here. My window overlooks the Great Park, which is very pretty by moonlight, and you may find the deer remind you of your rural home. I am Major Dove, of the Household Cavalry.'

I accepted his arm and we set off towards the Great Park. I was trembling slightly, but I could feel that he too was very nervous. When we came to a handsome brick mansion, he fumbled awhile with keys, and soon we were ensconced in a cosy top-floor apartment, illuminated by gas. The room smelled wonderfully of maleness: leather sofas and chairs, teak tables and shelving festooned with swords, canes, and all sorts of military bric-à-brac. There was a cabinet full of shiny leather-bound books, which I inspected with polite interest as he busied himself with champagne and glasses. Outside in the park, I could see the deer slumbering peacefully on the dark grass, under a wondrous moon.

The books were unfamiliar to me, but their titles

179

left me in no doubt as to their contents! *Miss Flaybum's Academy*, *The Adventures of Lady Whippingham*, and the like. They were all works of erotica, of the flagellant tendency! I had certainly found the right client.

We sat and drank champagne for a while, making small talk – mostly his – about the military life and the splendours of London society. Beneath the bravado he seemed lonely. He missed his wife and daughter, and so on. At length he said shyly:

'I noticed you admiring my library, Miss Cumming.'

'It is a very interesting collection, sir. I am sure there is much instruction to be gleaned from its pages. Do you show it to many young ladies, sir?'

'No . . . there are not many ladies in Windsor with sufficient discernment, Miss Cumming. Perhaps *you* have.'

'And what makes you think that?'

'Why, a woman is like a horse, don't you know. You can always tell good breeding,' he said with a smirk.

I knew what sort of game to introduce.

'Sir, I find that distasteful!' I cried in a pretend rage, and picked up my cloak and cane. 'I shall take my leave, sir.'

'No!' he exclaimed in confusion. 'Please let me make amends for any impropriety! You mentioned five pounds, and here it is, to show my good faith.'

And he thrust a lovely crinkly banknote at me, which I took with a disdainful pout and, lifting my skirt, tucked it into my stocking top, affording him a tempting view of my bare thigh.

'Hmm!' I sniffed. 'You think honour worth a mere five pounds? I believe you deserve to be punished for your insolence, sir.'

180

'Please – no!' he cried, and knelt before me, then kissed the point of my boot.

'Would you rather have it known in Windsor that you have insulted a lady to her face?' I sneered. 'If you are a man, you will accept my punishment for your offence, Major Dove.'

'I accept, Miss Cumming. Punish me if you must!'

'Very well,' I replied, after pretending to think. I thrust the point of my boot right into his mouth and he licked it fervently!

'Get up, you dog, and remove all your clothing. I want you naked, sir, for I am going to thrash you.'

'Please . . . no . . . be kind . . . be gentle!' he babbled as he rapidly undressed, then stood before me naked, awaiting instructions like a hungry puppy. His prick was quite large, though not as large as some I had serviced, and nowhere near as big as Freddie's; but quite tempting, especially as it began to stiffen noticeably under my stern inspection.

'Hmm!' I snapped. 'I see your member is as insolent as its owner. Do you always become stiff before a beating?'

'N – no, Miss,' he stammered. 'But I have never been thrashed before, not by a lady, I mean.'

This was, of course, a lie.

'Well, such unruly behaviour' – I whacked his cock with the tip of my cane, upon which it rose to its full height – 'deserves a double punishment. I was going to give you three cuts on the bare backside, but now I think it shall be a full six.'

'If you insist, Miss. I submit to you.'

'Of course, I shall need a further five pounds, for with all this use, my walking cane will be ruined and need replacing!'

'Yes . . . yes!' He scrabbled in his wallet, and soon a second fiver joined its partner in my stocking top.

It was most gratifying to have money thrust at me by a naked slave, with a bobbing stiff cock!

'Good,' I said, all businesslike. 'Now, Major, you may bend over the sofa, and I am going to give your bum a tanning it will never forget. Six juicy cuts from my cane. Do not protest, for you well deserve them! Nice and slow, and as tight as I can make them.'

'Yes, Miss Cumming,' he blurted, and bent over the sofa, allowing me a fine view of his taut, muscled buttocks. 'Thank you for being so understanding.'

'Well, let us get one thing straight, Major Dove,' I continued. 'My cane is no fool, and she does not like being told untruths. When you told me you had not been thrashed by a woman before, that was all rot, wasn't it? Tell me the truth, you bad boy!'

And I swished my cane merrily so that it whacked the sofa an inch from his waist, which made him sigh deeply.

'Very well, Miss,' he murmured.

'You are quite comfortable?'

'Yes.'

'Then you may tell me your story as I punish you. I love a good story. ONE!'

And I brought the cane down hard.

'Gosh!' he said and swallowed. 'Well, there is not that much to tell. Let me think. Yes, my nanny used to spank me, you know, when I was little. She pulled down my drawers if I was naughty and slapped my bottom, and I must confess I enjoyed it, so that I was often naughty on purpose.'

'I am not talking of mere spanking,' I said sternly, 'I am talking of proper punishment. Tell me about your first taste of a woman's cane. TWO!'

'Mm! God! That . . . that would have been at my boarding school. I used to get the cane from the head-master, like all the other fellows, and from the prefects too, and I didn't like it one bit. But one weekend, when I had committed some breach of the school rules, I forget what, I was to be thrashed, and I went to the headmaster's study as usual, and found that he was not there. His place had been taken by the matron, Mrs Danvers. She was a handsome woman, about thirty-five, I think, and all the boys had a pash for her. She explained that she would be giving me my punishment, since she was the only senior member of staff present that weekend, though I found this rather odd, I must admit. Anyway, she said she had been told to give me six of the best.'

'And when she told you that, did your penis stiffen, Major?'

'Why, yes! How did you know?'

'A guess. THREE!'

The Major's breath came now in short, strained gasps.

'Oooo ... well, she told me to bend over, and stood beside me with the cane, you know, and my head was very near her bosom and I could smell her perfume, all lovely and flowery, and I must admit, my, my manhood was near bursting. She saw that and became very angry, although I think she was only pretending, and told me I was wicked, and since I was to get six, I should have to take them bare.

'I was terribly embarrassed, but she took hold of my belt and unfastened it, and in a jiffy she had pulled down my things round my ankles. I felt so afraid, because I had never taken the cane on the bare bum before, but my penis was still stiff as a board.'

'It seems to be stiff now, Major. Do I remind you of your matron?'

'I don't know.'

'FOUR!'

'Oh! Oh! Yes, perhaps, Miss. You have me all

183

confused. You are so beautiful, Miss Cumming, yes, a little bit like her, so cruel, yes, oh yes, a lot like matron!'

'And what happened?'

'Well, she caned me all right, six of the juiciest stingers you can imagine. It smarted like the blazes, and I felt all choked. But when it was over at last, she took my head and pressed it against her bosom, and I could feel her breath very strong under her white starched apron, and smell that lovely perfume. She stroked my hair and comforted me with all sorts of cooing softnesses, and then she unbuttoned her blouse so that her breasts were naked for me, and she put my lips to them, making me suck her nipples, which were so big and hard and stood up like sweet cherries. And then –'

'FIVE!'

I began to unbutton the top of my blouse.

'God! Oh! Ooo! Yes, then she put my hand on her blue apron, between her legs, and made me rub her there gently, while she touched me on my stiff penis, and stroked it, and tickled my balls, and then she took a silk hanky from her pocket, lovely and scented with her woman's smell, and she put it on the tip of my penis, rubbed hard, and then – then I spent, Miss. I spurted my spunk as her sweet hand rubbed my cock and my face was in her breasts, and I rubbed her between her thighs and she moaned as my juice came from me . . . Oh, Miss Cumming!'

'SIX!'

I threw aside my cane and with my blouse open and breasts bare, I pressed his face against me, then took hold of his stiff cock and rubbed the swollen glans with the tips of my fingers until I felt him shudder, and a lovely hot jet spurted from him into my cupped hand.

'Oh, Miss Cumming,' he panted, 'what a fine filly you are! I have never been punished so beautifully!'

I allowed him to kiss my boots again before donning his uniform, and then we resumed our places on the sofa to continue enjoying our champagne, with no evidence that anything had taken place, except for his flushed visage and moist, adoring eyes.

I had gained a most valuable insight, or confirmed what I already knew, namely that many men love to be caned by a woman. In beating a man, a woman touches him in a most intimate and sensitive place. The rod is an extension of herself, and in using it she shows that she cares about him enough to inflict pain.

And by the same token, I now love *my* buttocks to be beaten by a loving woman, or a puissant man.

We chatted a little more, like old friends. The Major told me about his wife, Thalia, and their daughter, both of whom he loved dearly. His wife was a 'fine filly' but unfortunately 'wouldn't take the crop', and was prepared to administer it to him grudgingly if at all.

This is a very common complaint amongst married gentlemen, who are obliged to seek comfort elsewhere, and frequently, as the Major ruefully admitted, in quarters less than salubrious.

At length I said that it was time for me to go.

'Are you long in Windsor, Miss Cumming?' he asked hopefully. 'For I am often naughty and insolent, you know.'

'I must return home tomorrow,' I replied. 'But I intend to be in London frequently, Major, so you may give me your card and I will perhaps consent to let you attend me.'

I took one of his handsome gold-embossed cards, and prepared to take my leave.

But suddenly, on a mischievous impulse, I turned

185

my back to him and bent over, at the same time lifting my skirts high so that he could see my panties. His eyes popped, as, my head turned to him and my mouth creased in a mocking smile, I peeled down my panties. He could see my bare arse, but not my cunt, and he was quite bewitched when I handed him the panties. They were sopping wet from my own excitement, and I let them dangle by his lips before dropping them into his lap.

'A memento, Major,' I said, allowing my skirts to fall again.

'Why . . . Miss Cumming! I see from the stripes on your lovely hindquarters that you are no stranger to punishment yourself!'

Indeed, the marks of Freddie's birch had not yet faded from my skin.

'That is for me to know, and you to find out, sir,' I retorted. 'But your question shows that the impertinence has not yet been thrashed out of you. I order you to wear my undergarment on parade every day for a week. On our next meeting, if you have obeyed, I may consent to chastise you properly . . .'

14

Business in Town

After a hearty breakfast of bacon and eggs, Freddie and I left the Cloisters Hotel and deposited our cases at the railway station. Then we strolled over Windsor Bridge into the pretty somnolence of Eton village. The college stood majestic at the far end of the High Street, which was more or less the only street, since the college seemed to be the only reason for the village's existence.

At the college gates, a curious spectacle awaited us. From a top-floor window protruded the head of a boy slightly younger than Freddie. His neck was pinioned between window and sill, and his face was contorted in tearful pain, like one of the gargoyles on the great mediaeval cathedrals, intended as warnings against demons. It was evident that the boy was being flogged, for we could hear the clatter of feet on floorboards, and then a fierce crack which made the window shudder as the boy jumped in shock. A crowd of Eton boys had gathered below to watch the spectacle with great merriment. Freddie looked rather pale.

I asked one of the top-hatted boys what was going on.

'Just a new boy. They need to be taught manners, the little swine! Just look at him blubbing, like a gel!'

'Were you not a new boy yourself, once?' I asked.

'That was last year,' he replied scornfully, 'and *I* could take a good six without blubbing, on the bare bum too.'

But I counted eight strokes before the tormented wretch was released, and in view of the crowd, who jeered and threw oranges or apples, was made to kiss the cane that had thrashed him.

'I am not sure I want to go to Eton, Miss,' said Freddie rather uncertainly. 'It seems a cruel place.'

'Nonsense, Freddie,' I cried brightly, 'why you will soon come to enjoy it, and when you are senior, you can thrash and bully those smaller than yourself! You are no stranger to discipline, my boy.'

'But that is *your* discipline, and very precious to me.'

'Well, chin up, and be brave,' I smiled, as I delivered him into the lugubrious hands of the college servants, and made my way quickly back to Windsor Station. As I passed the Victoria Barracks, I could hear the troopers on parade, and I wondered if Major Dove had been to Eton. How I pitied my French cousins, unlearned in the sweet chastisements of our great English public schools!

I caught the nine o'clock train to Waterloo, which took me past the leafy suburbs of south-west London – Colnbrook, Isleworth, Twickenham, all decked in their tender autumn foliage, and as far as Richmond on the river, where I got off the train.

I then took a connecting train for the short journey to Wimbledon, where I arrived shortly before eleven, and left my baggage in the station depository.

I would meet Freddie at seven in the evening, in the Great Western Hotel at Paddington, where we would dine before boarding the overnight train to Exeter; this left me a day to conduct my clandestine business.

It was with great joy that I found myself once more

in Wimbledon, the nearest thing I had to a home. However I had no intention of making a sentimental visit to St Agatha's, my old school, which I had departed so suddenly not long before. When I did choose to make a visit, it would not be a sentimental one.

First, I went to an estate agent near the station, where such establishments generally abound, and explained that I needed a small house to rent for three months, until I could find a suitable property to purchase. I made up some fiction about returning from South Africa with a great fortune, to look after my widowed mother, but the agent paid more attention to my stockinged legs, which, with my skirt daringly unbuttoned to the thigh, I was careful to cross and uncross for his inspection, as my hand toyed with all the banknotes in my purse. After a good luncheon in the Railway Hotel (which he paid for) I took possession of number 323 Worple Road, a pleasant thoroughfare at the bottom of the hill, on the way to Raynes Park; St Agatha's of course towered at the top of the hill, beside the common.

My next call was to the Bank of West Surrey, where I desired to open a current account. I told the manager, Mr Dryden, much the same story, embroidered with some stuff about an inheritance.

Banks are like courthouses; they try and look as distant as possible from the sordid transactions which are the reason for their existence, namely money and crime. The Bank of West Surrey, a cathedral-like affair on the Broadway, was no exception.

'This is slightly irregular, Miss Cumming,' said Mr Dryden. 'You see, we require character references for the opening of an account.'

'Money is money, where I come from,' I exclaimed, 'and needs no character references. In South Africa it is the banks who must furnish references, to prove they are honest!'

'Well, really!' he blurted, not knowing whether to be perplexed or angry. I hitched up my skirt a foot or so, and crossed my legs with a flourish.

'I shall be a most profitable customer, Mr Dryden, and shall have frequent occasion to consult with you on my financial affairs. Perhaps I seem forward; it is just that in South Africa, we colonials do business in a more direct and forthright way than in the mother country.'

'I don't doubt it, Miss Cumming,' he stammered, as I raised my skirt quite coquettishly, allowing him to see my garters and my panties, and a good glimpse of my creamy bare thigh skin. And for a fleeting moment, I parted my thighs so that he had a brief glimpse – accidental, of course – of paradise; namely my panties pulled tightly around the swelling of my mons.

Suffice it to say that ten minutes later I had my money safe in the Bank of West Surrey, and was the proud possessor of a chequebook, with Mr Dryden, quid pro quo, the possessor of a very noticeable erection, which was probably as much a novelty to him as the chequebook was to me.

It remained to pay a visit to the faithful Mr Izzard. I took a cab up to Wimbledon village, and stopped before his pharmacy. He beamed with joy and surprise as I entered the shop, and I permitted him to remove my gloves for me, which he did with great delight, covering the soft leather with kisses both before and after removing them.

I explained my plans to him, adding that I was in rather a hurry just at the moment, but that he would certainly see a lot of me in the months and indeed years to come, if things worked out as I expected. I felt I could relax with this nice little man, and as we sat I made sure he saw a lot of me then and there; I kept my legs tantalisingly open, so that he had a tempting view of my thighs and my panties too. He smiled almost beatifically.

'What exciting plans, Miss Cumming! Such opportunities both financial and scientific! I have such intricate and wonderful appliances in mind, which will serve your purposes most admirably, I am sure.'

'Then please go ahead and construct them, Mr Izzard,' I replied, 'for I can assure you I shall be your very best customer. But be honest – it is not just my business plans that excite you. Are you not a tiny bit enamoured of this place between my thighs, you naughty man?'

He blushed profoundly.

'Why, Miss Cumming – it is a work of art, as you very well know. *You* are a work of art, and your beauty will be your fortune.'

'It is very kind of you to say so,' I said, and gently I took his trembling fingertips and guided them to my quim. I brushed his fingertips along the moist surface of my panties, and then permitted him to remove them.

'You may keep them for your collection, Mr Izzard,' I said regally, 'and I can assure you there will be lots more.'

'Thank you a thousand times, dear lady,' he blurted, as he showed me to the door. 'You are so kind to your humble and obedient servant!'

'I, Mr Izzard? Kind?' I said, smiling.

That evening Freddie and I dined sumptuously at the Great Western Hotel, and had a bottle of wine, which he enjoyed. He was quite enthusiastic about his prospects for Eton, and seemed to have put the morning's distressing episode out of his mind. Of course I did not confuse him by telling him that I had no intention of letting him go to Eton, but had other plans!

After dinner, I suggested we took a stroll, and we sallied out on Praed Street. It was not long before I spied the handsome tart who had spoken to Freddie the previous evening.

'Do you like her, Freddie?' I asked slyly.

'Yes, I suppose she is good-looking,' he replied diffidently.

'In that case, I want you to fuck her,' I said.

'What?' he cried.

'For me, Freddie. Here is some money: go and engage her services, and we shall go to her room, and you shall fuck her while I watch. It is for my pleasure.'

Well, we soon found ourselves in the tart's modest but cosy room nearby, and after I had discussed prices and practices with the girl, whose name was Marlene and hailed from Glasgow, we lost no time in getting down to our lustful business. She had no objections to having an avid spectator – on the contrary, she thoroughly approved, for she could gain more 'bawbees' from the transaction. She seemed quite uninhibited, and was even quite good at feigning orgasm, as Freddie fucked her twice in the cunt and once in the anus, which seemed a matter of indifference to her. I sipped the wine I had purchased at a vintner's beforehand, and watched with great excitement as Freddie's powerful loins stroked the girl quite mercilessly.

Eventually, Freddie excused himself to go to the lavatory, and I was able to talk intimately to Marlene. She was like many gay girls, reduced by hardship to flee home and enter a life of sin, but still dreaming of respectability – some day. I explained to her that respectability could only be bought with money.

'I suppose gentlemen ask you to do some strange things at times,' I said.

'Aye, they are a queer lot, men,' she said, philosophically, 'and women too. But I never refuse to do anything, not if the bawbees are right. Some of them want to be whipped, and whip me, and that, and some of the men want ... well, they want me to do my business all over their faces or pricks. Isn't it odd? It is always the richest swells who want such humiliation. Folk talk of filthy lucre – perhaps they feel guilty at having so much of the dirty stuff, and crave to be dirtied as a punishment.'

'Well, well,' I said thoughtfully. 'You say you take the whip as well as administer it?'

'Surely!' she laughed. 'At two shillings a stroke! Why I have an arse like leather, after all the lashings I had from the dominies at school. If you can take the Scottish tawse, why your English cane is child's play.'

'Even on the bare bottom?'

'Poor Scottish lasses cannot afford to wear drawers, Miss!'

'This is something I should like to put to the test, Marlene, for I might have a proposition for you, which will considerably improve your station in life. I hope you have no objections to my administering the whipping myself?'

'For two shillings a stroke,' she replied grinning, 'I would be whipped by the devil himself. I do it for ladies too – it is all the same as long as the coins sparkle. Now just tell me how you want to take me, Miss.'

'Back on the bed, I think, Marlene,' I said, and took my cane from my bag.

Marlene took four of my tightest cuts on her bare

bottom without even a groan and without flinching. I marvelled at her power of endurance, and Freddie watched approvingly, especially when she bounced to her feet afterwards with a rueful grimace.

'Well!' she exclaimed with a smile. 'You have certainly had your money's worth, Miss, for I don't think I have ever had such a hard tanning.'

'What if you were to be tanned regularly, Marlene? Not by me, but by gentlemen, perhaps ladies, who pay far more than you are currently earning? Would you like to work for me, in comfortable quarters, with an excellent class of client; food and lodging of the finest?'

'Yes!' she cried without hesitation. 'It is nearly winter, and the street is a harsh place then.'

As she dressed, I outlined my plans, and said I would be in touch with her.

'There are other gay girls in this lodging house, Miss. Should I ask them if they are interested too?'

'The more the merrier, Marlene,' I replied. 'I think you know exactly what my requirements are. Girls who are handsome, clean, businesslike, and above all, versatile.'

'I know exactly what you mean, Miss,' she said with a wink, as she counted the money I had paid her.

I was well satisfied with the day's business, and as the night train to Exeter clattered westwards, I rewarded myself with my own treat, which was a session of glorious fucking to the rhythm of the rails with my indefatigable young buck. And when I fell into a happy, sated sleep, I dreamt that the train itself was a great tool, its smokestack spurting in an inexhaustible hot spend.

15

Milady's Boudoir

'It is time to think of your future, Miss Cumming,' said Lady Whimble, pouring herself another glass of port.

'Indeed, Milady,' I said, sipping coffee. It was a blustery wet day, the wind whipping the branches of the bare trees outside, and the scent of winter in the air.

'You have no objection, I hope, to staying with us until Christmas. After that, I dare say you will wish to seek another post as governess, since Alfred will be away at Eton. I can perhaps help you there, some good friends of mine in Wiltshire, the Volumenes, have a young whippersnapper like Alfred who needs some taming.'

'Thank you, Milady,' I replied, 'I am most grateful.' The name Volumene, though uncommon, seemed slightly familiar.

'Good,' she continued rather vaguely. 'It is coming up to Hallowe'en, you know. We always have a little celebration, which I am sure you will enjoy.'

'Hallowe'en,' I said. 'In London, we had Guy Fawkes night.'

'It is much the same thing, except that it is not for children. All the adults of the village come together to celebrate, with much merry-making, in Sally's Wood, which is the, ah, traditional place. The vicar organises things; he is very fond of Hallowe'en – it is one of our oldest Cornish rites.'

She smiled indulgently. 'He always insists that I act as Mistress of Ceremonies, saying that it is an old custom, for the lady of the Great Hall to preside. It is great fun, if rather chilly, for we have to meet at midnight! But the fire keeps us warm.'

'I look forward to it, Milady. Will Freddie be there?'

'No ... no, not Freddie. It is for grown-ups,' she answered with a slight frown. Suddenly, to my great surprise, she stood up and stretched herself like a cat, revealing a springy, youthful body which gave no sign of the crippling arthritis. I was too polite to make a remark, but she said:

'Do not be surprised at my sudden agility. The arthritic pain comes and goes, and sometimes I feel as lively as a young girl: a young girl as lithe and graceful as yourself, Miss Cumming. In fact, you remind me a little of myself when I was your age; not in physical appearance, for we are not alike, but in demeanour and poise.'

'Well, you flatter me, Milady,' I answered.

She leaned towards me and absent-mindedly stroked my hair. In doing so she allowed the loose silk robe to fall slightly forward, and I was afforded a glimpse of her breasts. I looked down and saw that beneath her peignoir she was quite naked.

'If I may say so, Milady, I think that maturity has only served to ripen your beauty,' I purred diplomatically, and she blushed.

'Why, thank you, Miss. Of course, I do not possess a figure like yours, with those full young breasts, and such a perfect bottom, which quite puts my boyish derrière to shame!'

'But I envy you that slim figure of yours!' I blurted.

'Hmmmm . . .' she said sceptically. 'How can that be so? You make me curious, Miss Cumming. It would be – amusing, to compare in front of the mirror's impartial eye.'

'Well, that is easily arranged, Milady,' I replied with a chuckle, 'for I cannot let your curiosity go unsatisfied. If you wish to look at me, I am not one of those girls who think the naked human form indecent. In fact I could not help noticing that beneath your peignoir you are . . . at your ease.'

'Oh,' she said airily, 'I cannot be bothered to dress in the mornings.'

'Then allow me the honour of attending your toilette, Milady.'

'Why not indeed? Perhaps you would care to follow me?'

Lady Whimble's languid demeanour soon disappeared after she had locked the door of her sumptuous boudoir behind us.

With a flutter of excitement, I began to undress. Her eyes devoured me as I removed shoes, stockings, garters, quite slowly and with teasing coquettishness. Then my chemise, my blouse: she gave a little gasp as she saw my big nipples standing quite stiff, with my golden rings hanging from them. At last, with a flourish, I peeled off my green silk panties and stood *au naturel* in front of my curious employer!

'I hope you approve, Milady,' I said softly, with a gleam in my eye.

'Oh, I do, I do,' she said. 'But we must compare, mustn't we?' and she let her silk peignoir slip from her body.

She reached out and playfully put her fingers through my nipple rings.

'So charming,' she whispered. 'And a ring . . . down there too. It is really quite exciting. I suppose it is the fashion in London now. How prettily the ring sits against your lovely bush! I have never seen one so thick. I have nothing but a little downy moss, like the first sprouting of a young girl. I cannot believe that mink is real, and I am quite jealous of you for having it!'

I decided to finish with false modesty. I took her hand from my breast and placed it firmly on my mink.

'There, Milady, it is quite real.'

'So much hair for one so young,' she said dreamily. 'I must stroke it; there, you don't mind. And those luscious bubbies, why, I could kiss them.'

She caressed my teats, lifting them up as though weighing them.

I put my hand on her slim, firm breasts, feeling the big nips which stood up like walnuts.

'Your teats, so slim and delicate, are very lovely, Milady,' I whispered.

'Oh, how nice,' she sighed as I rubbed her nips. 'Well, let us look in the glass, dear miss.'

We stood in front of the looking glass clasping each other's waists; with my eyes half-shut, I could imagine that I held a lovely boy to me, a slim, musky image of Freddie. I put my hand to her arse and stroked it, letting my fingers tickle the base of her spine.

'Oh,' she moaned. 'I like that.' Her fingers slipped easily into my wet cunt, where they brushed my clit, which was by now quite stiff. I placed my hand on her own cunt, which was silky and wet to my probing fingers.

'Please do kiss my bubbies, Milady,' I said, 'I should love you to.'

She knelt, and her mouth captured my left nipple, ring and all. Her tongue darted expertly over my engorged nip, and sent tingles of pleasure to my excited clitoris.

'Your lips are so tender,' I sighed. 'I should love to feel them – down there . . .' and without a word, she knelt fully and transferred her mouth to my throbbing clit, which she tongued with giddying tenderness. Her hands clasped my buttocks, kneading them, with her thumbs stroking my cleft.

'What a lovely firm arse you have,' she murmured, her eyes staring up at me and seeming to pierce me with her lust. Her lips glistened. 'I must kiss it, too.'

I turned, and at once felt her eager tongue licking the cleft of my buttocks; then her hands spread my cheeks wide and she flicked her tongue like a small piston against my anus bud. I gasped at the infernal tickling pleasure and my cunt was a river.

'Why, Miss Cumming,' she said, as she smothered my arse with kisses, 'what are these? I know you are an expert in disciplining my unruly son – but it seems you are no stranger to the cane yourself!'

I still bore the faint marks of Freddie's birching, at Damehole Point that passionate night, but I decided to be cautious.

'Oh, they are old wounds, Milady. From my last birching at St Agatha's.'

'It must have been awfully savage! Your poor back and bottom. Oh, let me kiss them better.' And with her hands clutching my tingling breasts, she licked me all the way up my buttocks.

'Alfred can take a sound birching, Milady,' I gasped, 'and I consider myself a match for any boy.'

'You were flogged naked, Miss?' she asked, her mouth biting my neck and ears, while with slow, maddening strokes, she frigged me between the thighs. I felt as though I should melt!

'Yes, Milady,' I stammered.

'And Alfred?'

'I have flogged him naked, Milady.'

Abruptly, she turned round and faced me.

'Miss Cumming, I must ask you, please, will you whip *me*, whip me as you have whipped my son.' I must have looked startled, for she continued. 'Please . . . I beg you. Whimble used to thrash me – I mean, he thrashes me when he is here – and I miss it so. It is a secret between us, yes?'

'Of course, Milady,' I replied.

'I must be punished,' she said simply. 'For I can only spend if I am punished.'

'I consent to punish you,' I said, and placed my hand on her cunt. Now I gasped in real surprise, for her clit had swelled and stiffened until it was at least two and a half inches long, like a tiny boy's prick!

'A deformity . . . a shame,' she moaned. 'You will not tell?'

I could not begin to guess at the demon of shame which had driven this poor, beautiful woman to throw herself into the arms of evil. But at that moment I felt nothing but tenderness and compassion for her.

'It is *beautiful*, Milady, and you must not think otherwise,' I cried, and knelt to take the stiff red clit all the way into my mouth, where I tongued and sucked it until she gave a little strangled cry of ecstasy.

Suddenly, I released her, and forced her down on her bed, face down and with thighs spread. I took a cane from her rack.

'I must warn you, Milady,' I said sternly, 'that where punishment is concerned, I do not play games.'

'This is no game, Miss,' came her muffled reply.

'I will hurt you most dreadfully.'

'Please . . . hurry.'

200

I was as good as my word, and relished every jump, every squirm of that taut boyish flesh. I counted six, and then threw aside the cane! Taking her by the hips, I flipped her over on her back. Her eyes were closed; she was panting as I straddled her. I felt her clit slip like a boy's cock right inside my cunt, and I rode her in a gorgeous clit fucking, until we both cried out in orgasm.

'You *will* stay until Christmas, Miss Cumming?' she said afterwards, as we dressed. 'Or perhaps even longer. I am sure the Volumenes can wait for a new governess.'

'There is the question of remuneration, Milady,' I said, all businesslike again. 'A guinea a week is modest as a stipend.'

'Hmmm ... shall we say thirty shillings a week? There will be extra duties, of course.'

'Which are?'

'You shall be my discipline mistress. I shall require a sound whipping once a week.'

'No more?' I asked.

'If necessary. You must open your thighs for me, girl, and let me fuck you in your sweet wet cunt with this deformed clit of mine.'

'Thirty shillings a week ... backdated, and it is a bargain.'

'Hm! You are a harsh young minx, but you have a bargain. You will stay, then?'

'Agreed, Milady,' I lied sweetly.

16

Selene's Wood

It was a chill autumn just before Hallowe'en that
year. I noticed that the cooling of the weather was
accompanied by a frostiness in the village folk. My
lustful transactions dwindled, and eventually ceased
altogether, so that I was living on capital, a truly
dreadful thing! Miss Chytte and I were constant companions, our relationship having by mutual consent
passed from business to friendship. And her financial
affairs were no less parlous than my own.

'My takings are almost nil,' she said glumly, as we
cuddled by the fireside one evening after a particularly vigorous loving session. 'It is something to do
with Hallowe'en, and the approaching winter. The
villagers become withdrawn and surly. Or perhaps . . .
perhaps they suspect something, about us, about our
discovery at the vicarage.'

'Anything is possible in this nest of vipers,' I said.
(I had not told her of my new relationship with Lady
Whimble, for fear of muddying the waters with jealous upsets.) 'Anyway, I think it will shortly be time
for us to make a move.'

'To London?'

'Yes. But I want to leave *en beauté*, or gracefully,
so it should be after Hallowe'en, for Lady Whimble
has invited me to some sort of celebration in the
wood, at midnight, and I suppose I had better attend.
You will be there, I suppose?'

'No! No!' she replied fiercely, 'and it would be best for you to feign a diplomatic illness on that occasion, Mistress. There is no good in their sinister rites.'

'Have you never thought of alerting the authorities, Miss Chytte – the constabulary?'

'They are part of it! And not just here in North Cornwall, but at the highest levels!'

'In that case let us make our escape while they are all at their devilish celebrations. Freddie will not be there: we can take the coach to Exeter, and then go by the first train to London. There is nothing to retain us, and the sooner we are away the better, for you are right: with the vicar in charge of the festivities, I sense that no good, perhaps even the profoundest harm, will come my way.'

And I explained to her the arrangements I had made in Wimbledon.

'A cosy little home of our own! 323 Worple Road, how nice it sounds. Mistress, I am yours to command!'

I saw that I had been shrewd to discontinue her payments for my disciplinarian attentions; one should not do business with friends, if they are to remain friends. It remained to sort out the problems of Freddie, and a solution – not entirely unexpected – was not long in coming.

A letter was delivered for Lady Whimble, and it bore an Eton postmark. Freddie had told me that a judgement on him had been promised by the College no later than 31st October, Hallowe'en itself. The morning of Hallowe'en arrived, and I made it my business to intercept the post. I took the Eton missive from the silver tray in the hall, and took it up to my room, where I steamed it open. I almost jumped for joy. There was no place at Eton for Freddie.

The provost expressed regret at the curious, not to

say, depraved, turn young Whimble's education had taken, presumably under some satanic French instructor!

I did not know the meaning of the word gamahuche until young Whimble made frequent use of it, and I am convinced that like the rest of his depraved vocabulary, it should have no part in the formation of an English gentleman's character, was one of his milder expostulations.

I did not reseal the letter, but kept it, thinking that the less Lady Whimble knew at this stage, the better. Letters do get lost in the post, and a duplicate would surely follow, so that I could apprise Freddie of the situation in my own good time.

As it happened, I was not allowed that time.

I pleaded influenza as a reason for not attending the Hallowe'en festivity, and took to my bed quite early that evening. Very late, there was a knock on my door, and Lady Whimble entered. The room was dark. I was fully dressed, my things packed, ready for a 'moonlight flit'. Lady Whimble stood in the doorway, silhouetted in the pale moonlight that bathed the stairway behind her.

'I am so sorry you cannot be with us, Miss,' she said. 'It is already eleven o'clock, and we are about to depart. You will be all alone here – Alfred is out at his sports, his midnight riding – but I think you know all about that, Miss.'

Alfred was indeed out on horseback. Our plan was that when the household was clear, he should return and take Miss Chytte and myself to Exeter in the coach. I thought at that time that it would be best to leave him at Rakeslit, with instructions to join me later, and clandestinely: his alibi of midnight riding would exonerate him from any suspicion of helping my hurried departure.

'I am not sure what you mean, Milady.'

'I think you are. Damehole Point, Miss Cumming? That must mean something to you. I know all about your activities with my son; the countryside has eyes and ears, Miss Cumming, especially under the moon. Your sluttish behaviour with the Chytte girl I could condone, for she is only a tea-slopper, fit for harmless amusement, and besides, she is Sapphic like us. But to betray me with my own son . . . You must pay the price.'

I leapt out of bed, my heart chill.

'How can I have betrayed you, Milady,' I cried, 'when our own relations did not begin until you invited me to your boudoir? Not until then! Whatever transactions may take place between Freddie and me are none of your business, Milady!'

Lady Whimble screamed.

In response, Dorkins and Sally burst into my room. I tried to cry out, but Sally had my mouth rapidly gagged with one of my own stockings (my best silk ones!), while Dorkins pinioned me with cruel, strong arms – an embrace which in happier circumstances I should heartily have welcomed. Then Sally proceeded to rip my garments from me, until I was naked; my kicking and squirming to no avail, and helpless in the terrifying grip of my captors.

'Well, now, Miss Cumming,' sneered Lady Whimble, 'you shall not need any of your fine frippery at our little ceremony. I must say you had on a lot of clothes for a sickly woman, and I wonder if you were planning to leave without saying goodbye. It is no matter; your naked body is all we require for our celebrations, and you shall be warm enough, I assure you. What a ripe young body it is, to be sure! We shall have bumper crops next year in our fair county of Cornwall, after you have danced for us!'

Her words struck a chill in my heart. What hellish fate lay in store for me? Lady Whimble reached out and touched my naked breasts, squeezing them painfully and rubbing my nipples between her fingers so that I cried out in protest.

'What, so sensitive?' she said. 'And yet you are no stranger to the lash, young lady. If my fingers cause you such discomfort, then you will find matters disconcerting indeed when we take you to Sally's, I mean, Selene's Wood, where you shall be guest of honour.'

With that, a pad of chloroform was clamped over my mouth; my lungs filled with the sickly fumes, and I fainted. When I awoke, I thought myself in a scene from Dante's Inferno, a poem of which I supposed these rustics had not heard. I was naked, and tightly bound to the alder tree; my fingertips touched another's; and I looked to see Miss Chytte similarly trussed on the other side of the massive trunk.

All around stood naked men and women, their bodies obscenely daubed with green, ochre, and blue dyes. They held daggers, staves and smoking candles, and wore masks of leaves and woven mistletoe. Despite their gaudy disguises, I thought I recognised most of them – the whole village was assembled for its grisly rite of Hallowe'en, in whose obscene traditions, as old as time, I was about to be unwillingly initiated. I reflected that the average Londoner, blessed with every advantage of our nineteenth-century civilisation, cannot begin to guess at the benighted folklore which holds sway in our rural provinces, once one has passed the last station on the Metropolitan Line.

A bonfire in the shape of a pyramid belched stinking smoke. The company stood within the confines of the pentagram which I had earlier observed on the earth, and I saw the vicar himself leading the proceedings, chanting a litany in a language which was no earthly tongue. He wore leaves and berries on his head and his body, accoutred with the horns and tail of a goat, was smeared with mud.

The men of the village all had erect penises – some, I must say, stiffer than others – and the women passed among them, chanting and dropping scalding wax on their cocks, at which they roared with savage glee. The vicar's horrid white cock stood too, rigid and baleful in the moonlight and the glow of the fire.

'Selene, goddess of all Cornishmen!' he cried.

'And Cornish women!' interjected a petulant woman's voice, which I recognised as Prunella's.

'And Cornish women too,' said the vicar crossly. 'Bless our ancient rite and make our old county, which we all love so much, blossom anew with a bountiful harvest!'

Lady Whimble then appeared, holding her tall wand, and naked like the rest, with a mask of roses. (I had noticed that some of the rose bushes at Rakeslit seemed to have lost some flowers.) Her body was daubed with mystic signs: circles, stars, the sun and moon, and the old Indian symbol of the swastika. Her eyes gleamed as she addressed me.

'The moon is an exacting mistress! For you, Miss Cumming, perhaps a novelty; one of your fashionable London conceits. But here in sweet Cornwall, we possess memories older than you metropolitan flibberti-gibbets! You and your Sapphic friend, who, under our noses, have presumed to indulge in blasphemous rites, shall now be chastened by our own, noble rite, for the good of our land!'

She waved her wand menacingly, and I shuddered

as I imagined what was to come. Were Miss Chytte and I to be flogged so mercilessly that we expired, a tortured sacrifice to fertilise the earth of Cornwall and produce turnips for evermore? How I longed at the moment to be trotting up Bond Street in a hansom cab, surrounded by shopping!

'What shall you do with us?' I cried, in terror of her answer. 'If I am to die, please do it quickly. And release Miss Chytte, for she is innocent and has done you no harm. If there is any wickedness to be purged, then I take it all on myself.'

Lady Whimble cackled mischievously.

'You foolish girl,' she cried. 'You are not to die, you are to become one of us, a true Cornish woman! Chytte and Cumming, you have arrived in our midst outsiders, but when you have undergone your initiation, you shall remain with us forever, as true daughters of *Kernow*!'

Although it is always a relief to be told that one's life has been spared, I was not sure in this case if the transaction was entirely favourable.

'First,' continued Lady Whimble, 'you shall be thrashed. Yes, a proper whipping, with my sacred rod!'

And she brandished her magic wand, which swished menacingly in the turbid air.

'I shall take the whipping for both of us,' I cried. 'Leave Miss Chytte.'

'Nonsense!' sobbed Miss Chytte. 'My hide is tougher than hers. Do it to me alone!'

'Silence, you squabbling whores!' roared Lady Whimble. 'It is unseemly for daughters of Kernow to behave thus. When you are chastened, you shall be as sweet and pure as any maiden here.'

At that point I bit my tongue to avoid making a rather obvious comment.

'How many strokes must we take?' I asked, swallowing hard.

'A Cornish dozen, girl, will sting you into obedience!'

My heart sank. This obviously referred to some ancient tally of torture which might run into hundreds of strokes that would be beyond even Miss Chytte's endurance.

'H . . . how many is a Cornish dozen?' I quavered.

'Eleven, of course!' shouted Lady Whimble, and proceeded to flog Miss Chytte with vicious strokes of her heavy wand. The cane descended hard on her bare back, then applied its caress to her buttocks, and I heard Miss Chytte sighing in pleasure. I was glad Lady Whimble knew only half the truth about our 'rites'.

Then it was my turn to be flogged, and I braced myself. All the time the crowd was howling with glee at the torment inflicted on Miss Chytte's naked body, and the portion I was soon to receive. I did not relish my Cornish dozen, but I knew that I could take it. And I began to realise that the chanting and hooting of these rustics was not as sinister as it sounded, that in fact it was in a large part mere bravado.

I decided to call Lady Whimble's bluff.

'Milady,' I said haughtily, 'be so good as to tell me what follows my whipping.'

She put her face close to mine, and said with a grimace of lust: 'You shall be as the earth, my girl. You shall receive the seed of every man in the village, while the moon looks down on you, and accepts our tribute. One by one, the menfolk shall approach your bottom, frisky and glowing from my cane, and they shall anoint you in quim and nether hole. You shall know them all . . .'

I did not wish to mar the proceedings by pointing

out that I knew most of them already, so I contented myself with a guffaw of scorn.

'Why, Lady Whimble, you did not need to go to this trouble. I am honoured – I cannot speak for Miss Chytte – but I would gladly have attended your rites, if properly invited.'

'What?' cried the vicar, taken aback. 'But the tradition – a virgin must be taken by force from the sinful land of Devonshire, and broken to our ways.'

'Well, Mr Turnpike, I am not from the sinful land of Devonshire, and as to my virginity or otherwise, I think you are fit to answer that question.'

'It does not *have* to be Devonshire,' he mumbled, blushing under his mud.

'Enough?' I cried imperiously. 'Release me from my bonds, Lady Whimble. There is no need of them. I shall gladly kneel to take your Cornish dozen, and not a whimper shall cross my lips. And then, I propose to be the sole sacrifice. Miss Chytte is a tender flower –'

'No I am not!'

'– And a whipping alone is enough to break her into your – into *our* Cornish ways.'

'The seed must anoint you!' thundered the vicar.

'Let the seed anoint me,' I replied. 'I shall take the spurt of every man here, in my quim, in my bumhole, aye, and in my mouth too!'

The chanting faltered and gave way to a buzz of excitement.

'Now whip me, and let our doughty menfolk use me as they will!' I cried.

The vicar nodded, and Lady Whimble cut my bonds. Proudly, I knelt, doggy-fashion before her and received the tightest caning I had ever known. How it smarted! Every lash stung like a thousand nettles, and I could not help squirming and trembling as the cane stroked my bare back and buttocks. But I took my punishment without a cry, my eyes on Miss Chytte who smiled at me, and I must confess my fortitude was due to vainglory in no small part, and the desire to impress my friend.

'Well,' I cried merrily after the last stroke had laid its fire on my naked arse, 'I hope your Cornish cocks, gentlemen, can tickle my cunt and bumhole more than your Cornish dozen!' (Although I admit that my voice did quaver a little, for my lacing had been damnably tight, and my bottom knew she was smarting from the attention of an expert!) With that, these brave rustics sheepishly formed a queue, and I cried: 'Come on, then! Who's first? My cunt is wet and hot for your cocks, my fine fellows! Are they stiff enough to pleasure me? For the offering is as naught unless I have stiff, pretty cocks filling my holes, and my mouth too! A dribbled, sullen seed is no good in our rite, it must roar from your balls with vigour like hot milk from a cow's udder.'

'Now, gentlemen,' shouted the vicar. 'Follow me!'

Thankfully, Turnpike did not apply his attentions to my body, but to Lady Whimble's, while Mrs Turnpike obediently held her wand. The vicar and Lady Whimble were soon writhing in the mud, helped on by a few juicy strokes of the wand on the vicar's pumping bottom, as the rustics gazed in awe.

I admit that I did too; not at the vicar's fervent efforts, but at the wholehearted lovemaking of Lady Whimble, who squirmed and squealed and clawed and bit like a wondrous maddened animal, her body a furnace of pure inhuman lust. I turned to look at the assembly, and in truth I was rather enjoying myself. I liked being the centre of attention, as any girl does! And the thought of being fucked in anus and cunt by one cock after another made me wet in my

211

slit. Many women will admit coyly that their fantasy is to be a luxurious 'gay girl', to enjoy being fucked by innumerable men in succession, so that their bodies are reduced to their cunts, as the men's bodies become nothing more than one eternally stiff prick, the balls endlessly replenished with hot spunk to anoint the hungry woman.

'Who is to be first, or rather which three?' I called. 'For I shall take you in my bum, in my cunt, and in my mouth! I'll suck you dry, gentlemen! Will it be you, Mr Treglown? Or do you need me to stool on your manhood before he can stand? Mr Bragg? Why, your cock is as limp as one of your Cumberland sausages. Mr Tannoc, won't you put a hot crusty roll in my oven? Mr Flett, sir, I want your cucumber, not that little radish! Yes, gentlemen, your masks are no disguise, for I know you all by your cocks!'

This taunt had the desired effect of breaking their hesitation, and soon I was dizzy with pleasure as stiff cocks poked me in both my nether holes, while my tongue and lips worked greedily on shafts of delicious hot meat, all of which I sucked to splendid rigidity before emptying the balls and swallowing every last drop of the hot sperm. Some of the younger men, including, to my pleased surprise, Dorkins, came back for second helpings of my body, although strictly speaking I suppose it was I who took the second helpings. From time to time I looked at Miss Chytte and grinned, and her initial repugnance at my non-Sapphic enjoyment of this glorious multiple fucking gave way to something like wistful envy. All in all, I reckoned that my sweet Selene was getting good value from her Cornish flock, and that with the help of my willing body (how *good* it was to be fucked so hard, and so much!), the fields of Cornwall should yield turnips beyond the wildest dreams.

Fired by my example, I like to think, the ladies of the village determined to have their own portions from their menfolk, and soon the wood, which I had thought so sinister, was a sea of rutting bodies, bouncing and slamming and sucking like a sea of frenzied codfish.

I saw Dorkins' Sally gaily taking Mr Treglown in her arse; Prunella being energetically spanked by the good Mrs Turnpike, while she sucked Mr Flett and was buggered by Mr Tannoc, and I realised that at last I was privileged to attend one of the orgies which my Ancient Greek textbooks had mentioned with such embarrassment. My cunt was soaked with dripping sperm and my own floods of love juice. I resisted the temptation to touch my throbbing clit, for I knew I should explode with pleasure, and sink exhausted to the ground. The sensation of having two cocks fuck me at the same time, separated only by the thin wall of elastic flesh between my cunt and my anus, was quite blissful, and when the joy of filling my mouth with a throbbing stiff cock was added, I thought myself as near seventh heaven as it was possible to get, in Cornwall. I was almost tempted to throw in my lot with these crude folk, whose earthy pleasures were so much to my taste, but reflected that such a scene was repeated only once a year, and steeled myself in my resolve to return to London, where I could experience whatever I pleased as often as I pleased. I did, however, feel that the vicar's influence was in no way benign, and that if freed from it, these simple folk could enjoy their coarse pleasures untainted by his unhealthy penchant for 'art' and the thrall in which he held them. While I was pondering this question, a stiff naked cock presented itself for my inspection prior to entering me, and I gasped in surprise, for I knew that lovely penis in every curve, every magnificent swelling of tight skin. It could only be . . .

'No!' I cried as I looked up, and saw the grinning face of Swivey! 'Not you . . . ugh!'

'Ain't I clean enough for you, Miss?' he spat, and indeed he did seem cleaner than his normal rum-soaked self, his muddy skin being delicately daubed rather than the accretion of centuries. Then I looked at that penis again, and could not believe that its gorgeous throbbing beauty could be attached to this wreck of a man. For that cock was none other than my dear Freddie's!

There was a lull in the proceedings, as my erstwhile partners recuperated from their generous spurtings, their womenfolk trying to coax their pricks back into life, and I was alone with Swivey in the smoky fire-light. The vicar was busy fucking his own wife for a change, while Lady Whimble enthusiastically be-laboured his pumping arse with her wand. I looked up at Swivey's grinning face again, and the truth dawned on me.

'I would know that cock anywhere,' I stammered.

'You should,' he said, bending close to me as he touched my quim with its throbbing tip.

'You . . .!' I gasped as he entered me. 'Oh God, fuck me, for that is the most beautiful cock in the world.'

He thrust deeper inside me, and began to ram his swollen bulb hard against the neck of my womb. His gnarled fingers found my stiff, tingling clit, and stroked it with the touch of a feather, which made me moan as my juice gushed from my trembling cunt.

'Yes, yes, fuck me . . . fuck me, my lord, fuck me, Lord Whimble!'

'Ah, yes,' he panted. 'I knew you and my boy were at it, and how jealous I was! I only get a sniff of cunt

214

once a year, and I wanted it to be *your* cunt, Miss. God, how sweet and wet you are!'

His accent was no longer the rustic croak of Swivey the 'outside man', but the clipped voice of an officer.

'You won't give me away?' he moaned anxiously as he fucked me.

'No, Milord,' I replied, gasping. 'But what . . .?'

'Ah,' he sighed, 'the life out east did for me. The girls, and the opium, and the drink. Disgraced for a native girl, booted out of the regiment, surviving by my wits in the stews of Delhi and Calcutta. The drink took me, as it has done so many. At last I got back to England, and my features had coarsened so much that no one, not my wife, not my boy, could recognise me! I'd invented some story, you see, about being killed in action, and forged papers, sending them money whenever I could scrape some together and letting them believe it was my pension. I came back here – I could not stay away from them, though they don't know me. Just to be near them, and to be in my beloved Rakeslit, is happiness enough.'

'Oh keep up that sweet fucking, Lord Whimble,' I moaned, 'and diddle my clit as hard as you can, for I am going to spend, if your Lord . . . ship . . . please!'

As I writhed in a gorgeous spend, I heard Lord Whimble grunt and buck fiercely as he spurted his noble sperm, hot and wet inside my quivering purse, and I glowed with pleasure, twice blessed, to have taken the seed of both father and son!

'It's not a bad life, really,' said Lord Whimble, reverting to his Swivey voice. 'For where else would an old wreck like me get a sniff of a girly once a year?'

At that point there was a fearful roar, and billows of phosphorus smoke, and a horrid creature burst into our midst. It had the shape of a man, but in the murky light seemed to be a goat, complete with horns, tail, and cloven feet. Everyone, including the vicar, fell to their knees in awe.

'Arrrh! Urrrh! Oooorh!' howled the goat, unmistakably a Cornish goat. 'I am the Great Panjandrum of Cornwall, Selene's favourite pixie, and you will do what I say! Arrrh! Urrrh! Oooorh!'

'The sacred pixie!' gasped the crowd. 'The Great Panjandrum!'

'Selene is displeased,' said the goat. 'Do you think her negligent, that she needs such barbarous rituals? Go back to your homes, you deluded fools, and pay no more heed to this false prophet, with his blasphemous carvings and pictures!'

The goat delivered a hearty kick to the prostrate body of the vicar, then picked up Lady Whimble's wand and began to lash his back with great vigour. 'Begone, impious filth!' he roared. 'Know that I have destroyed your museum of sinfulness. Yes, I have eaten everything in it! I am all-powerful, the omnivorous pixie who eats mountains, aye, and people too! I'd eat the lot of you except that you're all Cornish! Go back to your clotted cream, you knaves!'

The crowd wailed and cried for mercy.

'Cast this faithless charlatan from your midst!' thundered the goat, as he whipped the vicar's bottom with a lively rhythm, and the vicar fled squeaking away, followed by Mrs Turnpike. I must say I felt sorry for the pickle the nice Mrs Turnpike's loyalty had got her into, but it just shows that being dependent on men can get a girl into all sorts of bother. As they disappeared yelping into the night, the goat's attention fixed on the trembling body of Lady Whimble. He gave her five juicy lashes on her bare bottom, to get her attention, then bellowed:

'As for you, false priestess, you shall mend your ways. I myself shall take the two offerings to Selene, for she will be well pleased with this succulent girl's flesh, but first, with the pixie power invested in me, I give you in marriage, to this man!'

So saying, the goat took Swivey, or Lord Whimble, by the arm, and propelled him forward.

'Do you take him?' cried the goat. 'It is solitude that has made you mad, woman. A good man will restore your health and sanity!'

'I do, oh almighty pixie,' stuttered Lady Whimble.

'And you man, known as Swivey?' said the goat.

'Rather,' said Lord Whimble. 'I mean, I do.'

The goat was busy unfastening Miss Chytte from her bonds.

'You may kiss the bride,' he commanded, although Lord Whimble needed no commanding, for his magnificent cock was already hard again as he pressed it against his wife's body to the cheers of the assembly. I thought it a rather efficient and touching form of wedding ceremony, without all the pomp and circumstance which is such a drain on the purse. But I did not see the consummation which was obviously going to follow, for the goat scooped up Miss Chytte and myself in his powerful arms, and carried us at the trot away from that scene, whose ominous beginnings had turned out so pleasantly.

When we were well away from the wood, we came in sight of a coach and four, whereupon the goat put us down and pulled off his head.

'Whew!' he said. 'It's hot in there.'

'Freddie! My angel,' I said, and fell into a ladylike swoon.

Freddie had not broken everything at the deserted vicarage, and we paused to collect such prints and paintings as we could carry, including the painting of St Agatha's torments, to which I had taken a fancy.

'I always suspected my goatskin would come in handy,' said Freddie thoughtfully as we neared Rakeslit Hall.

'Pack your things, Freddie,' I ordered. 'You are coming with us to London, this instant.'

'They are already packed,' he said.

'Get your luggage, then, and don't forget a few bottles of brandy from the cellar, and some cigars if you want,' I said. 'Then we'll go to Miss Chytte's, and over the moors to Exeter for the first train to London this morning.'

'How romantic,' said Miss Chytte.

'What about Eton?' said Freddie, frowning. 'Mama will be a bit disappointed.'

'Don't worry. You were not going to Eton anyway,' I said, and then explained. 'I have better things for you to do.'

'Yes, *please*, Mistress,' he crowed joyfully.

'Tell me Freddie, did you know that Swivey was . . . I mean . . .?'

'Well, Mistress, I suspected for a long time,' he said thoughtfully. 'And then when I saw his manhood, I knew.'

'So did I,' I said. 'It is the image of your own.'

'Runs in the family. It's called the "Whimble Whiplash" ', he said rather smugly.

'Well, Freddie, I saw Miss Chytte eyeing the Whimble Whiplash with something like admiration,' I said firmly. 'And so I think it is time she had a lesson that not all love need be Sapphic.'

'Oh, Mistress . . .' cried Miss Chytte, blushing.

'Freddie will stop the coach in a suitably romantic spot on the moors, Miss Chytte,' I said sternly, 'and he will fuck you!'

'Oh!'

'Oh!'

'And you, Miss Chytte, will be fucked and enjoy it! You will be called on to perform far more wondrous duties in London. That is an order!'

'Yes, Mistress,' chorused my happy slaves.

17

Return to St Agatha's

It was so sweet to be back in London! The very names, Old Oak, Westbourne Grove, Acton Town – they were music to my ears, and when we got down from the train at Paddington, I felt that all the cares of the world had lifted from my shoulders. My body still smarted dreadfully from my ordeal, but I was back in the metropolis, among friends, with money and a home of my own!

I told Freddie and Miss Chytte to wait for me in the tea room at the Great Western Hotel, while I ventured forth into Praed Street. It was just after two o'clock, and Marlene was at her usual station. She smiled in recognition.

'Hello there, Miss, have you come for business?'

'I have, Marlene, not the quick business you have in mind, though. You remember the job I spoke of?'

'I do, Miss. You don't mean –'

'Yes. It starts today! We are going to Wimbledon, my friends and I, and I invite you to come with us.'

'Wimbledon? Isn't that the country, with trees and cows and suchlike?'

'More or less. Are you coming?'

'Yes! And my dear friend Deirdre is willing too, Miss, if there is a place in your house for her. Can she come? She is young, ready for anything. Irish – a convent girl, and very lustful.'

'Assuredly. But hurry. Do not worry about leaving your rooms, for I will have tenants for them before nightfall.'

I told her to meet me at the Great Western, and she hurried off back to her room in Norfolk Place in search of Deirdre, and to assemble her belongings, which, as I suspected, did not amount to much.

I settled down to wait, with Freddie and Miss Chytte, over a lavish tea with all sorts of delicacies: smoked salmon, potted shrimps, game pie, and even oysters. It was not really tea, strictly speaking, for we allowed ourselves to become merry with wine, and were laughing and joking as though our ordeal had never happened, when Marlene reappeared in her best finery, with her suitcase. She was accompanied by a girl of quite extraordinary voluptuousness, dressed in tight white satin, with gloves and a hat, as though she were going to Royal Ascot, or to church.

Marlene curtseyed to me, and said:

'May I present Deirdre, Miss,' and her companion curtseyed too.

Deirdre was very beautiful, and I told her so. She smiled, showing dazzling white teeth, and said that all Irish girls were like that. I said I was sure she was the loveliest Irish girl *I* had ever seen, and with good reason.

Deirdre was a negress!

'Deirdre's Papa was from Kingston, Jamaica,' said Marlene. 'He was on a banana boat, you know, and Deirdre was brought up by the nuns in Phibsboro.'

I did not see the connection between banana boats and Phibsboro, but extended my hand, secretly delighted at having this ripe young beauty in my service, and bade her welcome.

'Sure, it's a grand thing meeting yez, Ma'am, so it is,' said Deirdre.

* * *

221

'Why, Cumming!' cried Miss Tubb – now sporting a golden wedding ring, as Mrs Lowe – the headmistress of St Agatha's. 'What a pleasant surprise! You are just in time for tea, and I trust you will join me.'

'Gladly,' I replied.

'And this must be young Alfred Whimble, he is the very image of his father.'

We went into the headmistress's apartments, where she invited me to make myself comfortable.

Freddie and I were installed on a sofa, the very same one over which I had bent to receive my strokes of the cane, so long ago.

'I will have tea provided for your servants downstairs,' said Mrs Lowe.

'They are not my servants,' I replied. 'They are my business associates, and I should like them to have tea here. I expect Mr Lowe to join us, for what I have to say will be of interest to him as well as you.'

'Yes . . . yes, of course,' she said, flustered. 'I just thought –'

'You thought that Deirdre here was some sort of maid,' I interjected with a sweet smile. 'Well, I hardly think she is maid material. She is much better than that. Why, she might make an excellent matron here at St Agatha's, don't you think?'

Mrs Lowe emitted an uncertain giggle.

'You always had a keen sense of humour, Cumming,' she said.

'It is *Miss* Cumming now, Mrs Lowe,' I snapped, and we sat in a somewhat fidgety silence as the tea things arrived. At length Mrs Lowe said:

'Have your friends been in London long, Miss Cumming?'

'They are well acquainted with the streets of our city,' I replied. 'They too, are governesses, of a sort.'

At that point Mr Lowe entered, greeted me with

some surprise and much discomfort. I motioned him to sit down, for I had not much time to waste on this wretched pair of connivers.

'Marlene and Deirdre are whores, you see,' I continued. 'Just like you, Mrs Lowe, and just like me.'

She went pale, then her face reddened with anger and she rose.

'This joke is in very poor taste, Cumming, and I think you must leave at once.'

'Sit down, Mrs Lowe,' I rapped. 'It is you and your husband who must leave, and this very afternoon. But first, allow me to present you with a small gift.'

Freddie placed the parcel he was carrying on the table, and undid its wrapping. Inside was a photograph album.

Mr and Mrs Lowe stared at it, fearfully.

'Some pretty photographs, to bring back old memories,' I said.

'This is monstrous,' hissed Mr Lowe.

'But how do you know, if you have not seen the contents?' I said. 'Besides, they are no more monstrous than your calculated theft of my trust money, sir!'

I opened the book and flicked through the pages.

'Yes,' I continued sardonically, 'you and all your friends are there. The plates, of course, are in a safe place, and I can have as many prints made as I wish. I am not sure that the Bar Association would be impressed, Mr Lowe, nor the Headmistresses' Conference, madam. I have taken the liberty of already sending photographic proof to Lloyd's of London, attesting to the athletic prowess of your chum, Mr Volumene . . . there is of course Scotland Yard, not to mention the scandal-hungry gutter press. Well, Mr Lowe, this is all rather unforeseen, isn't it? You thought that by now I would be a flayed corpse, rotting in the devil tree of Sally's Wood, didn't you?'

'What do you want?' croaked Mr Lowe, ashen-faced.

'Not what do I want, dear sir,' I said cheerfully, 'but what is going to happen.'

I drew a sheaf of documents from my bag, which had been drawn up by a solicitor that morning, after our first happy night in 323 Worple Road. Mr Lowe went red as he scrutinised the papers.

'You want us to . . . to *sell* St Agatha's?' he blurted. 'For a consideration of . . . *nothing*?'

'Yes.'

'St Agatha's is worth at least a hundred thousand pounds!' he cried.

'A good bargain, I think,' I said, 'considering the amount you stole from my trust fund. You will note that you also undertake to pay the rent on rooms four and six, at 27 Norfolk Place, London, for the next month, so that Marlene and Deirdre do not forfeit their deposits with the landlord. And to show you how kind I am, I have provided you with a pleasant set of rooms to live in, right at the heart of the metropolis.'

'What do you mean? Rooms?' stammered Mrs Lowe.

'Why at 27 Norfolk Place, of course!' I cried jovially. Then my voice hardened.

'Sign, both of you,' I hissed. 'You have no choice.'

Mrs Lowe burst into tears. Mr Lowe reached for his pen with the vigour of a dead man, and I knew I had won. Trembling, they signed.

'Please do not make us go at once,' pleaded the erstwhile headmistress. 'What will the school think?'

'You need not worry what the school thinks,' I said. 'For as the new headmistress I will make sure they do not think much of you at all. But you do not need to go just at once – say in half an hour or so. There is a debt I must repay.'

I nodded to Freddie, who pinioned Mr Lowe and held him helpless.

'Repayment of debts, even long-standing ones such as mine, is a condition of good business practice,' I continued. 'You will please bend over this sofa, Mrs Lowe, and adjust your dress. That is, lift up your skirts and show me your bare bottom, so that I may repay the debt I incurred some years ago, when you gave me three strokes of the cane, most cruelly and without justification. Mr Lowe will no doubt be pleased to witness.'

'You are mad!' she shrieked. Marlene slapped her.

Marlene then held her by the ankles, while Deirdre, giggling, forced her to bend over the sofa and sat on her head. I lifted her skirts and petticoats, and drew down her bloomers, to reveal a ripe, somewhat flabby arse. And on this I laid three vicious cuts of her very own cane, relishing her every squeal and shudder.

After three, she was shaking and sobbing uncontrollably.

'Let me go, let me go, you bitch, you slut,' she screeched.

'You have had my three returned, Mrs Lowe, but, silly me, I had forgotten the interest on the loan!'

And I lashed her twice more, to complete the juiciest caning I had ever delivered.

It did not take long to hurry the disgraced and woebegone pair from my premises, and when their carriage had disappeared from view, we raised our teacups in a toast.

'My Lord, and ladies!' I said. 'Welcome to St Agatha's!'

* * *

As I expected, the abrupt departure of Mr and Mrs Lowe did not cause too much confusion, and neither did my equally abrupt annexation. I was the mistress of St Agatha's, owning it lock, stock and barrel. Of course I was not going to interrupt the efficient running of the school, I was too sensible for that, and besides, when I had access to the books, I saw that the place was making a handsome profit, or would have, if the Lowes had not siphoned off most of the income for themselves. I remembered most of the staff and girls, and knew which ones I could trust and which I could enlist to my purpose. My first, and indeed only dramatic action in my first days as headmistress, was to improve the quality of the school meals to a very luxurious extent! Any uncertainties girls might have can always be dispelled by the provision of sumptuous teas.

My reasoning was this: what better cover could there be for a house devoted to the arts of discipline than a girls' school, where severe discipline was the order of the day in any case? Visitors came and went every day: parents, tradesmen, school inspectors. The school was well furnished with wings, outbuildings and so on, to be diverted to my erotic uses. Gradually, the number of pupils would dwindle, the younger classes would be discontinued in favour of the mature girls of the fifth and sixth forms ... and I would be sure to pick girls that I could recognise as sympathetic, perhaps eager to earn a little pocket money by assisting or even participating in my scenes of voluptuous pleasure. The school charter was clear – the school was a business, like any other, and could be bought and sold as Miss Tubb, later Mrs Lowe, had bought it before me.

There was much to be done. Meanwhile there was ample funding in the school treasury to keep us all in comfort for the near future. My rented house in Worple Road served as a cosy home, although I divided my time between it and the headmistress's house at school.

Mr Izzard was a frequent visitor to the school, where he came to discuss business with me, and I also invited him to tea on occasions, at Worple Road. I used to invite Mlle Gryphe as well, for I liked the dear soul, and thought it would cheer her up to get out from time to time, and I must say she did know how to dress up.

Apart from her, I kept in service those mistresses I thought would be useful or obliging, and gave them a slight increase in salary, while I dismissed with a gratuity those I thought too curmudgeonly for my business purposes. Dear Mlle Gryphe was obviously pleased to see me again, and gushed with enthusiasm when I told her very vaguely of my plans for the school. She noted with interest that Mr Izzard seemed to be involved.

I amused myself by typing up the *Adventures of Yvette* into a full-length book, intending it for use as a French text for the fifth and sixth forms. (Yvette ends this episode in her life married to a lascivious American rail baron, whose greatest amusement is to tie her with thongs to the track of the Chicago–New Orleans express, and rescue her at the very last minute before she is chopped in half.)

I gave the typescript to Mlle Gryphe, somewhat mischievously, I confess, and to my amusement she not only professed herself delighted with it, but also annotated it with copious notes, exercises, vocabulary, and so on. She hinted rather dreamily that Yvette reminded her of herself when young, for it seemed that she had had *beaucoup d'aventures érotiques*.

So I was not altogether surprised when in due course the Wimbledon and Merton Advertiser announced the engagement of Mlle Solange Gryphe, of Aix-en-Provence, and Mr Albert Edgar Izzard, pharmacist, of Wimbledon High Street.

I often had occasion to think of my tumultuous experiences in Cornwall, which seemed an age away. I thought of those villagers as poor lost souls. I had taken their money and given them my body for a few brief moments, but there was nothing I could do or could have done for their peace of mind. They were not guilty in accepting their ancient pagan heritage and its odd rituals, but deluded.

The photographic plates were safely stored; I never looked at them, nor discussed them, nor showed them to anyone else.

I will relate in further pages what happened to us all at St Agatha's and beyond. But I must add a piquant little anecdote which will give the reader a hint of events to come.

One evening, with a full moon beaming through my window, there came a knock at the door of my study. Miss Chytte peeped in.

'A gentleman to see you, Miss Cumming. He would not give his name, saying that he knows you and wants to surprise you.'

'Well, let him come,' I said, curious.

The door opened wide, and in strode a handsome gentleman of early middle age, with a military bearing. He was accompanied by a young girl of about sixteen years, who possessed a quite astonishing English rose type beauty: raven-haired, with a lovely swelling bosom and a tight full bottom to match, and pouting, arrogant red lips.

'Headmistress,' he cried, 'how pleasant to see you!'

I smiled, and motioned them to be seated.

'It is about my daughter, Veronica. I wonder if there might be a place for her at St Agatha's? She is a bright girl, but headstrong, you see. Takes after me, a very devil! She needs discipline, Miss, the stronger the better.'

'Why, I am sure we can accommodate her,' I said with a very friendly but teasing smile. 'I can assure you that Veronica will be *thoroughly* disciplined here at St Agatha's.'

'Splendid!'

I picked up a springy yellow cane from my rack and stroked it absent-mindedly as I eyed the handsome father and daughter.

'Of course,' I murmured, 'in matters of discipline, school policy is that parents should be involved just as much as their daughters.'

I tapped the cane handle with my fingertip.

'In every way . . .'

Veronica creased her lips in a gorgeous sullen pout; her father's eyes sparkled.

'I suppose you'd like me to sign some papers?' he said eagerly.

'Yes indeed, Major Dove.'

And Selene shone down on me.

NEW BOOKS

Coming up from Nexus and Black Lace

Sherrie by Evelyn Culber
May 1995   Price: £4.99   ISBN: 0 352 32996 3
Chairman of an important but ailing company, Sir James is having trouble relaxing. But in Sherrie, seductive hostess on his business flight, he has found someone who might be able to help. After one of her eye-opening spanking stories and a little practical demonstration, money worries are the last thing on Sir James's mind.

House of Angels by Yvonne Strickland
May 1995   Price: £4.99   ISBN: 0 352 32995 5
In a sumptuous villa in the south of France, Sonia runs a very exclusive service. With her troupe of gorgeous and highly skilled girls, and rooms fitted out to cater for every taste, she fulfils sexual fantasies. Sonia finds herself in need of a new recruit, and the beautiful Karen seems ideal – providing she can shed a few of her inhibitions.

One Week in the Private House by Esme Ombreux
June 1995   Price: £4.99   ISBN: 0 352 32788 X
Jem, Lucy and Julia are new recruits to the Private House – a dark, secluded place gripped by an atmosphere of decadence and stringent discipline. Highly sexual but very different people, the three women enjoy welcomes that are varied but equally erotic.

Return to the Manor by Barbra Baron
June 1995   Price: £4.99   ISBN: 0 352 32989 0
At Chalmers Finishing School for Young Ladies, the tyrannical headmistress still has her beady eye on her pretty charges; the girls still enjoy receiving their punishment just as much as Miss Petty enjoys dispensing it; and Lord Brexford still watches breathless from the manor across the moor. But now there's a whole new intake for Miss Petty to break in.

The Devil Inside by Portia da Costa
May 1995   Price: £4.99   ISBN: 0 352 32993 9
Psychic sexual intuition is a very special gift. Those who possess it can perceive other people's sexual fantasies – and are usually keen to indulge them. But as Alexa Lavelle discovers, it is a power that needs help to master. Fortunately, the doctors at her exclusive medical practice are more than willing to offer their services.

The Lure of Satyria by Cheryl Mildenhall
May 1995   Price: £4.99   ISBN: 0 352 32994 7
Welcome to Satyria: a land of debauchery and excess, where few men bother with courtship and fewer maidens deserve it. But even here, none is so bold as Princess Hedra, whose quest for sexual gratification takes her beyond the confines of her castle and deep into the wild, enchanted forest . . .

The Seductress by Vivienne LaFay
June 1995   Price: £4.99   ISBN: 0 352 32997 1
Rejected by her husband, Lady Emma is free to practise her prurient skills on the rest of 1890s society. Starting with her cousin's innocent fiancé and moving on to Paris, she embarks on a campaign of seduction that sets hearts racing all across Europe.

Healing Passion by Sylvie Ouellette
June 1995   Price: £4.99   ISBN: 0 352 32998 X
The staff of the exclusive Dorchester clinic have some rather strange ideas about therapy. When they're not pandering to the sexual demands of their patients, they're satisfying each other's healthy libidos. Which all comes as rather a shock to fresh-faced nurse Judith on her first day.

NEXUS BACKLIST

All books are priced £4.99 unless another price is given. If a date is supplied, the book in question will not be available until that month in 1995.

CONTEMPORARY EROTICA

THE ACADEMY	Arabella Knight	
CONDUCT UNBECOMING	Arabella Knight	Jul
CONTOURS OF DARKNESS	Marco Vassi	
THE DEVIL'S ADVOCATE	Anonymous	
DIFFERENT STROKES	Sarah Veitch	Aug
THE DOMINO TATTOO	Cyrian Amberlake	
THE DOMINO ENIGMA	Cyrian Amberlake	
THE DOMINO QUEEN	Cyrian Amberlake	
ELAINE	Stephen Ferris	
EMMA'S SECRET WORLD	Hilary James	
EMMA ENSLAVED	Hilary James	
EMMA'S SECRET DIARIES	Hilary James	
FALLEN ANGELS	Kendal Grahame	
THE FANTASIES OF JOSEPHINE SCOTT	Josephine Scott	
THE GENTLE DEGENERATES	Marco Vassi	
HEART OF DESIRE	Maria del Rey	
HELEN – A MODERN ODALISQUE	Larry Stern	
HIS MISTRESS'S VOICE	G. C. Scott	
HOUSE OF ANGELS	Yvonne Strickland	May
THE HOUSE OF MALDONA	Yolanda Celbridge	
THE IMAGE	Jean de Berg	Jul
THE INSTITUTE	Maria del Rey	
SISTERHOOD OF THE INSTITUTE	Maria del Rey	

JENNIFER'S INSTRUCTION	Cyrian Amberlake	
LETTERS TO CHLOE	Stefan Gerrard	Aug
LINGERING LESSONS	Sarah Veitch	Apr
A MATTER OF POSSESSION	G. C. Scott	Sep
MELINDA AND THE MASTER	Susanna Hughes	
MELINDA AND ESMERALDA	Susanna Hughes	
MELINDA AND THE COUNTESS	Susanna Hughes	
MELINDA AND THE ROMAN	Susanna Hughes	
MIND BLOWER	Marco Vassi	
MS DEEDES ON PARADISE ISLAND	Carole Andrews	
THE NEW STORY OF O	Anonymous	
OBSESSION	Maria del Rey	
ONE WEEK IN THE PRIVATE HOUSE	Esme Ombreux	Jun
THE PALACE OF SWEETHEARTS	Delver Maddingley	
THE PALACE OF FANTASIES	Delver Maddingley	
THE PALACE OF HONEYMOONS	Delver Maddingley	
THE PALACE OF EROS	Delver Maddingley	
PARADISE BAY	Maria del Rey	
THE PASSIVE VOICE	G. C. Scott	
THE SALINE SOLUTION	Marco Vassi	
SHERRIE	Evelyn Culber	May
STEPHANIE	Susanna Hughes	
STEPHANIE'S CASTLE	Susanna Hughes	
STEPHANIE'S REVENGE	Susanna Hughes	
STEPHANIE'S DOMAIN	Susanna Hughes	
STEPHANIE'S TRIAL	Susanna Hughes	
STEPHANIE'S PLEASURE	Susanna Hughes	
THE TEACHING OF FAITH	Elizabeth Bruce	
THE TRAINING GROUNDS	Sarah Veitch	
UNDERWORLD	Maria del Rey	

EROTIC SCIENCE FICTION

ADVENTURES IN THE PLEASUREZONE	Delaney Silver	
RETURN TO THE PLEASUREZONE	Delaney Silver	

FANTASYWORLD	Larry Stern	
WANTON	Andrea Arven	

ANCIENT & FANTASY SETTINGS

CHAMPIONS OF LOVE	Anonymous	
CHAMPIONS OF PLEASURE	Anonymous	
CHAMPIONS OF DESIRE	Anonymous	
THE CLOAK OF APHRODITE	Kendal Grahame	
THE HANDMAIDENS	Aran Ashe	
THE SLAVE OF LIDIR	Aran Ashe	
THE DUNGEONS OF LIDIR	Aran Ashe	
THE FOREST OF BONDAGE	Aran Ashe	
PLEASURE ISLAND	Aran Ashe	
WITCH QUEEN OF VIXANIA	Morgana Baron	

EDWARDIAN, VICTORIAN & OLDER EROTICA

ANNIE	Evelyn Culber	
ANNIE AND THE SOCIETY	Evelyn Culber	
THE AWAKENING OF LYDIA	Philippa Masters	Apr
BEATRICE	Anonymous	
CHOOSING LOVERS FOR JUSTINE	Aran Ashe	
GARDENS OF DESIRE	Roger Rougiere	
THE LASCIVIOUS MONK	Anonymous	
LURE OF THE MANOR	Barbra Baron	
RETURN TO THE MANOR	Barbra Baron	Jun
MAN WITH A MAID 1	Anonymous	
MAN WITH A MAID 2	Anonymous	
MAN WITH A MAID 3	Anonymous	
MEMOIRS OF A CORNISH GOVERNESS	Yolanda Celbridge	
THE GOVERNESS AT ST AGATHA'S	Yolanda Celbridge	
TIME OF HER LIFE	Josephine Scott	
VIOLETTE	Anonymous	

THE JAZZ AGE

BLUE ANGEL NIGHTS	Margarete von Falkensee	
BLUE ANGEL DAYS	Margarete von Falkensee	

BLUE ANGEL SECRETS	Margarete von Falkensee	
CONFESSIONS OF AN ENGLISH MAID	Anonymous	
PLAISIR D'AMOUR	Anne-Marie Villefranche	
FOLIES D'AMOUR	Anne-Marie Villefranche	
JOIE D'AMOUR	Anne-Marie Villefranche	
MYSTERE D'AMOUR	Anne-Marie Villefranche	
SECRETS D'AMOUR	Anne-Marie Villefranche	
SOUVENIR D'AMOUR	Anne-Marie Villefranche	

SAMPLERS & COLLECTIONS

EROTICON 1	ed. J-P Spencer	
EROTICON 2	ed. J-P Spencer	
EROTICON 3	ed. J-P Spencer	
EROTICON 4	ed. J-P Spencer	
NEW EROTICA 1	ed. Esme Ombreux	
NEW EROTICA 2	ed. Esme Ombreux	
THE FIESTA LETTERS	ed. Chris Lloyd	£4.50

NON-FICTION

HOW TO DRIVE YOUR MAN WILD IN BED	Graham Masterton
HOW TO DRIVE YOUR WOMAN WILD IN BED	Graham Masterton
LETTERS TO LINZI	Linzi Drew
LINZI DREW'S PLEASURE GUIDE	Linzi Drew

– –

Please send me the books I have ticked above.

Name   ....

Address   ....

             ....

             ....

             .... Post code ....

Send to: **Cash Sales, Nexus Books, 332 Ladbroke Grove, London W10 5AH**.

Please enclose a cheque or postal order, made payable to **Nexus Books**, to the value of the books you have ordered plus postage and packing costs as follows:

   UK and BFPO – £1.00 for the first book, 50p for each subsequent book.

   Overseas (including Republic of Ireland) – £2.00 for the first book, £1.00 for the second book, and 50p for each subsequent book.

If you would prefer to pay by VISA or ACCESS/MASTER-CARD, please write your card number and expiry date here:

....

Please allow up to 28 days for delivery.

Signature   ....

– –